# SORDID

D1522422

## AVA HARRISON

*Sordid: A Novel*
Copyright © 2018 by Ava Harrison
Published by AH Publishing

Line Edit: Write Girl Editing Services, Lawrence Editing, www. lawrenceediting.com, Love N. Books

Content: Jennifer Roberts-Hall, Becca Mysoor

Proofreader: Marla Selkow Esposito

Formatting: Champagne Book Design

Dedicated to those who fear walking in the shadows.

# PROLOGUE

## Grant

M Y SHAKY HAND HOVERS ABOVE A DOCUMENT THAT could sever my already fragile relationship with my family. I watch as it trembles, knowing I shouldn't be doing this. I should walk away from this deal. It's not right. This need for vengeance isn't me. It might have been once, but something inside of me has changed. Ever since last week when I spoke to Spencer at the hospital, *I've changed.*

"What are you waiting for?"

Chelsea's voice grates on my nerves, threatening to destroy the little composure I have.

"Just give me a minute," I snap.

"What's there to think about? Sign the damn papers, Grant. You don't have a choice. You stand to lose more than Spencer."

The way she spits his name gives me pause. She's always hated him. Hated them all. She's a viper, ready to pounce on anything and everything my family possesses. And right now, I'm feeding her the prey.

"We need this property, Grant. If we don't go international and we allow Lancaster Holdings to expand before we do, we'll be sunk. Lancaster is growing too fast. We set this plan in motion, and we're already in too deep to stop."

She's right. Nothing can be changed. I chose this road a long time ago, and it's too late to turn back now. There's too much lost time. Once again, I allowed my pride to get in the way of everything. I've let time slip through my hands, dissolve like grains of sand in an endless desert until the years passed without a word. I watched those grains transform into mirages. Into something else. Something new. Something miserable.

I've watched from afar as others lived their lives. As they found love and happiness, while all I found was bitter disappointment. I'm not proud of who I am. Of who I've become. I was weak and foolish and failed myself.

And, in turn, I failed them.

My father was right, and I hated him for that. Loathed how right he was. So I became secluded from everyone. From my parents and from my brothers, Spencer and Pierce.

Built a wall.

I built a fortress until all that was left before me was an empty horizon of regret.

I have so many regrets, and it feels as if I'm drowning . . .

Suffocating.

Without a second thought, I lower my hand to the paper and sign.

# CHAPTER ONE

## Bridget

*Five months later*

T HREE DAYS.

Three, very long days.

Each second stretches out in front of me slowly. Painfully slow. It feels like an eternity. I know it's not. I'm just anxious for it to begin. For my life to begin.

The future is not something I ever used to worry about. I've never really thought about where I'd be and what I'd be doing in ten years, or even five. To be honest, I never really thought where I'd be five minutes from now. But everything has changed. I'm finally ready to live. I'm ready to start my job, and eventually, I'll take over the world. All I have to do is wait.

And it's agonizing.

I'm stuck. My life is on pause. But in three more days, I'll finally start the job over at Barkly Media. Even if it's only an internship, I can't help the excitement that courses through my body. It's as if every molecule of my being is brimming with it. I'll prove to myself, and to everyone who thought I'd fail, that I'll succeed. The first step toward the rest of my life. The first step to being more than just Bridget.

Bridget...

The daughter who's always been second, *and then third*.

The girl who's followed in her sister's footsteps her whole life.

For as long as I can remember, it's been that way. At first, I was just the kid sister of Olivia, but then there was Lynn. Don't get me wrong, I love Lynn and Olivia. Truly, I do. But it'll be nice to have something of my own for once. The drama these two have brought into my life has been unbelievable at times. Now, with them both settled and happy, I can focus on me. And that's just what I plan to do, starting with landing the perfect internship.

Sure, I graduated from UCLA only a few short weeks ago, but I had no time to waste. In the marketing industry, securing a job in Manhattan is close to impossible. Starting as an intern, learning the ropes, and securing the connections I need would land me a job, eventually. Or at least, that's what all my professors promised me back in school. *It better be.* Having to do summer semester has set me back, which means I need to work harder to prove myself. Not only to my employer but also to myself. I want to prove I can stand on my own two feet.

I'm mid-daydream about my first day when I notice I missed my phone ringing. Reaching out, I swipe the screen and play back the message. Cassandra from Barkly Media wants me to call her back. I press the call back button and wait for her to answer.

"Barkly Media," a woman says through the phone.

"Hi, may I please speak to Cassandra?" I reply while nibbling on my lip.

"This is she." Her voice is ice cold.

"Hi, Cassandra. This is Bridget Miller," I stammer as I sit down on my bed and wait to hear the reason for her call.

"Hello, Bridget. Thank you for calling back so promptly. Unfortunately, I regret to inform you that we will not be needing your help at this time." She says a few more things, but I can't make out any of her words as my whole world drops down from underneath me.

*It's over.*

My stomach clenches as the realization hits me.

My dream job is gone.

I want to tell her a lot of things. I want to tell her that I need this job. That it's a necessity. That it's a goddamn *lifeline.* I want to add that I just put down first and last month's rent on a studio apartment. But of course, I say nothing at all. Placing the phone down, I let out the breath I'm holding.

*Hello, Bridget, Miss 3rd place. What are you going to do now?*

Pacing, I find myself gnawing on the inside of my cheek. I'd wanted to do this on my own, but as I pace back and forth, I realize it's time to admit defeat. I pick up my phone and dial my sister's number. As much as I hate asking for help, time is of the essence, and I don't have time to let my pride get in the way. Olivia will know what to do. The phone rings once before she answers.

"Hey, babe. Everything okay?"

"Yes. I mean no. I mean . . . " I stop and let out a long exhale.

"Well, which is it? You're confusing me." Olivia laughs breezily.

"I don't know," I huff. "I lost the job," I admit with a sigh.

"How about you start from the beginning and tell me everything."

"Fine. I got a call, and the job at Barkly Media fell through."

"I'm surprised you even got that job," she mumbles under her breath.

"What's that supposed to mean?" I snap.

"It means, that you waited until the very last moment to choose a major. And the very last moment to apply. Are you surprised it didn't pan out?"

"I mean . . ." A long gust of air escapes my mouth. "I guess not, I was just hoping—"

"I know. Listen, We all make mistakes. Bridge, what did you expect?" I want to object. I want to say that I've worked my ass off to get this far, and it's not fair that I'm being compared to her mistakes. Olivia was not one to give lectures. Not too long ago she had overdosed on cocaine and ended up in rehab. I've tried so hard to not live in the shadows my sisters have cast from their own discretions, but no matter

4

how hard I try it still hovers over me.

"Are you listening to me?" I give my head a little shake and realize that I had, in fact, drifted off into my own mind. "What did you say?"

"I said I would handle it. Let me talk to Spencer, Bridge."

"No. No way. I'm not working for your boyfriend." I know I'm being petty, but all my life everything has been about her. I wanted something that was mine. Just mine. Not scraps she gave me. And that's what working for her boyfriend would be—scraps.

"You wouldn't have to work with him."

"I just . . . I just can't work for The Lancasters. I appreciate you even thinking about it, but no. It's fine. I'm fucked, but it's fine," I groan.

"What if you didn't have to work for him? What if I could get you a job somewhere else?"

"Olivia, there is no way anyone is hiring this late in the game. I appreciate it, but unless a miracle happens . . ."

Olivia chuckles on the phone. "Oh ye of little faith. Tell me now, do you have faith in me?"

"Of course I have faith in you. You're my sister. But how is having faith in you going to help my situation? Unless your modeling agency suddenly opened without you telling me, and even then, I wouldn't work for you anyway."

"Beggars can't be choosers but no. I haven't opened yet, obviously. But I do think I have a job for you. One that will give you good experience to use toward something else."

"You do? How? I already told you that me becoming

your slave will not help with my life." I chuckle, but there is no mistaking the sarcasm in my voice. That very option is something I could very well see Olivia suggesting.

"What if I told you I just heard that this fantastic temp agency is looking for some new blood?"

"I'd say tell me more."

She laughs at my comment. "When I was looking for an assistant to start getting my agency in gear, I worked with the Karen Michelle Temp Agency, and the owner mentioned she is looking for new staff. They are extremely picky and very hard to get into, but she owes Spencer a favor or two. I bet I can get you in with them."

"Are you sure?" My voice has taken on a slightly higher pitch as it always does when I try to contain my excitement.

"Yes."

"That's amazing. Although, I doubt they'll take me. There are probably millions of people trying to apply." My voice dips again as reality drops down on me. Just because she has a contact, doesn't mean I'll get a position. "But if I get it, I'd love you forever."

"I will warn you, she's not warm and fuzzy. She's a shark. The kind that sniffs for blood and pounces at the first sign of weakness. If anything, she'll make you want to drink, but she does have the best clients."

"That's not a problem, I don't need warm and fuzzy. I just need a job."

"You know Mom and Dad won't—"

"I rented an apartment. I moved out. I'm not taking

money from them, so I can put up with a shark as long as I'm getting paid. Make the call. Please."

"Don't say I didn't warn you." She chuckles.

"Duly noted."

"Okay, I'll text you the details a bit later."

"Thanks and again, I fucking love you!"

"Forever?"

"Forever."

An hour later and I've already received a text from Olivia telling me to be at the temp agency she and Spencer have been working with at eleven. My lips part and a strangled gasp escapes.

Shit. It's already ten.

I only have an hour. Where did the time go? Peering down, a slew of curses pour out of my mouth in rapid succession. I'm still in my goddamn pajamas. Of all the mornings I could have chosen to be lazy, this isn't the best one. Or maybe it's for the best. The less time I have to prepare, the less I can stress about it.

Without a minute to spare, I'm running through my apartment, pulling clothes over my head until I'm naked and in the shower. Once out, I dry off and dress into what I can only hope is something presentable—in other words, something I don't have to iron. Before long I'm running out the door and making my way to the agency. When I finally arrive, it's five minutes to eleven.

Breathe.

I can finally breathe.

I give my name to the receptionist and sit down in the lobby to wait. It's only then that I realize I know almost nothing about the agency. How am I supposed to seem serious and prove to them that they want me when I don't know anything about who they could potentially place me with?

I queue up trusty Google from my phone and learn they have the coolest clients ever. Placements are usually in fashion, TV, or luxury hotels. My mouth hits the floor when I see they work with Marie Claire, Vogue, and Gucci, and my lips part into a large smile at the idea of landing a job doing marketing for a fashion house. That would be a dream come true. I'm going to owe Olivia big time.

"Karen is ready to see you now," the receptionist says while standing. "Let me show you to her office."

A few seconds later, I'm walking into a brightly lit corner office with floor-to-ceiling windows facing Park Avenue. The room is sterile and void of all emotion, with white walls and white furniture. The focal point is a large Lucite desk, and sitting behind it is a middle-aged brunette with a tight smile. It's so small I wonder if she's had too much work done on her pristine face to even crack the surface.

"You must be Bridget," she grits out, and it's obvious she's not happy to have me here.

*So it's not just the effects of too much filler and Botox.*

"Spencer Lancaster gave me little information about your credentials." There's no dismissing the complete disdain in her voice.

A war starts to wage inside me. I want to tell her where

she can stick her pretentious ass, and that I don't need her job or her handout, but I know that's just my pride talking. So I can grin and bear it and tolerate this woman's abuse or . . .

This is the lesser of the two evils.

Sucking in my cheeks, I respond, "That's probably because I don't have any. I was supposed to work at—"

"Hand me your résumé." She holds out her hand impatiently.

Fumbling through my bag, I locate the paper in question. Job-wise it's pathetic. I don't have to look to know that. I have little experience. But it doesn't matter. I know what I have to offer. I'm smart. I have fantastic grades. I'm a natural leader. Let's just hope Karen can see past my lack of experience. But who knows. She might not just to spite me. Olivia warned me this morning on the phone that this woman was a shark, but she's so much worse. Maybe a piranha. The way she clicks her tongue and rolls her eyes as she peruses my résumé has me wanting to snap back and tell her why I'd be perfect for any job. I sit up tall, trying my damnedest to show her without words I'm worthy.

"I can do anything. I know my résumé is limited, but I promise you—"

Karen cuts me off with a shake of her head. "You have no experience in anything. This résumé is shit. I can't work with this," she grates while waving my résumé in the air. "Fucking Spencer."

She says the last part under her breath.

"What is it you want to do in the future?"

"Marketing. I-I haven't thought much past that."

She scoffs. "You don't say." She purses her lips. "Doesn't matter now. If you want to succeed in any high-profile marketing position, you need experience, and since I owe Spencer, you're now my problem to deal with."

My eyes widen, and my hope begins to climb. Is she saying she'll help me? I'm about to ask when she lasers me with her large caramel eyes.

"Do you know how hard it is to even earn a marketing internship at a magazine or a fashion house?"

I shake my head.

"No, I didn't think you did. If you did, you would have worked every summer of college."

She has me there. Instead of working, I'd decided to double major. Anyone else might have been impressed by that, *but not Karen.*

"Which you didn't. Any other person with your experience—or lack thereof—would've been shredded upon arrival. Alas, you know the right people. Lucky for you I'm good at what I do, so I'll get you placed."

I try to control the smile that's threatening to spread across my face. Something tells me Karen wouldn't be impressed. "Thank you. I'll work hard."

"You better not make me regret this."

"I won't. I swear."

"I expect you to work your ass off so we can leverage it to a full-time position, and I expect to make a sizable commission from this . . . misfortune."

I ignore her words, happy to have this opportunity and not willing to mess it up before it begins. Regardless of whether she was coerced, she's going to help me get my life started, and for that I'm grateful.

I'm ready.

A week later, I'm walking through the doors of the world-renowned Axis Agency. The space is phenomenal just as Karen promised. Facing the water, the huge loft space has a beautiful view of The Statue of Liberty.

I arrive early, eager to start, but surprisingly, I'm not the first one there. Standing in the middle of the pristine white loft space is Matthew Lawson, the owner. He looks different than the photos online. He appears to be shorter in person than his pictures suggest and has significantly less hair. Not that it matters what he looks like. From all my reading, he's supposed to be a genius. He's known for his cutting-edge ideas, brilliant delivery, and return on investment for his campaigns. He's so famous they even talked about him in my lectures. He's also supposed to be impossible to work for, not that it will be a problem for me as I'm a lowly temp. No way will I be placed anywhere near him.

He must hear my heels tap against the floor because he looks up as I enter. His pupils dilate and he runs his gaze from my feet up to my eyes. A chill runs up my spine, but it's the wicked smirk that bothers me most. It's as if he's undressing me, and it feels like spiders are crawling up my body. Being anywhere near this man gives me the creeps. Not that it matters. I'm sure this is the first and last time I'll see him.

"And what do we have here? You must be my fresh"—his words linger and bile forms—"assistant. I'm very excited to meet you. I'm Matthew Lawson. Here, at Axis, we're a small, *intimate* company. You can call me Matt." He winks, and the emphasis on the word intimate isn't lost on me.

Shit, I'm supposed to be his assistant. As great an opportunity as this is, the way he watches me has me on edge. "Hi, M-Matt, I'm Bridget. I-I'm excited to be here, too," I muster, but I'm so damn unhinged, I actually stutter.

"Come with me. I need to have you sign a few papers."

Together we walk into his office. With him in front of me, I do everything I can to pull my skirt as far down as possible.

---

Out of breath from trekking up the stairs to my apartment, I pull out my phone and dial Olivia.

"How was your first day?" she asks before I can even say hi. I knew the moment I got home I had to call her as she'd be dying to know how my job went.

I groan at her question. "I'm never going back."

"Bridge . . ."

"The place is goddamn awful. I walked out."

"You quit? On your first day?" Her voice echoes in

surprise through the phone.

"Turns out he's a pig. I refuse to work for him."

I don't tell her the full story. I don't tell her that as I was signing intake papers, he stepped up behind me and I could feel that he was hard through his pants. I'm certainly not going to tell her that every time we bumped into each other, his body brushed against mine in a sickening manner that made me feel unsafe. So I just tell her he's a pig and hope she doesn't question what I mean.

"So, what are you going to do now?"

I let out a sigh of relief. She's not mad. After what she did for me, I'd hate for her to be upset with me.

"I'm not going back."

"Bridget, I know he's a dick. Unfortunately, a bunch of men in his position are like that. I wish there was something I can do." She sighs. "I'd love to give him a piece of my mind—"

"I know, and I love you for it, but it's fine. I just won't go back."

"I totally understand. I'd do the same thing, but Spencer and I pulled some serious strings to get you in with this agency. You have to at least call them and say you're sorry and see if they'll place you somewhere else."

"I know, I know. Karen's just scary."

"Time to grow up, Bridge."

"Fine, I'll call. But after that, I'm going to open a big bottle of wine and drown my sorrows."

"I know it sucks, but you already said you aren't going to

ask Mom and Dad for help, which means you have to get a job. You cannot burn bridges along the way. Take it from me. If you burn too many bridges and your options are limited, you might find yourself in a horrible situation."

I know she's referring to her own life, but her warning rings loud in my ear. Both my sisters have gotten themselves into trouble. And even though they've changed their ways, I still feel like I need to prove to myself and my parents that I'm not like them.

"You're right, and I'll take care of it. Listen, I'm starving and want to grab a bite." I walk toward my fridge and pop it open, searching desperately for some inspiration on something to nosh on.

"Okay. Don't drink too much."

A giggle escapes. My sister knows me all too well.

"Yeah, yeah," I respond in a mocking tone.

"Love you, Bridget." Olivia chuckles.

"Love you, too."

When I hang up, I grab a small container of ice cream from the freezer. I feel defeated by my day. Karen isn't going to take this well. If I still have my life at the end of this, it'll be a miracle, but Olivia is right. I need to grow up. With that settled, I pull out a spoon from the drawer and scoop into the mint chocolate chip container. It's cold and refreshing and makes everything better . . .

*Almost.*

# CHAPTER TWO

## Bridget

HALFWAY THROUGH MY ICE CREAM FEST, MY FRIEND Brian texts me, asking me to meet him at some sick party being held at the hottest new lounge in the Meatpacking District. After having a day from hell, a drink is sure to lift my spirits. My options for the evening are limited. Drown myself in sweet confections or try to be social and forget. Brian's cute, and with all the bullshit over the last day with Axis, and being sexually harassed, having a drink and flirting—hell, maybe even taking it further than flirting—sounds like the perfect distraction I need. But now as I stand here all alone and waiting, it's the worst idea in the world.

With a lift of my hand, I bring the shot of tequila to my mouth and down it in one long gulp.

"Rough day?" the bartender asks.

"Rough life," I respond, and he lifts his eyebrow for me to expand on that statement. "Basically, I had to walk out on my dream job because my boss was a chauvinistic pig. Staying there would have had trouble written all over it."

"Damn, that sucks. But look at the bright side. At least you aren't that guy." He nods, motioning at the guy on the dance floor making a complete ass of himself. He's gyrating around to his own rhythm, one that does not match the beat of the music.

I throw my head back on a laugh as the man breaks into the running man. "This is true. Things can always be worse."

He smiles and pours me another shot. "On me."

By the time I down it, he's moved on to the next patron, so I take the time to look at my phone to see if maybe Brian texted. Nothing.

"Did he stand you up?" the bartender asks over his shoulder as he pours a pint of beer.

"How do you know I'm waiting for a guy?"

The corners of his eyes crinkle and I can't help but deflate at the prospect that everyone around me knows I've been stood up. Today has been a spirit crusher, and it just keeps getting worse. All I needed was one night. One freaking night to try to forget, but no.

"It's his loss," the bartender says with a small smile.

I smile back, my grin never reaching my eyes.

Standing to go, I look across the room and spot Brian. I scrunch my nose as I watch him kissing some hot blonde with a skirt that looks as if it could easily pass as underwear. *Clearly, Brian's all but forgotten about me.* I really shouldn't care, but I do. It's just one more rejection I can't handle. Not today. Without another word, I throw my credit card onto the bar. The bartender lifts it from the counter and heads over to the register to close out my tab. As I wait, my head turns around the space to search for the nearest exit. I need to get out of here before I break down.

As soon as I have the bill squared away, I head toward a side exit. I shiver when the burst of chilled air assaults me. My arms wrap around my body, clinging tightly, trying to stave off the tears. It's no use. I swipe a stray teardrop from my cheek and hurry my steps, eager to get as far from this place as possible. I'm rounding the corner when I collide with a hard body.

"Whoa there," a throaty, masculine voice curls around me. Hands grip my shoulders to steady me. "You came awful fast around that corner." The man chuckles.

I don't say a word. What's there to say? If I speak, I might break. A whimper escapes my mouth instead.

"Hey. Are you okay?" He removes his grasp, leaving me vacant and unsteady without it.

The man bends down so we're eye to eye. My breath hitches and butterflies take flight. Even in the dark I can tell this man is attractive. No, that's not the right word. He's beautiful, absolutely gorgeous, and here I am having a meltdown in his arms. Fabulous fucking day.

"Can you hear me?" He is pulling me out of my inner ramblings. I search his eyes, unable to discern what color they are, but they're large and expressive. Right now, he's clearly concerned, and that thought has me coming to my senses and backing away.

Wet rivulets cascade down my face and I try to swipe

them away. "I'm fine."

"Did someone hurt you?" he asks, his friendly tone taking a possessive cut, that's rough around the edges. Almost scary. *I would not want to cross this man.*

He doesn't know a thing about me, but he's acting like he's ready to go toe to toe with whoever has me in this state. My head cocks to the side, and I take him in, my curiosity piqued. He's breathtaking. Tall and lean, easily six foot three. He runs his fingers through his unruly brown locks, and suddenly, I imagine my own hands brushing through them. My face warms to what I believe is a crimson blush.

"I'm really sorry. I didn't mean to run into you," I offer, trying desperately to resurrect my current state. He probably thinks I'm a crazy person. I run into him and then I don't speak for what feels like an hour while he assesses my state of unrest. It's humiliating. Especially given how well-put-together he is. Dressed from head to toe in what looks to be a fine Italian suit pressed to perfection and fitting his body like a glove. My mouth stands agape, and it's not until he chuckles at my perusal that I'm brought back to Earth.

*Pull yourself together.*

"I'm fine. I've just had a really bad night," I offer as a lame attempt to move the conversation forward.

"Me too. Is there a guy back there I need to have a word with?" the stranger offers, smirking as my eyes widen.

"No. I mean, yes, but no. It wouldn't be worth speaking to him. His tongue is lodged down some busty blonde's throat. It's fine, though. I wasn't really into him anyway. I just had a bad day and was looking forward to some decent conversation, drinks, and a night to forget, ya know? It's my fault for caring. I shouldn't." My recount of the night explodes from my mouth in a waterfall of word vomit. When I'm uncomfortable, I ramble. It's always been a nervous tic.

"Anyway, I should've stayed home and worked on my apology to this temp agency I'm currently working with. I up and left a high-profile client today because he couldn't keep his hands to himself, and now Karen's going to kill me, but that's my problem, not yours, and anyway . . ."

His eyes are wide.

"Slow down. Who put their hands on you?"

I stare, dumbstruck. One simple phrase from a stranger and I'm completely paralyzed in place. Nobody in my life has ever shown that much concern, and this is a total stranger. "I . . . It . . . It was just this guy I was working for. Nothing happened. I left." My head hangs in shame.

"Hey . . ." He tilts my chin upward so I'm staring directly into his caring eyes. "You don't have to be embarrassed about someone else's actions. He clearly upset you, which means you had every right to walk out. Don't let this Karen woman make you feel like you did something wrong."

This man has me glued to this spot, completely off-kilter. He listened to every word I spewed. Has anyone ever done that before? *Not for a long time . . .* Not since all the shit hit the fan with my family when I was back in high school. Ever since my senior year, everything has been about my father having an affair on my mom. Or about my best friend, Lynn, actually being the product of said affair. Just as life finally calmed down, and maybe I'd be noticed and appreciated for my own merits, everything was about Olivia and her partying and drug use. It's been so long since I've not been compared to my sisters and their flaws and someone paid attention to just me; I can't stifle the need to bask in it.

"Okay," I whisper, not knowing what else to say.

"You're cold." He rubs his hands up and down my shoulders. "Let's get you somewhere warm."

His arm comes around my shoulder, pulling me into him. The scent of peppermint and wintergreen assault my senses in a wonderful euphoria. I sigh. It doesn't go unnoticed based on the light chuckle coming from the stranger. I snuggle into him without thinking and almost immediately come out of the fog he's had me in.

I stop in my tracks and whip around until I'm facing him. "Wait. Where are you taking me? I don't know you." It sounds ridiculously stranger-danger, but not so much after getting sexually assaulted by Mr. Lawson. I might as well wear a Me Too neon shirt. This stranger might be nice and handsome, but wasn't Jeffery Dahmer the same way?

His hands come up in surrender. "I'm just trying to help. You were upset, and it seems like you could use some company. I thought we could go get a drink." He shuffles on his feet.

I groan. "I'm sorry. I'm acting erratically. It's just been one hell of a day."

"Like I said, I get it. My day has been one for the books

too." He drags his straight teeth along his lower lip and fire shoots to my core. It's so sexy I can hardly contain a whimper. This man is like nothing I've ever seen. "I think we could both use a drink."

"Just one," I say, convincing myself more than him.

"We'll see." He winks cockily, and I'm a goner. "So, Miss . . . ?" His invitation hangs in the air, waiting for me to pluck it, press it into my chest and RSVP the hell out of it.

"Bridget. Just Bridget." Not a good time to give him my last name. Again. Stranger-danger.

"Bridget." He tries the name out, smiling. "Let's go."

"Are you going to tell me yours?" I protest.

"Maybe."

I laugh. He does, too. It feels good, and for the first time today, I don't feel like a truck ran me over. "Grant."

Even his name is sexy.

"All right, Grant. Lead the way."

He could tell me we're headed to hell, and I'd go without a fuss at this point. It's stupid and irresponsible, but I couldn't care less. I don't have to be perfect tonight. I don't have to compare myself to anyone. No one knows me here. *He doesn't know me.* I can be whatever I want to be, even if that means having an impromptu drink with a complete stranger.

We don't walk far before we approach a tall brick building. A door I didn't even see opens and a tall, smartly-dressed man steps out.

"Sir. Welcome. Your table is ready for you."

"Gerald." He tips his head down, and apparently that's his version of thank you. "I'll have a plus-one this evening."

"Of course, sir."

The gentleman named Gerald moves aside, ushering us through the door. A dimly-lit lounge greets us. There are private booths surrounded by white satin drapes and tables littered throughout the room. The place is moderately full with several of the tables still open.

"Right this way," Gerald calls. He leads us to one of the more private sections with white drapes obscuring our view of the other patrons. With the night I've had, privacy is welcome. "Can I get you something to drink?"

"What will it be?" Grant asks.

"A shot of tequila," my inner college girl blurts out.

"Gerald, two shots of Don Julio 1942." Grant surprises me, not batting a sexy eyelash.

"Sir." Gerald nods before walking off. I turn around to Grant with a smile that hurts my cheeks. "Don Julio? Who are you trying to impress?"

"You," he says simply, his eyes meeting mine, nonchalant and challenging. My heart is in my throat, my pulse hammering against my neck. This. Man. Then he continues, "You're upset. You need something worth drinking." *Cyanide sounds like a good idea.* But of course, I keep my snark to myself. Miss 3rd place, remember?

"I'm fine, really. I just needed to get out of there."

Our shots arrive in record time. Grant raises his glass to me. "To bad days and better nights." His voice turns husky on the word nights, and it makes my stomach warm with innuendo.

"I'll drink to that."

We clink glasses and tip them back. The liquid is smooth going down my throat, slowly melting away all the tension that was still harboring in my shoulders. As I'm lowering my glass to the table, my eyes catch Grant's. Feeling unnerved, my gaze drifts, and I watch as his throat gulps down the liquid. The motion is so sexy I find myself swallowing in response. The room heats, and I can't shake the awkwardness at having this beautiful man sitting across from me. I literally ran into him, while crying over a guy I had no real interest in.

He waves to the new waitress. "Another."

After our second drink, I'm much looser. We've talked about nothing in particular, but it's nice to let go and have fun for once, especially after my job debacle. He brought me to some swanky club that's for members only. High roller members from the looks of things. It's nothing but fancy suits and tumblers of pricey scotch. I might have gone to private school and grown up wanting for nothing, but this is a whole new level of wealth. I'm out of my element, but the man next to me manages to make me feel like I belong here.

"So, tell me what happened. Maybe a bit slower this time." He smirks, and heat spreads through me. First from embarrassment from my rambling, but soon it transforms into something else. Understanding. This stranger with piercing green eyes looks at me like he understands. And the thought warms every molecule in my body.

"Oh, where to even start." I look off toward the drapes, trying to avoid eye contact. It's dark in our enclave. Only candlelight illuminates the space. They flicker like little fireflies on a warm summer night.

"The beginning is always a good place." Grant's deep voice pulls me from my thoughts, and I look up at him. We lock into a stare, and I swallow before speaking.

"It's been a rough day."

"We established that."

I smile. "You said you've had a rough day, too?"

"Yep. It's been a series of rough days. Hell, it's been rough months. Fuck it, *years*."

"I was basically sexually harassed at the workplace if it makes you feel any better," I blurt out, and he sets his glass down.

"What do you mean, *basically*?"

"I got a job through a temp agency, and the guy was horrid. I left, but the problem is that it's the Karen Michelle agency, and Karen Michelle is the *best*." I roll my eyes. "But enough about me. What about you?"

"You did the right thing in leaving. Karen will have to deal with it unless she wants one of her clients to have a lawsuit on their hands. Sexual harassment is no joke, Bridget, and you shouldn't make light of it."

"I'll deal with it. Just not tonight." I beg him with my eyes to drop the subject. He catches the drift by lifting his tumbler to his mouth and taking a gulp of the amber liquid. "So, what's your deal?"

He groans. If he thought he was getting out of sharing, he's sadly mistaken. "I'm having some interoffice conflict."

"What does that even mean?"

"Too complicated to explain."

"Well, I've probably had one too many to understand anyway."

As I say the words, the lightheadedness rushes in. The drinks have been flowing like water as we've talked and enjoyed each other's company.

"As have I."

"So, let's not discuss it anymore. Let's have another drink." I laugh. One more drink and his hand has found a resting place on the back of my chair. "Tell me something about you," I demand playfully.

"Hmm . . . let me think." He taps his chin. "I don't have a lot of time to watch television, but when I do, I like to watch reruns of *Cheers*."

My brow rises. "*Cheers*? Like the old bar show?"

"The *old* bar show? It's a classic, Bridget."

"Classic is the keyword here," I deadpan, but I can't stop my gaze from running over his every feature. He's older than me. A few small creases etch away at his forehead, but they don't take away from his devastatingly handsome face.

He chuckles, and tiny lines form on the outside of his perfectly delectable lips. "Well, I'm older than you, it would appear."

"You don't have to age yourself by admitting you like

*Cheers.*" I bite my lip to stifle my chuckle.

"Hey"—Grant laughs—"you bruise my ego."

"Don't worry, pops. You've still got it going on." I wink.

"You don't say."

Grant's hand has moved from the back of my chair to my leg. I'm not sure when that happened, but the motion of his hand rubbing lightly against my exposed flesh has tingles shooting through my body.

Our eyes meet and heat pools behind his pupils. The lust is so thick in the air I can barely breathe. The need to touch him is intense. He leans into me, his mouth dangerously close to the shell of my ear.

"Want to get out of here?" My body shivers from the feeling of his words tickling my skin.

"Sure," I rasp. It's as though I'm in a heady trance, and leaving with him is my only option. Everything about this is wrong. On a normal night, this wouldn't be happening. On a normal night, I wouldn't leave with a stranger. But this isn't a normal night. Lord knows I have no idea where it will lead, nor do I care.

He takes my hand turning abruptly, leading us out of the room. "This way," Grant orders, his voice low and husky, dripping with a raw sexual undertone that makes it impossible not to agree.

"Okay."

The rough pads of his fingertips trace a pattern against me, making me feel hot. Needy. Together we set out, his gait faster. His long strides pull me with him, out of the bar and down a back hall. I follow him down a long corridor, and then out a door that leads outside. Brisk air kisses my skin, and I realize we're in the back alley.

"Where are we—" I'm pushed against the wall, forcefully. The hard edge of the brick bites my flesh.

"I want you," he grates roughly. "Say yes."

"What?" The word escapes on a breathy whisper as it takes everything in me to remain controlled. I'd only have to lean in a few inches and our lips would touch. I'd taste him. The thought sends a jolt to my core.

"Bridget," he groans. "Say it. Tell me you want this. I'm losing patience not being able to kiss you, but I don't want to be like the other asshole you've dealt with today. Say yes. I won't take what's not given freely."

"Yes." The word comes out harsh, desperate.

"Fuck," he growls as his mouth descends. His tongue slides in, taking possession of all that I am.

I want every part of this man.

His hand slides up my side, leaving goose bumps in its wake. I'm electrified by his touch, emboldened by his arousal. I shouldn't be allowing a stranger to have me pinned against the wall. I shouldn't be going down this path. A war wages in my mind, but when determined fingers pull at my panties and cup my core, the battle is lost. He parts me. Slides his finger. Then another.

I need this.

My only choice is him.

My kisses are filled with desperation. All thoughts are of

him claiming me, of his body pressed against mine, of how it would feel to have him inside me. A pleasure pain builds as he finds the sensitive spot and torments me. The friction of his ministrations has me clawing at him.

I need more.

So much more.

"Please," I plead against his mouth. Pulling my lips away, we lock eyes. "Please." I want him to take me. To fuck me against the wall in the back alley. I need him. The force of his movements increases.

I can feel it.

I can taste it.

The world around me fades away. All noise ceases as I chase my high. I'm almost there.

Undone.

"Fuck," he growls, yanking his hand away, leaving me vacant and needy. "Fuck, fuck, fuuuck." He pulls frantically at the root of his hair. I watch confused as Grant slams his fist into the wall. My eyes round in horror as I now know that's not lust in his voice. It's regret.

"I can't do this," he mutters as he walks away, leaving me baffled and alone.

*What did I do wrong?*

Only everything.

# CHAPTER THREE

## Grant

W HAT THE FUCK DID I JUST DO?
How did that happen?
How did I let myself go so far?
I've officially lost my ever-loving mind, that's how.

My bones scream in pain. Glancing down, I notice that there's blood on my knuckles. Shit, things got out of hand real fast.

It started harmlessly. She ran into me and took my breath away. She was upset, and she needed *me*. It's been a long fucking time since a woman has needed me and it felt good. It didn't help that she's beautiful. At that moment, I'd never seen anyone so gorgeous, so sexy, yet so innocent at the same time. I think I needed her as much as she needed me.

*Fucking idiot.*

I watched as she went from being desolate to only moments later embracing letting go and throwing her head back and laughing. How she let go with such abandon after what she'd been through had my blood boiling with jealousy.

Every once in a while moments of weakness and self-doubt crept in. She hid it well under the sarcasm and tough exterior, but it was there. Her jaw ticked. She bit her lip. The look in her eye told me she was unsure of what to do or say next. I knew the look. The confused feeling that must have run through her body. So I went against every moral I had, every rule I'd ever set, and dragged her away from prying eyes.

And the moment we were alone, I was lost to her.

When her gaze met mine, those same eyes I'd watched dance in wonder looked at me as if I were the only man in the world, and I wanted that to be true. I wanted it so badly that I needed it to be. So I took her. I shouldn't have, but I was desperate for her. Desperate for the feelings. The feel of her.

*God . . .*

The feel of her in my arms. It's been too long since I've had a woman in my arms. I was drunk on it. Drunk on her. Her warmth. The way she pressed against my hand, her body urging me to take her. To fuck her. To take what I wanted. It's been so long since I've felt that. Something so pure and tangible and wanting it to be mine. But in the end, I couldn't. My fucking conscience had got the better of me. It killed me to pull away, but as I took with no regard for anything but my basic needs, I became everything I hated. And deep down, as much as I hated the idea, I knew what I had to do.

So I left.

Pulling myself out of the sordid memory, I run my hands through my hair.

Fuck.

Fuck.

Fuck.

Now what do I do? I don't know the girl, and I never have to see her again, but will she be okay? Despite every voice in my head shouting no, I can't help it. I'm a lot of things, but I'm not a prick to people who don't deserve it.

I push the door open, and I'm met with an empty alley. *Shit.*

I'm sure she's fine. Pissed, but fine. Letting out a huff of air, I make my way back down the hall and into the lounge. I plaster on my fakest smile, straighten my back, and let the mask fall. I need to leave. Coming here was a bad idea.

"Grant," I hear from behind me and glance over my shoulder. A woman I once dated in college is standing there. Her heavily injected lips pucker, and she pushes her fake breasts together, giving me an ample view of her cleavage. Monica is just as fake as she was the last time I saw her. She reaches out to touch my arm.

"Monica." I look down at her hand, then give her a pointed look. She can't be touching me like that. No matter how much she wants me, it's never going to happen. Monica, as beautiful as she is, could never make me sway.

It was wrong of me to go there with Bridget, but I couldn't help it. She was so enticing . . .

I almost faltered in my resolve.

*Almost.*

# CHAPTER FOUR

## Bridget

I DON'T REMEMBER HOW I GOT HOME LAST NIGHT. MY BRAIN was in a fog of alcohol mixed with humiliation. What I do remember is the irony of the fact that I once made fun of my sister Olivia for making out with a stranger and now not even a year later, I've done the same thing. I guess as much as I try to not follow in my sister's footsteps, I do. The only difference is Olivia fell in love with her stranger and I was left with the trash. The memory makes me wince.

*He rejected me.* But worse than the rejection was the look in his eyes. Haunted. Tormented. A look in which it was obvious that not only did he hate what he did, but he hated me for it. As if it was my fault that it happened. As if I forced him. Just thinking about it has my head pounding. What is it with men taking advantage of me? He didn't exactly force himself on me. I came willingly, but the way he left . . .

It was shitty.

Between my hangover and last night, I need a distraction. Picking up my cell, I fire a text over to Lynn.

**You around?**

I pray she is. After yesterday, I need my best friend. I need to vent, and maybe scream, and Lynn is the only person who will fit the bill to make me feel better.

Lynn: **Yep, Carson is gone all day.**

I breathe out the pent-up oxygen I didn't even know I've been holding.

Me: **Want to hang?**

Lynn: **Time and place?**

Me: **72 Diner? I could use some greasy food.**

Lynn: **Ha. Hungover?**

Me: **You have no idea! What time?**

Lynn: **One hour?**

Me: **Great. See you then.**

Knowing I'm going to spend the day with her has my corded muscles uncoiling. I need someone to talk to about what transpired at the lounge last night. More importantly, I need a pep talk in how to handle the situation with Karen. As much as I've tried to push it aside, I can't do it any longer. Everything from yesterday has me realizing more than ever that it's time to grow up.

An hour later, I find myself in a small, dingy booth sitting across from my sister. My head is pounding, and I can barely muscle up the energy to lift my mug to my mouth. Lynn, on the other hand, is grinning away at me as she sips a cup of hot coffee and nibbles on a french fry. I want to smack the smirk off her face. Why did I think coming here was a good idea? The people around us are way too loud. The place is too bright. God, all I want right now is to be still in my bed.

"You know, I'm trying not to laugh at you, but it's hard. You're pulling the funniest faces," Lynn says.

"Why would you laugh at me? You're my sister, and right now you're supposed to be supportive in my time of need."

"I know, but I can't help myself. Watching someone with a hangover is just so much better than experiencing it yourself. I was feeling miserable last night when I got into bed with my book before ten. But now I'm feeling quite pleased with my decision."

"Cruel. So cruel." I wince. "So, what am I going to do about this whole situation?"

"You mean the romantic one in which you kissed a handsome stranger out by a dumpster?"

"Real funny, asshole. There was no garbage."

"Girl, you were probably so hot and bothered you didn't even notice the stench." She winks at me. "But for reals, what are you going to do?"

"Nothing. I'll never see him again."

"Well, he sounds like a whack job. Good riddance," Lynn offers in support.

I chuckle. "Yeah, that's one way to describe him. One minute he's kissing me like his life depends on it, and the next he's running off in anger. I know I was tipsy, but I definitely didn't imagine his complete change in demeanor. Was the kiss that bad?"

"I doubt it. I've been told by a good many people that you happen to be a good kisser."

"You have? Like who?"

Lynn laughs. "I don't know. I just said that to make you feel better. But I'm sure you're a good kisser."

"Good to know."

Lynn lets out a long sigh. "I need a good kiss. I swear it's been forever."

"How long has it been?" I raise an eyebrow. "Because unless it's been over a week, it can't be worse than getting kissed by someone who runs away afterward."

She looks down at her food.

"How long?"

"About an hour."

"Whore. What the hell, man? An hour."

"Yeah, Carson is really neglecting me." She grins.

"Stop rubbing it in."

"Sorry. As for you, the man was clearly delusional. Like I said, he sounds like a bit of a weirdo. Honestly, Bridge, don't worry about it. You have way too much going on in your life to worry about some sociopath who makes out with you and then leaves you high and dry. He probably can't get it up anyway." She brings her cup to her mouth and takes a sip of her brew. "Want my suggestion on what to do?"

"Sure."

"After this, head to Barney's, buy a new outfit, and kick some ass."

"That's all well and good, but I'm kind of on a budget. Internships and temp jobs don't exactly pay worth a damn and, well . . . I don't even have a job at this moment, remember?" I purse my lips.

"Have you talked to Karen?"

"Hell no. She's worse than Miranda Priestly."

"Who?" Lynn's eyes widen in question.

"*Devil Wears Prada—duh.*"

"Of course, your cultural references will be from a chick flick. She sounds scary."

"Frightening. And FYI, it was a book first."

Lynn leans toward me, giving me her no-bullshit smirk. "Here's some tough love. Suck it up, buttercup, and have the talk with her. At the end of the day, her client was in the wrong, not you."

"You're so smart."

She winks and dives into her plate of fried grease.

She's right, and I know I need to own my decision. Scary or not, I need a job.

———————•◦•———————

Hangover and all, I find myself sitting across from Karen. The sneer on her face has my back going ramrod straight. She's definitely not happy.

"What the hell do you think you're doing walking out on the Axis Agency? You will go back there today and explain this was all a misunderstanding. He's a legend. The best in the business. I can't afford to piss him off."

"I can't ever go back there. He—"

"I don't give a crap what he did. He's the most influential

person in marketing. Piss him off, and there goes every chance of getting a full-time job. If he decides you'll never work in marketing again, guess what? You'll never work in marketing again. That's how this business works." She clenches her jaw while drumming her nails on the desk. "If it weren't for your sister and Spencer Lancaster, I'd never place you anywhere."

I hate that the only reason I'm even getting a job is because of Olivia and her boyfriend. I hate that my own merits aren't enough. But what am I going to do? Normally I'd say something, but in this case, she's right. I know she's right. In the marketing industry, securing a job in Manhattan is close to impossible. Coming in as a summer intern, learning the ropes and securing the connections I need would have landed me a job come September. Or at least, that's what all my professors promised me back in school. Instead, I had to do a summer semester and missed my chance at most fall internships. When I landed Barkly it was a dream come true, but that fell through. My options are limited now, and I can't afford to burn any bridges. Because as much as I adore my parents, I refuse to mooch off them any longer.

"I'm sorry you feel that way," I finally answer. "I'm a hard worker, but not in situations that make me uncomfortable. If I need, I'll press charges. That's how serious I am about never returning there."

Karen remains stone-faced but doesn't say a word. We embark on a staring contest. I know these rules. The first to break eye contact loses. I refuse. I won't back down. Grant's words from the other night replay like a mantra over and over again, acting as my anchor.

*You did the right thing in leaving.*

"Leave. I need to think about how to handle this situation," Karen says, turning away and effectively breaking our contact.

My fingers press into the skin on my forearm, the sharp bite of my nails silencing me. The urge to defend my decision is all-encompassing, but I know better. And as much as it hurts my pride, I stand and exit.

I did hold firm, and she did lose the battle of wills, but does it matter?

# CHAPTER FIVE

## Grant

IT'S BEEN TWO DAYS SINCE THE BAR, AND I CAN'T GET Bridget out of my mind. I know it's a dangerous game I'm playing, but I can't control it.

I pick up the phone and call the head of security for The L. "Mr. Lancaster," he answers.

"Miles, I'm going to need you to look into someone for me."

"Not a problem, sir."

"Her name is Bridget. She mentioned that she was working at a marketing firm but had to walk out. The temp agency she got the job through was the Karen Michelle Agency. Get me the details."

"On it."

I place the phone down, anxious to hear what he has to report. This girl has made me a weak and desperate fool. It's not the first time I've been a fucking idiot where a woman is concerned. You'd think I would've learned my lesson.

I should call back and tell him to forget it. I should, but

I won't. I need to know something, *anything* about her. Maybe just a kernel of information will be enough to stave off the curiosity because that's all it was: a passionate moment outside a bar with a stranger. A stranger who was desperate just as I was.

Yes, just one more piece of her is all I need. Information will curb the hunger.

*Fucking idiot.*

---

I'm sitting at my desk a day later, and everything is grating on my nerves. Spencer keeps calling. Ever since we had our little "heart-to-heart" after his girlfriend, Olivia, overdosed, he's been waiting for me to talk to him. When he called months ago, it was right after Chelsea convinced me to bid on a property she'd found out he was interested in purchasing. He wanted me to tell him why I outbid him. But at the time I wasn't ready to talk about the past. Hell, months later, I'm still not ready to talk to him. For so long my objective has been to destroy the legacy my brother stole from me, but now that resolve has changed. Something changed that day on the phone. When he yelled at me, telling me his girlfriend had just struggled for her life, I've never felt like a bigger asshole. His words hurt. Hearing the pain in his words hurt. But when his voice dropped and he said, *"I want my brother back,"* any residual fuel to hurt him faded away.

I do want to talk to him, though, but so much time has passed I wouldn't know what to say. Plus, the timing isn't ideal right now. Between The L, having to monitor Chelsea and this damn girl I can't get out of my mind, I'm like a live wire or a raging inferno ready to explode.

Speaking of, I still haven't heard back from Miles, and I'm beginning to get pissed about that too. How long does it take to find out something about someone? The last few times I've called, he hasn't been around, almost like he's avoiding me. Even worse, he's out of the office for the next few days, so I won't be getting any answers any time soon. Which pisses me off. *Shit.* The need to know more about her is taking up way too much of my time. I can't be acting like this. With the opening of The L looming, I need to get my shit together. We aren't getting nearly as much press as I'd like, and if this isn't successful, I'll hear Chelsea say I told you so. She'll make my life a living hell.

My phone starts ringing again, and it's Spencer . . . *again.* It's not normal for him to call back-to-back like this. Chelsea must have done something.

I send Spencer to voicemail, refusing to deal with this now. I'll have to speak to Chelsea before I call Spencer.

Storming into her office, I see her typing away. She's still as beautiful as when I first met her. She exudes sensuality with every breath she takes. At one time I was completely enthralled by her full lips, by the passion in her deep blue eyes, but now I see through her façade. I see the bitch beneath the surface.

"What the fuck did you do?"

"Well, good morning to you, too."

"Cut the bullshit. Tell me now."

"I went ahead and did what you were too much of a pussy to do."

"I told you to drop it. I told you no more bidding against Lancaster Holdings."

"You were fine with me bidding on Manchester and St. Barts, so I decided it was in the best interest of this company to not listen to you. Now, if you have nothing else to discuss with me . . ."

"You will cease all acquisitions. Do you hear me? No more bidding. No more purchases. You will leave my family alone, Chelsea."

"Why would I do that? This is what you wanted. What was best for The L. Or don't you remember storming into my office at The Lancaster the day you found out your father sideswiped you with Spencer, demanding revenge? Funny how short your memory is right now. One visit with your brother and you're singing a different tune. Well, don't worry, Grant, my memory is long enough for the both of us. And I'll get my satisfaction."

She's right. Chelsea and I might not get along, but we've always seen eye to eye on the ruin of The Lancaster, the destruction of everything that should have been mine. But after seeing Spencer and speaking to him, that goal just doesn't seem so important anymore.

Growing my business is one thing, but doing it at the

expense of my family is another. The reasons behind my bitterness were my own doing. I see that now. Spencer isn't to be held accountable for my actions. I'm done doing shady business deals.

"I'm not singing a different tune. I still want to grow and expand. I just changed the method we use to do it. No more underhanded dealings."

"Only five months ago—"

"Stop it right there." I raise my palm in the air warningly. "I said no more, and I meant it. Leave Lancaster alone." My voice booms through her office as I turn on my heel and head to the elevator. Once alone, I let out the breath I'm holding.

She won't give up. It's not in her nature.

My hand bangs against the elevator door. *Fuck.* Until I can find a way to get her out of this company, I need to tread carefully. I take a deep inhale.

*Think.*

*What are my options?*

I can't afford a public battle now. I can't afford bad publicity for The L, and a public fight in or out of court will do just that. I need to keep my shit straight and figure out some other way to deal with Chelsea.

Grabbing my phone, I dial my attorney. "I want her out!"

"I'll see what I can do," he says, not even asking who I'm talking about. For the five years we've worked together—ever since I was ousted from Lancaster Holdings—he's known who I want out of my life. We try not to speak her name, but we both know.

Chelsea, the Chief Operating Officer of *The L*, and the biggest mistake of my life.

*My wife.*

# CHAPTER SIX

## Bridget

K NEE DEEP IN GOOGLING WAYS TO BEEF UP MY RÉSUMÉ, I don't expect my phone to ring. There's been no doubt in my mind that Karen wouldn't be calling, but there's the agency number on my phone.

"Hello," I answer, and I know my low voice gives me away. I'm nervous and scared of what she wants. It can't be good that she's calling so soon. A knot starts to form in my stomach, a feeling of impending doom hovering. If she can't find me a job, what will I do? I refuse to go to my parents for money. I refuse to admit I waited too long to get a job and now I'm desperate for work. For anything. I want to be self-sufficient. I don't want their help. I want to prove to them I can stand on my own two feet. I want to show them I'm not my sisters. I want to be *better*.

I love my sisters, but it'll be nice to have something of my own for once. Between Lynn having an affair with her high school teacher and Olivia overdosing, I've been vying for my parents' attention for years. Now it's time to focus on me—prove myself.

"Karen would like you to come to the office."

"Uh, okay."

"Can you be here within the hour?"

*Shit.* "Yes," I squeak.

"Great, I'll let her know."

With not much time to spare, I change into the power suit my mom had bought me right after I graduated from college. Nothing says stylish yet professional better than a fitted black blazer with a straight A-line skirt that falls a little above my knee. In this suit, I always feel like I can take over the world. With one last glance in the mirror, I square my shoulders and head out the door, eager to have my life begin.

---

I tap my foot nervously as she stares at me.

"I'm telling you now, if you ever want to work in this or any other industry again, you will *not* leave this next assignment early. I'm doing you a huge favor placing you somewhere else. Any other person I would show the door, you understand?"

I nod. We both know she's only doing this to avoid a legal battle, but who am I to complain. I'm getting another chance at a job. Another chance at proving I can make it in NYC on my own. To prove myself and not be compared to my sisters.

Her own head tips up in approval before she types frantically on her computer. She smiles, but the gesture is odd, not genuine at all, and I fear she's placing me with someone even worse than Matthew Lawson. *God, I hope not.*

"I've found the perfect job. It's not in marketing, but you aren't going to object, are you? It's also a longer gig."

"How long is it?"

"Minimum of three months, maybe six." She cocks her head at me.

"Where is it?" I ask, and a smirk lines her face.

"The L."

"The L?" My heart pounds in my chest.

"Is that going to be a problem?" the smug bitch asks.

*Is that going to be a problem?* Hell to the yes with "d'uh" on top. That's owned by one of the Lancaster brothers. The one who's estranged from Spencer. *What's his name again?* This has got to be a huge conflict of interest. From what I've heard—or haven't since Olivia wouldn't discuss—there's a major rift between Spencer and his recluse sibling. From what I've heard from her, she's never met him. He's rarely seen around town these past five years. Something about the imminent launch of The L, and brothers battling, but there weren't many details, not even a picture of him. He's like an elusive ghost, and every reporter is dying to sink their teeth into him.

I shouldn't take this job. But shit, I really don't have a choice. It's my last hope. "What's the position?"

"Does it matter?" She snickers.

"No," I admit sullenly.

"Good," she says in victory. She won. She knows it, and I

know it. "It's a temp position in HR, assistant work."

"I'm not really trained to be an assistant." I regret the words before they've even come out of my mouth. "I mean, it's perfect. Thank you for giving me this opportunity."

"They expect you within the hour for the interview. Although you have the job, they can still say no. So be on your best behavior. Don't embarrass me and whatever you do don't be late," she chastises.

Within the hour? I'm not ready to be interviewed. I'm not ready to try to convince them I'm right for the job. But as I look at Karen from across the desk, I just nod.

When I leave her office, I expel in relief. I hate the idea of working at The L, and I hate that I might upset Olivia. But if I can't afford my apartment, I'll have to move home with my parents. Yes, I'm sure they'd help with my rent, but I need to show them I can do this. That there's more to Bridget Miller.

———————— •◦•— ————————

Standing on the corner of Hudson Street, my mouth drops as I take in where I'll be working for the next few months. It's got to be one of the hippest and most cutting-edge hotels in the city. I know I shouldn't be this excited, but I am. This place is amazing.

I reel myself in. As much as Karen got me in the door, there's still a chance they'll tell me I'm not right for the job. I quickly get out my phone and type in the name of the hotel, then start scrolling.

I already know the hotel is owned by the brother of my sister's boyfriend. But other than the fact they have a turbulent relationship—to say the least—I know nothing at all about the family. Hell, I hardly know Spencer. The boys are supposed to be renowned for their looks and money, but there ends my knowledge. I only met Spencer the one time, and Lord, was I drunk. Story of my life apparently.

I locate The L in my search. Seeing the name Grant Lancaster and the words More Information has me furrowing my brow. Grant. That name has the effect of a tsunami on my system. The guy who left me in the goddamn alley was also a Grant. My cheeks start to flush with embarrassment. Being left hot and bothered has to go down as one of the most mortifying moments of my life. Not much can top that. Hopefully, my boss won't be as hot as the man from the other night because that would be torture. Worse than waterboarding. That man was way too hot. His lips as they branded my skin, too much . . .

I shake off thoughts of him having already spent too much time wasted on that man. I only have a few more minutes until they call me back into my interview. I need to find out more about The L. I'm just about to click the button to learn something useful when I hear my name being called out. I put the phone away. Hopefully, my bullshit meter is on high, or I'm pretty much fucked. With a giant smile on my face, albeit false, I wipe my sweaty hands on my jacket and make my way to the office. I haven't even made it through the door before the young pretty woman inside begins speaking.

"Thanks for coming on such short notice. I can't tell you how much we appreciate it. We're so happy to have you here." She smiles warmly. "I'm Paige."

I beam up at her. I can't believe she's thanking me. "Thank you. I'm thrilled to be here."

"Great. So, as a temp, you'll be working alongside one of us in this department," she says while typing fiercely on her computer. "Unfortunately, I'm not sure who you'll be assigned to, but they'll get it figured out over the weekend." She looks up. "Monday morning you can come straight here, and then someone will get you all situated. Do you have any questions?"

"Do you have any idea what I'll be doing? I'd love to pre-pare if at all possible."

"I have a feeling you might be working alongside me, which would consist of running errands, making copies, typical HR stuff. But we'll only know for certain on Monday. Are you fine with that?"

I wonder for a brief second what Paige would say if I responded with a no. That I'm way too overqualified to be someone's bitch, but honestly, I'd do anything she told me to at this point just to not have to swallow my pride and ask for help. "Of course. That sounds great. I'm happy to work anywhere within the hotel. So I'm officially starting on Monday?"

"Yes, Monday, eight o'clock. Straight to HR. Things are still a bit all over the place, so please bear with us. You'll need to fill out these forms today so I can process your ID card for

Monday." She rummages through her desk and hands me a few stacks of papers and then grabs a pen. "And here is a packet of paperwork you'll need to read and sign by Monday. We'll need all of that back before you can begin work. If you don't have any questions, you're good to go."

A minute later, I've filled out the forms and hand them to Paige while I stand.

"I'll see you Monday morning." I smile widely.

"Looking forward to it," Paige remarks before turning her focus back to her computer.

As I leave The L, I marvel at how easy the whole thing has been. Well, everything after the whole Axis debacle. Maybe Karen will soften to me yet. Doubtful. Surprisingly, I'm starting to feel better about this despite my earlier reservations. The L might not be a nightmare after all, as long as Olivia doesn't have a fit. I can't give my sister enough thanks for setting this up, although I'm sure she wouldn't be thrilled to know she placed me right in the path of her man's estranged family.

I spend the next hour walking around the hotel, trying to gather my bearings. I need to know that when I start on Monday, I'll feel confident and comfortable in my surroundings. The place is so big, but it has a nice flow to the layout, making it easy to navigate. I'm confident I'll be much better off here than at Axis. The hotel is beautiful, and it seems to be the perfect place for me to build my résumé. Hopefully, by the end of my position, I'll have made connections to take away with me.

I'm still smiling when I make my way outside. Turning around for one more look before I pass through the wide glass doors back into the hallway, I notice a handsome young man smiling back at me.

"You look happy." He chuckles.

I snap out of my reverie and grin up at the stranger. "Sorry, I'm in my own world. I just got a temp job here. I start on Monday. Hence the crazy smile on my face."

"Nice. I'm an intern here. I started a few months ago, and trust me, we need the extra staff. You'll like it, though. It's a cool place. I'm Jared, by the way."

"I'm Bridget. Nice to meet you. I've got to get going, but I'll see you around."

He quirks an eyebrow as his lips part into a sexy smirk.

I can't help but grin as I walk out. He's cute. This is gearing up to be a rather perfect position.

# CHAPTER SEVEN

## Bridget

MONDAY MORNING ROLLS AROUND, AND BEFORE I know it, I'm walking through the door to the HR department. Paige is already there to greet me. She holds the door to her office open and points to the chair.

"Good morning, Bridget. Glad you came back." She beams.

"I'm here and ready to go," I assure her with a smile.

"Right, hmm, let me see," she says while she riffles through some pages on her desk. "Ah, yes, here we go. Okay, so you were supposed to be in the HR department, but there's been some changing in personnel, and our COO requested that you be moved up to help on the top level."

"Top level?" I'm not sure what that even means.

"You'll be filling a position as an executive assistant in top-level corporate. It's quite a jump, but you seem the sort of woman who can handle that beautifully."

*I do?* I wonder if Paige is perhaps mistaking me for someone she spoke to in more depth. I doubt my résumé makes me suitable for such a position. Perhaps I should say something, but I don't have the time as Paige is already standing and directing me where to go. I look behind me and see that another woman is waiting to meet with her.

"O-Okay. Thanks, Paige. Anything I should know before I go up?"

I'm sure there's a whole manual of shit I should know, but they'll soon find out how unqualified I am to temp in the hotel much less for C-suite. I do quick work of smoothing out my skirt, hoping like hell I don't look like the mess I feel right now.

"They'll run through everything with you when you get there. Have a great day, and welcome to the team."

Her words don't do anything to soothe my unease, but I plaster on my fakest smile and move toward my new job. The whole way to the top floor I rein in my fidgeting and work on my breathing. I can do this. I'm Bridget fucking Miller, and I can do this. I keep repeating the mantra, hoping like hell it'll stick by the time I get there. Once I make it to the stairs, I'm already more relaxed.

I find the door with ease and smooth out my outfit one last time. *You can do this.* I straighten my spine and knock.

"Come in," a gruff male voice commands from the inside.

I open the door, and the world tilts. The floor falls out from underneath me, and I can't contain the gasp that slips through my lips when I spot the man sitting behind the big wooden desk.

*Grant.*

Looking even sexier than the other night . . . when he left me . . . alone . . . in a dark alley. Asshat. *Oh my God . . .*

This can't be right. Only it can.

It so. Goddamn. Can.

*Grant. Grant Lancaster. Grant-Fucking-Lancaster.* Oh, my God.

"What the hell are you doing here?" he scuffs.

"I . . . I work here." For several seconds, I stand there, openly staring at him while he stares back. My mouth is agape, and his is pressed into a hard, disapproving line. He clearly had no idea either.

"How did you get up here?" he demands.

"Paige sent me up from HR. She said I was to report here."

Grant picks up a folder and opens it. His lips pinch tightly. "Bridget Miller," he reads. "There's no way in hell this is happening. You can't work for me."

My stomach sours on multiple levels. The contempt in his voice has me feeling so small and pathetic. The look he gave me back in the alley floods my memory, and I feel like I could be sick. It's not bad enough that he humiliated me that night, but he's treating me like trash he discarded on the side of the road.

How did this happen?

How did I not recognize him?

How did I not know he was *the* Grant Lancaster?

"Please go back down to Paige and tell her I've discharged you. I'll write a decent exit letter for you, but you have to go."

"You kissed me," I say, because in truth I don't know what

else to say. I'm numb. Between his attitude and the fact that yet another freaking job seems to be going down the drain, I want to crawl into a ball in the corner and cry.

Grant's eyes widen, his brows furrowing in confusion and then anger. "For God's sake, close the door behind you. Do you really want everyone listening in on our conversation?"

I quickly shut the door and then sit in the chair opposite his desk. He glares at me, and I wonder briefly how he manages to remain so good-looking when he's so angry. And how, at a time like this, I can think about how good-looking he is. But how can I not? In the light of the day, he's even more perfect than he was on Thursday. In this light, I can see the green of his eyes. They're the green of sunlight on grass after the ice has thawed. Mossy and overgrown. Begging to be cared for. Or maybe the green of a tropical ocean during a storm. Troubled and reckless.

Shaking my head, I pull my gaze away from his hypnotic eyes only to have it land on his mouth instead. His lips. His lips are temptation and sin. They bring back a stream of memories of how they felt pressed against mine. Of how he tasted as he devoured me. *Fuck.* They make me want to lose myself in him all over again. I have to break away. Look somewhere else. My eyes focus out the window at the giant skyscrapers across the street from our building.

"Why are you still here?" he grates, pulling me out of my thoughts. Our gazes collide. His eyes are almost closed. They appear cold, hard . . . far away. But as far away as he seems, his stare still burns me as if I'm his enemy. As if I've done

56

this on purpose.

Not knowing what to do, I stay seated. Rooted in place. Completely frozen. Finally shaking my head once, I will words to come out of my mouth. "Maybe it's because I don't know what to do with myself. I'm confused. Or maybe it's because I *need* this job. Take your damn pick," I spit harshly.

"Did you know who I was all along?" he hisses.

"What?"

"At the lounge. Did you know it was me?" The words lash out and make me recoil. "Did you know who I was and that you were going to work for me, so you decided to flirt with me?"

"No." I feel anger bubbling in my chest, simmering quietly, but steadily, as the implication of what he is saying hits me. "I didn't."

"You clearly knew who I was. I can see it all over your face."

His harsh words and cold demeanor have me forgetting all about our time together. Right now I just want to slap the arrogant ass upside the head. "You have a very high opinion of yourself, Mr. Lancaster. Not everyone wants to snag a tycoon brother with a family that keeps the majority of New York's local tabloids alive." I roll my eyes, sarcasm oozing from every pore of my body.

"But yet just the other day you were panting all over my hand, asking me to fuck you," he lashes out.

I'm too shocked to speak, my mouth hanging open, unable to form words.

"You're just like all the other women. You knew it was me, so you tried to seduce me to get what you wanted. You use people for their money. You use people to get ahead in your life while you sit back and do nothing." His vile words snap me out of my stupor.

"Have you lost your mind?" I yell. "You are the one who kissed me, remember? I hardly even registered your existence. *You* offered me a drink. *You* took me out. *You* kissed me in a goddamn dumpster—thanks for that, by the way, way to boost a girl's ego. This is all on you."

Grant pulls at his hair, clearly frustrated. "As far as I'm concerned that night never happened. Do you understand?"

"I couldn't care less. That's a night I'd rather forget." The lie tastes sour on my tongue. "For the record, I didn't ask to be your assistant. I'm barely getting paid for this. I'm just a temp, and this is only to build my résumé so I can get a job worth having."

"So The L isn't good enough for you?" he sneers.

"Right now no. You're making it damn difficult for me to actually do my job. This was just assigned to me. Paige sent me up here herself. She said they're desperate, so when I quit in five minutes, you can deal with that shit show."

"You expect me to believe this is some ridiculous coincidence?"

"To be honest, I don't give a damn what you think. At this point, I'm pretty sure you're certifiable, and I don't have time for this." I turn to stalk out when his words stop me short.

"Stay."

Is this man on drugs? Between his insults and accusations, the last place I want to be is anywhere near him, but I stop despite my better senses. "Why? Tell me why I should stay to listen to anything you have to say."

"I just need to figure this all out. You're right, we are desperate for help, and Paige might kill me if I release yet another assistant."

I huff. "So you make a habit of pissing people off."

He lifts up his hand to stifle a long, drawn-out groan. "You're just like my wife. No wonder you're driving me insane."

# CHAPTER EIGHT

## Bridget

MY WIFE.
*My wife.*
*My wife.*

He has a wife.

He was married while he took me out to the back alley. When his hands touched me, he had a wife. A wife who might have been there at the lounge. A wife who probably had been there. Oh my God. A wife.

What did that make me?

Holy shit. This man—this adulterer—is angry at me for coming up to his office today. An office I was hired to work at. One in which I most certainly did not know he'd be.

"Are you even listening to me?" he asks.

I snap out of my reverie and look at him. He's glaring at me, but at the same time, his forehead is furrowed in confusion.

"You're married." There's no mistaking the bite in my voice. It drips over my words, making him flinch.

"Well, yes, but—"

"Every action that night you instigated, and now, somehow, you're mad at me? Is that really what's going on?" I speak with a calmness that surprises even me.

"Listen, you don't know anything. You have no idea what—"

"I don't know who you are. You might be a big shot here, but that doesn't mean everyone in the outside world knows who Grant Lancaster is. I wasn't meant to work at this hotel. I had another job all lined up, but they canceled it at the last minute. Not that it's any of your business."

"None of my business? I think it *is* my business how you ended up in my hotel."

"My options were slim, so when I got the opportunity to work at this hotel, I grabbed it. I literally ran over for the interview without even a chance to do my research. So I'm sorry if I don't know who the great Grant Lancaster is." I stand and shake my head. I don't need to be treated like this. "I'm leaving."

"Sit down," he says. "I need an assistant, and you need a job. That's all there is to it. Yes, I'm married. I'm also your boss, but I don't owe you anything more. So what's it going to be?" His words are like a million daggers slicing at every part of my being. They tear me down and leave me bleeding, but what can I do? He's giving me an option to stay regardless of what happened.

Closing my eyes, I consider my options. I could leave. I could. But then where will I be? I won't get another shot with

Karen. And truth be told, this is my best bet in proving how different from my sisters I am.

*I'm not different at all.*

The bitter irony hits me in the face. No matter how I try, no matter what I do, I'm destined to be exactly like them. Case in point, bumping into the stranger from the bar. The parallels are uncanny, this is what happened to Lynn. I'm a cosmic tragedy. Every time I try to be different, I just cement how similar to them I am.

*No. I am different.*

I can stand on my own two feet. My future is dictated only by me.

My chin lifts, and I meet his stare. The venom I just witnessed is replaced with another expression. One I can't place. I barely know this man. All I know is that he's married. He cheated on his wife with me, but I'm probably not the first or last. What happened that night was his fault, not mine. I'm not married, and I most certainly didn't know he was. He's in the wrong, and I can live with that knowledge.

"I need this job, and you need an assistant. Let's leave it at that."

# CHAPTER NINE

## Grant

I DIAL THE HUMAN RESOURCES DEPARTMENT.

"Hello, Mr. Lancaster. How can I help you?" Paige says through the phone. Her voice is low, timid, as if she knows I'm a ticking time bomb.

"Bridget Miller, who hired her?" The aggression in my voice is evident.

"Is there a problem with Ms. Miller, sir?" she squeaks.

"How did she come to work here?" I snap.

"Mrs. Lancaster hired her."

*What the hell?* Why would Chelsea hire Bridget Miller?

A sinking feeling rushes through me. Does she know about Bridget and me? Did she find out what I've done, and if she does know, how will she make me pay?

"Is everything okay, Mr. Lancaster? Do you need me to—"

"Everything is fine," I cut her off, hanging up the phone call before she can get a word in edgewise. I need to get to the bottom of this. How does Chelsea know Bridget, and why would she hire her? Slamming the phone down, the sound echoes through the room. Without a moment to waste, I head toward her office.

"Why are you hiring me a new assistant?" I shout as I slam the door behind me.

"Well, you needed one." She purses her lips. "Is she not to your liking?"

"How did you come across her?"

She smiles a malicious smile. How did I ever want this woman? "I have a friend who owns a temp agency, and she called me with a tip. The girl's sister is dating Spencer."

"What are you talking about?"

"Her sister, Olivia, is Spencer's new love interest," she purrs, and all the muscles in my back tighten.

"What are you up to?"

"Me? Up to something? Don't be silly, dear."

"I told you I was done. And I am done. I'm not sure what you're planning, but this girl has nothing to do with it."

"Of course she doesn't. I just knew you needed a new assistant, and when I heard you asked Miles to look into her, I found it . . . *interesting*. Was I wrong to assume she meant something to you?" She narrows her eyes at me, and I will myself to not give anything away. Not to give her the bait she needs to make my life an even bigger shit show. Because right now with everything else going on, with the impending opening of The L, a volatile Chelsea is not what I need. I grit my teeth and try to remain calm.

"Were you looking to hire someone, or was there another

reason you had the head of security for The L look into some girl?"

My mouth opens and shuts as I try to come up with a plausible answer.

"You have to admit, Grant, hiring her could be beneficial to our cause. She may have inside information. Is this going to be a problem?"

"I said we're dropping the shit with my brother, Chelsea. No more."

"Don't be silly. I don't want to stir up anything else. She just might know if he plans to retaliate. Don't make an issue where there isn't one. We don't want problems, do we?"

She has me. I can't afford to piss off Chelsea. Not now. Not yet. Maybe not ever. Maybe I did this on purpose. Maybe subconsciously, I wanted to get caught. To find a way out of the hellhole I'm in. But there's no way out. None that won't hurt Isabella. I made my bed. Now I need to lie in it, no matter how crappy the goddamn mattress is, and it's pretty fucking bad.

Once again Chelsea has ruined something that was just for me. She's blindsided me, and in turn, I've managed to offend the second person who made me feel something other than regret for the first time in years. Bridget was one moment just for me. For that one moment, I tasted bliss. In her mouth, I found it. But behind every kiss was a lesson. A bitter one. Reminding and reiterating the one thing I should have never forgotten.

Nothing comes without a price.

Most importantly no one can be trusted. Not even myself. I never should have trusted Miles.

Why did he tell Chelsea about my interest is Bridget? What's in it for him?

*I can't trust anyone.* Not even my own team.

There was a time I trusted my brother. He was the only person I could rely on. As my older brother, Spencer would have reminded me I had choices and could leave. Start over. But that was then, and this is now. He'd never understand. Everything falls into place for him. Nothing works out for me. Case in point, my new assistant. What am I going to do about this massive fuck up?

Fuck. I have to be at least ten years older than her. But when she was looking at me at the bar, and when we got outside and she was pressed against the wall of the building, all I could do—all I could think about—was how much I needed to be inside her.

I just agreed to work with this girl, but I can't do it. I don't have the strength. When she stands in front of me, all I'm reminded of is her taste. When she exhales in a huff, the moans that escaped her mouth come crashing into my mind. I should have told her to resign.

She's the one person who makes me feel. It's been so long. I never thought I'd feel that way again. The need. The desire. I thought that part of me had died. But she awakened an unquenchable hunger. It gnaws in my gut. Having her for even five minutes was too much. Trying to resist will be torture. Even now, I want to bend her over my desk and plunge into her heat. I want to taste the fire inside her. Bask in her. Empty everything I've held back into her. Lose myself in her.

*It can never happen.*

The door opens, and a very different Bridget walks in. When she first walked into my office today, the spark was there. But after I berated her, it's as if I ignited a fire inside her. She's determined not to let me get to her. I can see it, and damn if it isn't the sexiest thing.

"Mr. Lancaster. Here are the papers you asked for," she spits out.

She hates me, and fuck if it doesn't sting.

# CHAPTER TEN

## Bridget

THE FIRST DAY OF BEING GRANT'S ASSISTANT HASN'T gone well at all.

I saw a small glimpse of kindness in him the night I went to the lounge, and I kept hoping it would return, but it hasn't. Today has been awful and slow. All he seems to do is bark orders at me, and for the most part, he's sent me all over the hotel so he didn't have to be near me. At noon, with my stomach growling, I walk into his office.

"What time should I be eating lunch?"

He lifts his head, then looks over at his computer. I assume he's dismissed me, and I'm not sure what to do when he looks back at me.

"Did you bring something to eat?"

"Uh, no."

"Well, then, make your way to the restaurant and give them your work card. The food is free for those who work here. Why don't you know this?" he grumbles, still not looking up from his computer.

"I do know this, but I don't have a work card. They never gave me one."

A loud groan emanates from him, then he finally looks up at me. "Head over to HR and get one but be back here by one."

"Got it." I walk out.

I'm glad to get out of his office. But mostly I have no idea how I'm ever going to work with him. It's only been half a day, and already it's been like torture.

I make my way to HR and knock on Paige's door. "Hey, good to see you. I hope you're having a wonderful day." She smiles tentatively. "You've really saved our skin here."

"About that. Any chance there's anywhere else you can place me?"

"Is there an issue with Mr. Lancaster?" Paige's voice sounds surprised, but the pinched expression on her face speaks volumes. She knows damn well that working for that man is intolerable. I won't tell her the truth for so many obvious reasons, but I really need to try to get relocated.

"No, nothing's wrong. I just don't think I'm suited for that position, and I really don't want to let anyone down," I lie.

"I'm sure you'll do wonderfully. If Mr. Lancaster himself has yet to complain, you must be doing something right." Paige's face is hopeful. "There really isn't any other place I can put you that is more needed. Mr. Lancaster is in dire need of an assistant. Mrs. Lancaster placed you herself."

My stomach sours at the mention of Mrs. Lancaster.

"She did?" How ironic that of all the candidates she'd

choose me. It's absolutely insane.

"Yes. And whatever she says goes. She's amazing. You'll never meet anyone like her. She's a genius."

A sick feeling weaves its way through me. Hearing that Mr. Lancaster's wife is perfect brings back old feelings I don't want. The idea of him comparing me to her makes bile rise in my mouth. Is that why he stopped us? Did he kiss me because he was drunk and then realized I wasn't as perfect as his wife? I feel ill, but I don't want Paige noticing, so I give a tight smile and nod before changing the topic. "Can I get my work card? It's time for lunch."

"Of course. I can't believe I forgot. Let me print one out for you. It has a special barcode so you can't get them reprinted outside. Yours will be unique to everyone else's. They scan it at the staff restaurant to make sure you only use it once a day. It has a price limit, but it's quite high, so I doubt you'll ever reach it."

Perks. At least working for this asshole has some perks. "You don't know how much I like to eat," I force out.

Paige laughs, and my sour mood starts to lighten. "A woman after my own heart." She presses some buttons and stands. "Okay, here we go. If you're looking for suggestions, the pulled pork toasted sandwich is a winner."

"Thank you. I'll give it a try." I smile while walking backward out the door, finally feeling more like myself. "See you around."

I make my way downstairs to the restaurant that's designated for the staff and place my bag down on an unoccupied table. The place is busy. It's a cafeteria-style restaurant, so I head to the counter and order the pulled pork sandwich and a cappuccino. Once it's placed on my tray, I head back over to my table and sit down to watch the crowd around me. I've always been a bit of a people watcher. I love to concoct my own stories of what's going on in other people's lives. Also, not knowing anyone who works here, it's a great way to pass the time. As I go to take a bite of my sandwich, a familiar figure smiles and walks up to me. It's good to see Jared, and I relax into my seat at the idea of not being alone.

"Mind if I join you?"

I smile. "Of course not."

He places his own tray down and smiles. "So, first day. What did you order?" He glances over at my food.

"The pulled pork sandwich. Paige said it's amazing."

"Paige is right." He winks, and I peek at his tray.

I laugh. "We ordered the same thing."

"We clearly have good taste."

I take a bite and grin. "Whoa. This is amazing."

"This place has one of the best chefs in the city. His name is Porter Brown, but everyone calls him Portobello. They like to fuck with him."

I giggle. "Nice, I won't forget that one."

"So, how's the first day going?"

"It's . . . going." I wish it was flying. Or better yet—over.

He tilts his head. "Where did you end up?"

"I actually ended up in corporate. I'm with Mr. Lancaster."

"No shit." He chuckles. "I've never even met him. Word

around town is he's impossible to work for. He's been through three assistants this month alone. Apparently, he's very private. Never shows up to anything. Likes to sit in his penthouse office looking down his nose at us commoners." He shakes his head.

"Yeah . . . he's a peach," I groan. "Can't say the rumors aren't true."

"Wow, that sucks. It'll be excellent experience, though."

I reach for my mug and take a sip of my cappuccino, which is delicious, and shake my head. "If I can tolerate him long enough. He's not the friendliest guy in the world."

Jared laughs. "Yeah, I've heard stories. In business, he's a shark, and in his personal life . . . well, talking about his personal life will get you fired."

"Are people scared of him?"

"Absolutely. But that doesn't mean you have to be."

"Oh, I'm not scared of him. I just don't particularly like him."

Jared laughs. "Stick it out, and you'll have your pick of jobs."

"I'll do my best."

We spend the rest of lunch talking about all other aspects of The L. Jared seems to genuinely like his job, which is something.

After lunch, I return to the office in a better mood. Jared is a good guy, and I enjoyed his company. I'm feeling light and happy for a change until the moment I see Grant again. My bad mood returns instantly. He looks up at me, his gaze steely, then he looks down at his watch. I wasn't even gone an hour. I place my hand on my hip and wait for him to say something.

"Good lunch?" The sarcastic bite isn't lost on me. He acts as if going to lunch is something I shouldn't be doing.

"Yeah, it was delicious. Did you eat?" My retort is heavy on my tongue.

"I'm too busy."

"I would've brought you something. I can go now." I desperately want to get away from here and his temper.

"No, we have work to do," he says. "I can't have you sitting there all day. I'm going to set you up in the office across the hall with your own computer. I'll have a list of work for you to get through."

I'm relieved. I've been scared I'd somehow end up in his office, right in front of him. That would have been horrific.

# CHAPTER ELEVEN

## Grant

THE GODDAMN WEEKEND IS FINALLY HERE. I BARELY made it through the week with having Bridget as my assistant. Lucky for me, I gave her so much work she barely had time to breathe, let alone seek me out. You'd think after the hell I've been through, I'd be excited to be home, but right now thinking about seeing Chelsea I dread it even more than I dread seeing Bridget at work. But I'm home, so I should probably walk in instead of dragging my feet. There's no way around it. Seeing Chelsea is a necessary evil. Isabella is in there, and she needs her father as much as I need her.

"Baby, you're making me hot," Chelsea's voice croons into her phone. "Say it again."

I peak around the corner to see Chelsea laid back on the couch picking at her nails. If her head were turned toward me, I'd probably see her rolling her eyes at whoever is on the other line. Chelsea hates phone sex or any sort of foreplay at all. She's just a big fucking tease, and my guess is she's got the poor sucker on the other line eating out of the palm of her hand. I know too well how easily one can be taken by Chelsea's games. Poor bastard. I'm just glad she's not my problem anymore.

*She's your biggest problem.*

I cringe at the truth in those words.

Striding toward my whore of a wife, I stop dead in my tracks when I see our daughter playing at her feet, listening to every fucking horrible word her mother utters. My blood heats in anger.

"You want me, come get me," Chelsea says, scrunching her nose in disgust at her own words. She looks up at me, unfazed at being caught in the act. "Baby, I've got to run," she says while looking me straight in the eye.

The fucking nerve of this woman.

"I'm sorry. You go take care of that and think of me." She grins at me as though I give a shit about her games. I don't. I couldn't care less about whatever guy she's fucking behind my back now. It's the fact that she's doing it in front of our daughter that has me livid.

"Hello, darling. How was your day?"

"Daddy," Isabella says. "You're here." I look down at her on the floor and plaster on my fakest smile. No need to show her how angry I am.

"Hi, baby girl. Play with your dolls. Mommy and I are going to have a talk."

"Okay," she says, going back to her toys.

"Get up, Chelsea. Don't make me move you myself," I say

as quietly as I can, not wanting to scare our child.

She rolls her eyes but stands to follow me.

When we're out of earshot of Isabella, I lay into her. "Are you fucking kidding me? You have the nerve to do that in my house?" I roar.

"Did that bother you?" Her lips tip up in a cat-like smile.

"I couldn't care less about you. It's not like it's the first time. How many times has it been, Chelsea?"

"Wouldn't you like to know. If you don't care, then stop asking questions."

"Oh, I don't. This marriage has been over for a long time."

"Yes, it has," she snips. "This is a marriage of convenience, and that's all. I'd be happy to leave."

"Please. Do us both a favor and get the hell out."

"I could," she draws, "but you and I both know what that means for you. So, Grant, what will it be?" She trails her perfectly sculpted nails down my chest. I know what she's implying. The threat of her taking Isabella from me hangs heavy in the air.

"Stay for all I care then. But don't pretend you want Isabella. You continue to prove that all she is to you is a pawn. You don't love her. You only love yourself."

"Have it your way. But don't tell me who I can and can't fuck," she spits, turning to storm out of the room.

What the hell did I get myself into when I married her? My pride has done nothing but fuck me over royally. When will I ever learn?

The weekend crept by in a slow drawl. I couldn't wait to get back to work. Normally I would have been at the hotel, especially since we're opening to the public soon, but after Chelsea's neglect, I took the weekend to be with Isabella. Now it's Monday, and I'm back. I'd like to say I've been hard at work, but that would be a lie. Instead, I've sat here for hours thinking about nothing but *her*. When I walked in this morning all pissed about life, I took it out on Bridget, screaming, barking orders. The girl must think I'm a complete nutjob. Have I always been so horrible? Now I can't help replay each moment since she started working for me. The way her nose crinkles in frustration whenever I challenge her. The way she breathes deeply trying to stave off the words I know she wants to say but doesn't dare for the sake of her job. Fuck. She's exquisite when she's pissed, and I'm doing a bang-up job making her nothing but. I can't help it. Being an asshole is the easiest way to keep her at arm's length. If she gets too close, I'll cave. The flowery smell of her hair, the mint on her breath, I'll come undone.

Instead, I need to focus on the task at hand. I have a mound of paperwork to work through, and so far I've been staring at the same document for over an hour. Fuck. This distraction isn't good for business. I can't focus on legal docs, so I place it to the side and pick up the folder from my investigator.

I've hired someone to keep an eye on Chelsea and retrieve all her passcodes for me. I'm monitoring her company phone records, emails—anything to catch her in the act so I can build a case to throw her out on her ass. It seems like a good plan, but at the end of the day, I know it's worthless. She has me by the balls. I'd do anything for our daughter, and she knows it.

All I'm really doing is keeping an eye on her involvement where my family is concerned. If I'm two steps ahead of her, she can't really do too much damage, can she? I think that thought too soon. As I'm looking through the email logs, I stop short when I see an email to Karen, Bridget's recruiter.

Hello, Chelsea,

I'm sorry it's taken me so long to get back to you. I haven't spoken to Olivia Miller in some time, but she finally called today. From our conversation, it would appear she is not aware that Bridget has been placed with The L, and I can assure you the news of her working directly with Grant would not come as good news.

To follow up on our conversation regarding The Lancaster, they are currently seeking a new marketing director for their European market. I don't know what they are looking to do, but they are looking for someone with a very impressive résumé. Whatever they have planned, it's big.

I hope the tip helps. Looking forward to drinks soon.

Best,

Karen

I will myself to calm down. The worst thing that could happen is me snapping at the office. I've never put my hands on a woman, but I'd make an exception for her. She never fucking stops.

# CHAPTER TWELVE

## Bridget

I'M SITTING AT A RESTAURANT ACROSS THE STREET FROM THE hotel about to have lunch with Lynn. It's the first time she's come to visit me for lunch, and I'm excited to see a friendly face. An older woman walks over to our table. Her hair is white like a dove, and her face is etched with lines signifying years of hard work. She hands us our menus, and as she walks away, I start to fidget with the salt and pepper shakers. Lynn is my best friend, but right now I feel awkward. There's so much to tell her, and I don't know where to begin.

"So . . ." She points to the hotel. "That's where you work?"

I nod.

"It's beautiful from the outside."

"It is, isn't it? They sure know how to design a beautiful hotel."

"What's it look like from the inside?"

"Insane. It literally goes on forever."

"I need to check it out once it opens."

My brow rises in question.

"We all need a break every now and then. I like staycations." She shrugs.

"Noted," I reply before I start to fidget uncomfortably. As I'm about to try to change the topic, the waitress comes over and we both order. I think maybe the distraction is enough to get me out of my confession, but just as I'm coming up with something to say, Lynn beats me to the punch.

"What's up, Bridge? You seem off."

"I have to tell you something, but you can't tell Olivia."

Lynn's forehead scrunches. "I'm not sure I can make that promise," she responds as she pinches the bridge of her nose. "You know I'm not good at keeping secrets."

*You used to be.*

After Lynn lied to me for months about her affair with her teacher, I made her promise to tell me everything. Now she's an open book. The only problem is that now if I tell her about my job, I run the risk she might tell Olivia.

"It's really not a big deal. I, um, the hotel—" Anxiety knots in my shoulders and I lift my hand to massage the corded muscles.

"Just spit it out."

I hate that I have to tell her this. I hate that I've put myself in this position, but I did. And Lynn and I have no secrets. Not anymore, not since high school, so I need to tell her. "It's owned by Spencer's brother."

Her mouth drops open. "That's The L?"

"Yep."

"Shit."

"I know. Can you not say anything? I'm not sure what's going on. For all I know I'll be out of a job in a week." I grimace.

"Why? What's up?"

"You remember the guy I kissed?"

"Dumpster Dude?"

"Lynn!" But hey, brownie points to her for finding a catchy pet name for him.

She smirks.

"Yes, the guy in the alley. Well, he's, um . . . Grant Lancaster."

"Wait. Stop. The guy you made out with is Grant Lancaster? As in Spencer's brother?"

"Try to keep up, will you," I chide.

Her mouth continues to hang open as she takes it all in.

"Oh my God, he's your boss? You have the worst freaking luck."

"You're an ass."

"You really are screwed."

"Lynn," I warn.

"Fine. I won't say anything else."

"Can we change the topic now? What are you ordering? I'm buying today," I offer.

"What? No, you don't have to do that."

"I've been working at a hotel for eight days already. That's eight days that I've gotten free lunch. I think I can afford to buy yours today."

Lynn grins. "Well, I'm not complaining. So, eight days

already, huh? How's it going with dumpster man being the boss?" she belts out.

I cringe. Does she really have to be so loud? And here?

"Shh." I shake my head back and forth, and her eyes widen. "You're so loud. Plus, this really isn't a conversation to have here." I know I mentioned it first, but in hindsight, that was dumb of me. "A lot of employees eat here when they want to leave the hotel." I look around, but no one I recognize is here.

"He's a miserable bastard," I whisper. "That guy changes his moods more often than I change my underwear. Way more."

"Have you talked about what happened?"

I scrunch my nose. "We did. Briefly." Remembering our first encounter has me going rigid. "But it didn't go well."

"Oh, yeah," she says. "Why's that?"

The waitress chooses this exact moment to return with our food. Neither of us eats as Lynn just looks at me impatiently, waiting for my answer, her fork tapping on her plate as she waits.

"He's married."

With that, she drops her fork on the plate and the sound echoes around me like a freight train. My face warms, and I want to hide from her scrutiny.

"What the actual fuck! Are you serious?"

"I wish I wasn't." I push my hands through my hair, pulling at the roots. "It's all too much."

"What did you do?"

"What the hell could I do? I yelled. He yelled back. In the end, I conceded because as scary as he is when he's angry, Karen Michelle is even worse."

"Wow. I don't envy you, girl."

"Thanks," I say dryly. "Anyway, you can't breathe a word of this, Lynn."

"Promise." She chews on her lip. "Have you asked anyone about him? Does he cheat on his wife often?"

"I thought about it, but the last thing I need is for Mr. Lancaster to figure out that I'm asking around about him. He'll be even madder than before. Plus, I don't need anything fishy getting around to his wife. She works here too from what I've gathered."

"Oh shit. It's too much. Just remember, you won't be here forever. You're enjoying it, right? Other than the crazy boss drama?"

I consider the question. As much as me and my "crazy" boss don't get along, I do like the actual work.

"Yeah, I do like it here."

"You still want to get into marketing after this? Or do you like the hotel business now?"

I smile. "I still think marketing is the right job for me, but I'm liking the hotel business now. Who knows, maybe I can get a good recommendation and all my time here and having to endure hell will be worth it."

"Way to remain positive. You sound more mature already."

I stick my tongue out at her just to prove I'm still the

sister she's always loved.

I fill the silence by lifting my fork. After taking a few bites, Lynn groans in delight.

"If I worked across the street, I'd be here every day. No wonder you haven't quit yet. This food is amazing. Better than any sex a Lancaster could perform."

"Har, har, har. Really funny, but yeah. It's amazing, isn't it? I don't come here often, though. The food at the hotel is ridiculous. Oh, there's Jared." I wave through the glass window as he walks down the block.

"He's cute," Lynn says.

"He is. And he's a good guy. The two of us get along pretty well."

"And? Anything else?" She leans forward onto the table and smiles.

"What? You mean anything between us?"

"Well, yeah. He's cute. You're cute. Come on, man."

I laugh. "Definitely not. He knows he's cute. And he's not my type."

"Oh, yeah? Who's your type, exactly?"

I shrug. "Now, that's something I don't know. But it's not Jared, that's for sure."

We're almost finished with our lunch when I see Grant walking down the street toward us. My heart starts pounding in my chest. Please don't come here. Unfortunately, he does. He pulls the door open, and when he steps inside, he spots me. He narrows his eyes, and I meet his stare. Neither of us says hello. He walks in the opposite direction to a table

AVA HARRISON

on the other side of the restaurant. He's with two other men that I figure are part of the new hotel. I saw in the calendar earlier that he had a meeting to attend, but I didn't recognize the names, and he obviously decided to change the location because I would have never come here if he'd noted this restaurant.

"Oh, good," I say. "Mr. Lancaster is only starting his meeting now, and my lunch hour is almost up. Which means I get at least an hour of peace. I work better without him there watching what I do."

"Hang on a second. That guy who just walked in . . . *He's* your boss? He's the guy you kissed? *He's* Lancaster?"

"Speak softly!" I hiss. I look around, but nobody is listening.

"Sorry, sorry. But seriously, that's the guy?" Lynn asks.

"Yes," I groan.

"He's freaking gorgeous, and I hate to break it to you, but he really hates you. What's that all about?"

"Thanks, Lynn. Ever considered becoming a therapist? You have such a way with words." I shift uncomfortably in my seat.

"Do you like him?"

"What? No!" I move back in my seat and cross my arms over my chest.

"Oh my God, Bridge. You know you can't go there again. Right?"

I can feel my face warming. Damn my pale face! "No. Obviously. God, you're making me blush for no reason. I

86

don't like him. I actually hate him. I thought we covered that. He's emotionally unstable, and I definitely don't like him."

"Then why are you blushing?"

"Because I blush easily, you know that. It means nothing."

"No matter what, you sure have some good eye candy there for you."

I peek at where Grant is sitting and try not to get caught staring. He sits tall and assured, owning the room with his very presence. The meeting must be going well because he appears to be more relaxed than I've seen him since that night. As I watch his mouth move, I'm reminded of the kiss. I sigh, musing at how he's easily one of the most handsome men I've ever seen in my life. At that thought, his eyes meet mine. Neither of us turns away, and for one brief moment, the hostility seems to waver. In its place appears to be regret and . . . *longing?* He turns away, leaving me disappointed once again. There's nothing there but hatred, and I'd do best to remember that.

"Earth to Bridget. You can stop staring at the boss now. It's getting weird."

I turn my eyes to my sister and roll them for good measure. "Tell me everything about you and Carson."

Hopefully hearing about my sister and her perfect boyfriend will put all thoughts of Grant and that damn kiss out of my mind.

# CHAPTER THIRTEEN

## Grant

THAT FUCKING BITCH.

I pace my office. After my lunch meeting yesterday, I met with both my lawyer and the private investigator I'd hired to look into Chelsea. I never went back to the office. Instead, I surprised Isabella by picking her up and taking her to the Museum Of Natural History. Seeing her eyes widen with wonder at the giant whale exhibit made me forget all the shit I've been dealing with at work, but today I can't avoid it. The goal I've been dreading just came. One phone call, followed by copies of Chelsea's emails has me fuming. This shit keeps getting worse and worse. I need her gone already. Not trying to take over and ruin shit. I thought we'd reached an accord. Found a way to coexist. But boy, was I wrong. And like the idiot I've been for the last few years, I've once again grown complacent. She did her thing. I did mine. It worked. Until I finally fucking looked at her emails and call logs. It had never stopped. I just stopped looking close enough.

Not only is she messing with my life, but she's still

dragging my brother into this clusterfuck. The fact she had Bridget hired to spy on my brother is ridiculous. I've never even heard Bridget speak of Spencer. Chelsea has gone too far.

We are done. We might not get along—fuck, I might hate her—but in business, we always saw eye to eye—until recently. But this . . .

This I can't forgive.

I can't pretend this never happened.

She directly went against my orders. Without a second thought, I throw open my door and march down the hall and to the elevator, once on Chelsea's floor I barrel into her office. She lifts her head as I enter and plasters on her sadistic smile.

"What's your angle, Chelsea?"

"You'll have to be more specific."

"Don't play coy with me. I know you're up to no good with Bridget's recruiter."

"You're on a first name basis now, are you? Is she officially your side-piece?"

I slam my fist down on the desk, causing Chelsea to flinch. Good. "Don't you ever talk about her like that again. Do you understand?"

"You *are* sleeping with her."

"I'm not." I seethe.

She narrows her eyes and begins a steady tapping of her long nails on the desk. "If you're not sleeping with her, why the hell do you care what I say about her? She's a temp. A very young temp."

"I don't need you to tell me any of this. She's my employee. That's all there is to it. She isn't part of your game, and you won't pull her into it. Are we clear?"

"Crystal."

Without another word, I turn on my heel and stalk out of my wicked wife's lair. She's vile, and being in the same room with her is enough to choke the air right out of a person.

---

Between Chelsea driving me insane and Bridget in my space all the time, I don't know how I've made it through the last few days of hell. Every day I grow angrier.

I can't help but want Bridget. We've barely spoken, but just being in the same airspace as her makes me crazy. The visceral reaction I have to her is a workplace hazard. It's like a particular part of my body doesn't realize I can't touch her. But every time she saunters into the room and looks at me with her big blue eyes and full lips, I want to push her against the wall and finish what we started in the alley. Maybe it's just been too goddamn long since I got laid. Or even touched someone. It's been at least four years, but I know it's not that.

It's just her.

Kissing Bridget, touching her, unleashed a beast I'd buried deep inside me. Now it can't be quenched, and since there's nothing I can do about it, I'm just fucking angry about it. Angry that she's here to tease me, not that she knows she is. But with every sway of her hips, that's exactly what she's doing—teasing me. I'm angry that I'm weak.

Again.

I can't let my dick lead my life. I know how it worked out for me last time. The only good thing I have to show for it is Isabella. I'd never regret her.

Never.

She's the sunlight in my dark existence.

She is why I wake up. Why I come to work. Why I tolerate the abuse I subject myself to every day.

If it weren't for Isabella and The L, life would be different. I'd be bending Bridget over my desk right now and sinking myself into her tight—

A discreet cough pulls me out of my dirty thoughts. Fuck. Speak of the devil. How is she always so flawlessly beautiful? I know she isn't even trying. Her dirty-blond hair is pulled into a sloppy bun on the top of her head, and a pencil is tucked behind one ear. She looks like a sexy librarian with her pencil skirt and white button-down. A sexy librarian who needs to let loose.

I clear my throat and scrub my brain of the thoughts from moments ago.

"What do you want, Ms. Miller?" I hiss, barely able to maintain the hostility.

"I just wanted . . ." She pauses and bites her lip. The movement draws unwelcome attention to her mouth.

"Just wanted to . . ." I lead. My words come out harshly, but what does she expect when she's making me look at her goddamn lips? Lips that at this minute I want wrapped around my—

"I have the file you asked for." She lifts a folder in the air for emphasis.

"And did you get the pricing for all the viable options for the hotel?"

Her mouth drops open. Of course she didn't. I never asked her to.

"You never said—"

"I don't care that I never said anything. Learn to anticipate what's needed of you."

She mutters something under her breath that I can't catch.

"What did you say?" I stare her down.

She looks me square in the eye, pulls back her shoulders, and stands a little taller.

There she is.

The spitfire from the other day.

"I said," she pauses for emphasis, "I'm a temp here. I want to learn. So perhaps you should start teaching." She cocks her head to the left in defiance.

I stand and make swift work of moving in front of her. "You want to learn? What do you want me to teach you?" We're so close, I can feel her exhale of breath; I can smell her intoxicating scent. She smells like jasmine, exotic and heady. Like a siren leading me to my ruin. She better leave now, or I can't be held responsible for what I want to do.

"I, um, you should start by telling me what the expectations of the job entail," she mumbles, clearly affected by my proximity.

"Your first lesson is not to defy me." I lean in, needing her to leave, but wanting her to stay. My blood pumps furiously in my chest. I'm within inches of her mouth when she shakes her head once, pulling herself out of whatever trance she went into. She rights herself and then turns from me, walks toward the door, and slams it as she leaves.

Crossing the room, I grab a tumbler and pour myself a Scotch. That was too fucking close. I almost kissed her right here in the middle of my fucking office.

Idiot.

I need to get rid of her. I need her gone.

God fucking damn it.

The phone rings and I stalk back over to my desk. "Lancaster here."

"Grant." My lawyer's voice makes my back go ramrod straight. I've been waiting for this call.

"Lawrence. Have you been able to eradicate the thorn in my side?"

"Unfortunately, no, not yet. She screwed you big time. I'm not sure how exactly you got in this position, but I'll look into some other angles and get back to you."

I slam the phone into the cradle. The sound vibrates off the walls. That's not what I want to hear. The uncertainty of my company, my future, the life of my daughter are all hanging in the balance, and right now I'm helpless. I take another swig and place the glass down.

The liquid burns my throat. I shouldn't be drinking, but the hotel business isn't like most businesses. Being the boss has its perks. Grabbing the phone, I hit the intercom button.

"Ms. Miller, in my office now." I don't really need her, but I have this sick perverse need to torture myself and her. If I have to be miserable with her in my hotel, so should she.

Within a few seconds, she enters my office. Her chest heaves. The fabric of her blouse pulls tightly over her breasts. It's only been a short time since she was in here last, but I swear her shirt got tighter. How is that possible?

"You rang." She smiles, but regardless of the false smile, I recognize the disdain in her voice, and it infuriates me. So, being the dick I am, I can't help but goad her.

"Do you have the answers I need?" I bite out, fully aware there's no way in goddamn hell she could actually have the answers. "Most assistants interested in keeping their jobs would have been in here already." It's only been ten minutes since she was last in here.

She thrusts the file down in front of me. Pricing included. "Don't entertain any preconceived notion of my abilities simply because you've been between my legs," she hisses.

I can't find words to respond before she turns, dismissing me and walking out the door once more.

Well, that went well.

# CHAPTER FOURTEEN

## Bridget

THAT PIECE OF SHIT.

He wants me to fail, and why? So he can fire me? No. He can fire me regardless. He's the kind of bastard who just wants to make me miserable. He wants to toy with me. What the fuck was that? He was inches away from me. For a second I thought he was going to kiss me, but then, like every other time, the massive freeze descended.

No matter what I told Lynn, I can't lie to myself. My work environment is actually horrific, and to make matters worse, I have to stay. I'm completely out of options. I can't even call Olivia again and beg for help. She has her own problems. She just got out of rehab, and she's starting her own company. I haven't told her yet that I'm working for her boyfriend's enemy, but I'm not going to. She doesn't need any more drama in her life. Nor do I.

If I'm being honest, I don't want this to be about her right now. Everything is always about her, and for once in my life, I have something that's mine. It isn't much, a lowly temp job, but still. I'm working on a big project. A project that can change the outcome of my future. Do a good job on this, and I'm set. Work hard enough, and maybe I can convince Mr. Lancaster to give me a recommendation. Then I can get a better paying job with the prestige that would make my family proud.

Bonus . . . he'll finally be in my past.

It will take every ounce of strength and determination for me to make it the next few weeks here. Hell, the next few days. For all I know, Grant Lancaster is on the phone with the temp agency right now, serving me my walking papers. If he's not, it's a modern miracle, and I need to work extra hard to stop mouthing off when he annoys me. I need to bite my tongue, which is something I've never been good at. But I can at least try. I have to try.

Sitting back, I try to anticipate what he'll ask for next. I recollect my endless hours of school work and imagine that after he has the figures and budgets for the competition's marketing campaigns, he's going to want to beat them. He's going to want me to come up with better ideas, something more cutting edge to make The L shine. So that's what I'm going to do.

I fire up my computer and start my research. The L could have a stellar release, but whatever is going on internally is causing the hype to falter, and we aren't getting the press we need. With the opening looming we need to act and act now. It's not too late to make The L kickoff successfully, and the next time he hollers at me, I'm going to wow him. I'm going to make myself indispensable to the team, and then he can't get rid of me. I might not have wanted to work here at first, but now that I'm here, I refuse to fail. I don't care how big an asshole he is. This job could be just what I need to make a name for myself for the future. That's exactly what I'm going to do, *make myself indispensable.* I'll finally be able to let out my breath and stop walking on eggshells.

Yeah, that's what I'm going to do if I'm not fired. Make myself irreplaceable to him. How hard can that be?

# CHAPTER FIFTEEN

## Grant

I T'S BEEN TWO HOURS SINCE SHE WAS LAST IN MY OFFICE. Two long hours. I can't stand another minute of wondering what she's doing out there. Wondering what would happen if I beckoned her into the office and succumbed to the endless desire coursing through me. Why can't I get this girl out of my freaking head? She's a drug. A dangerous poison to me. She's young and fresh, not yet tainted by the nasty things life has to offer. I want to bask in her warmth. Lose myself in her naivety. What would it be like to not see the world the way I do? To live an illusion, if only for a moment. I need to get out of here. Leave the office.

These thoughts are dangerous. I can't think like this. There's no way out of the situation I'm in. Especially not now. Not with the hotel's grand opening looming in the distance. Everything rides on this. All my money hangs in the balance. Chelsea's greedy stupidity has fucked me. By bidding on properties, I'm leveraged to the max. If The L isn't successful, I could lose everything. But in the end, none of that matters. The part that matters is Isabella. If I lose every-thing, I could lose her, too. And without her, I'm nothing. I just have to work hard, keep my dick in my pants, and stop daydreaming about Bridget Miller.

Shit.

Even thinking her name has me angry. Picking up the phone, I call HR.

"Mr. Lancaster," the head of my human resources depart-ment answers.

"Paige. Any luck finding me another assistant?" I bark.

"Um, but you said there wasn't a prob—"

"I don't care what I said. There has got to be someone in this damn hotel who wants to work for me." I know full well I'm being an ass. It's not her fault I'm having a hard time not imagining fucking my assistant and that it's driving me in-sane. It's not her fault no one wants to work for me.

"I'm so sorry, Mr. Lancaster. Th-There are currently no candidates," she stutters.

Word has spread fast that I'm a ticking time bomb in the office. No one wants to transfer departments. Finding a suitable replacement is seeming impossible. Before Bridget, I had three girls quit on me. That doesn't include the com-pletely incompetent people I fired in the last month. Ever since I figured out what Chelsea did, how she continued to go after my brother's company even when I asked her—no, ordered her to stop, it's been war in the office. Lucky for me, Chelsea works three floors beneath me, so I can stay away from her. But that doesn't mean the tension isn't insane.

And everyone from the mailroom to the VP of Marketing is feeling it.

Hanging up, I dial Bridget.

"Connect me to Chelsea," I order.

I sit on hold. The music playing in the background grates on my last nerve. Tension courses through me.

"I'm sorry, she's not in the office. Would you like me to transfer you to her cell?"

"Yes."

The phone rings and rings. Where the fuck is she? Probably fucking lover boy, that's where.

"Sir, she's working from home today."

"Connect me to my house."

"Hold one minute, sir." Her voice is firm and unwavering, completely professional.

I'm asking her to connect me to my wife, and she acts like I don't know what she tastes like. As if I've never had my hand inside her. As if I haven't almost fucked her in an alley. The strength of this girl impresses me more by the minute. Bridget is an anomaly to me.

The phone keeps ringing and ringing. No one answers in my house, which is strange as Isabella's nanny should at least be answering. I bash the phone on my desk, put my coat back on, and rush out the door.

"Have all calls sent to my voicemail." I jet out the door and into the garage, pulling out at a speed that can't be safe for New York City streets. Thankfully, there's no traffic at this time of day in Tribeca, but I have to slow down or I'll never get there in one piece.

Forty-five minutes later, I pull up to my house in Connecticut. Living this far out is not conducive to opening a hotel, but when I married Chelsea, she insisted. She insisted on a lot of things, all of which were a bad idea now that the curtain has been lifted from my eyes.

The car is barely in park before I'm barreling out and heading inside. I'm only a few steps within the house when I start to search each room. Not only can I not find my wife, but where the hell is Margret? Heading up the stairs, I see my four-year-old playing in the playroom by herself.

"Where's your mother?" I snap.

"I don't know."

"Where's Margret?"

"I don't know, Daddy," she whispers.

"Why are you all by yourself?"

Her lip quivers and I realize my voice must be scaring her. I'm so used to reacting a certain way, sometimes I can't stop the anger that pours out of my body. I'm snapping, but it's not her fault the adults in her life are irresponsible. That they are too busy for her, including myself. I'm no better. I've been so wrapped up in opening the hotel that my own time with her has been few and far between.

A small tear falls from her face.

"How long have you been alone, baby?"

"I don't know." Her nose scrunches, and I kneel on the floor next to her. Now at eye level, I can see her eyes are welled with tears.

"Come here, baby." I pull her into my arms. "I'm sorry I yelled at you. Daddy is so sorry. Can you forgive me?"

"Yes," she whispers.

I hold her tighter. "Do you remember when you last saw Margret?"

"She put Bubble Guppies on."

Fuck. I don't pay this woman to put a TV show on for my kid and then leave. "Okay, baby. Do you want to come with me to find her?"

"No, Daddy, I want to watch."

"Okay." I place a kiss on her forehead and move to find her nanny. I'm not even halfway down the stairs when I spot Margret entering the house through the back door.

"Where were you?"

"I-I . . ."

"Yes," I say as I tap my foot rhythmically.

"I had to take a phone call."

I eye her suspiciously. "And you couldn't take this call in the house?"

"It . . . I . . ." she stammers, obviously trying to come up with an excuse why she's been caught.

"Yes," I spit out.

Her face goes pale. "I just wanted air."

"You wanted air, so you left my kid alone in the house?"

"I'm so sorry. It won't happen again," she says and rushes past. Something isn't right. When she moves past me, a smell lingers in the air. I'm about to ask her if she was getting high when the front door swings open and Chelsea saunters into the place as if she not only owns this house but also owns the world. Margret scurries up the stairs, and I hear the door to her room shut.

I turn my attention back to my wife. "Where have you been?" I fire off.

"Not that it's any of your business, but I had an appointment."

"You were supposed to be working from home."

She rolls her eyes. "Since when do you micromanage me?"

"Since you proved to me that I needed to. The L is mine and moving behind my back to acquire properties in the name of my company proves you need to be watched at all times."

She steps up to me, reaches out, and then her nails press against my shirt, digging in through the material against my skin. "Oh, dear husband, that's where you're wrong. The L belongs to us. Or did you forget? As your wife, I'm entitled to fifty percent of everything." Her words slither out like poison from a snake.

"No, Chelsea. I didn't forget." There it is, my life's work hanging over me. If I make trouble, she'll take half. I really am a fucking idiot. How I didn't see her for the money hungry bitch she is, is beyond me. But the wool was pulled real fast once I signed the papers binding her to me for life. We weren't even married a year before her true colors began to show. When my father threw me out of Lancaster Holdings, every last semblance of her façade came crashing down.

Chelsea and I met at Lancaster Holdings, where she was a secretary who'd worked her way up over the years. She was cutthroat, dedicated, and one of the smartest women I'd ever met. On top of being gorgeous, she was exotic. Sinfully beautiful. I had to have her and have her I did. We kept our relationship secret at first, but then she made it clear she wouldn't stay with me if I didn't take it to the next level. And that was when everything went to shit. Dad knew. He saw what I was too blind to notice.

But I was too goddamn blind to see past anything back then. Now I'm not. Now I see everything, and I hate how right he was.

I turn to watch Chelsea walking toward her room. She moved out of my room years ago. As the door closes, anger swirls within me. Never once did she even bother to check on Isabella. Isabella is just a means to an end for her. She isn't a mother. She only uses our daughter as leverage to get everything she wants from me, and I don't object. I can't. I can't risk losing her, and Chelsea is enough of a bitch to take her from me.

My life is spinning out of control around me, and I can't do a fucking thing to stop it.

# CHAPTER SIXTEEN

## Bridget

EVER SINCE MR. LANCASTER LEFT EARLY THE OTHER day, he's been broodier than usual. I don't let it bother me, though. I continue to act like business as normal. It's become a fairly easy routine. I hate Mr. Lancaster, and he hates me back. He barks orders, and I grin and bear it. Personally, I think it pisses him off when I smile at his rudeness. Maybe I shouldn't tease the beast, but it's too much fun. Eventually, he'll give up or fire me.

Sitting in my office in front of my own computer, I look down at my ever-growing to-do list. Today's email from Mr. Lancaster is even snippier than the last. Normally, he barks at me to come into his office to hear the list. When he's like that, I keep to myself. I welcome the emails, though. It's easier and makes the day go faster.

I wonder what is up his ass today.

I know I shouldn't care, but I can't help but wonder since it directly affects my day. What makes him so bitter to the world? Even after working together these past few weeks, there's little I know of him. I tried to get more information, but everything before these last few months is a mystery. There are years after his estrangement from his dad and when he was ousted from Lancaster Holdings that are a complete mystery.

As I'm just about to pack up for the day, I hear a cough from my door. Looking up, I see him standing there.

"You need to work late tonight," he snaps. It isn't a question. "We have so much to do before the opening of the new hotel, and I need you to finish these papers."

"For sure. I don't mind at all." I smile at him. *Kill him with kindness. Kill him with kindness.*

"Really?" He genuinely looks shocked.

Laying it on thick, I say, "Of course. Hey, that's what I'm here for, remember? The more I learn, the better."

"Thank you." He softens. "You're good at this. You have an eye for things that most people don't. I need you."

My mouth drops open at his bipolar personality. One minute he's yelling, now this? My cheeks warm and I hope he doesn't notice. "Um, thank you."

"Besides, you're very honest, and I need that right now."

"To a fault, at times," I agree.

"I prefer honesty. Trust me, it's always better in the long run."

I can't help but see the ironies of that statement. If only he had been honest in the beginning, all of this hostility could have been avoided. I think he's going to say more, say anything, but instead, he hands me a sheet of paper. He's all business again. But I suppose I shouldn't expect anything less from him. I look up, and he waves his hand.

"Carry on."

Dickhead Lancaster is back.

---

I'm sitting on my couch, replaying every minute of my day. The strange encounter with my boss and his split personality.

With a lift of my hand, I bring the glass of wine to my mouth. With each sip I take, my body loosens. Why does he have to be so handsome? Maybe if he wasn't it wouldn't be so hard to be near him. Instead, I constantly have to remind myself I can't think of him like that. But with my inhibitions lowered, I can't help but remember the first night I met him and how it felt. What would it be like if I had another moment alone with him? Would he kiss me again? Would he taste me? Would I taste him?

My breasts feel heavy. As if they need to be touched. The thought of Grant's caress has my core clenching with anticipation. But he's not here. It's just me, and I'm desperate for relief. How long has it been since I've come? Since I've had someone fuck me.

Too long.

Closing my eyes, I imagine what it'd be like if I weren't alone right now. If my hands weren't mine, but his instead.

*"Take off your clothes,"* he'd order, and I'd have no choice

but to obey.

My nipples pebble and peak under my shirt. With a lift of my hand, I grasp and knead my breast through the thin material, pulling and pinching each nipple as if they were his hands.

*His teeth.*

Every nerve ending inside me is on full alert, my core tightening desperately in need of being filled. So I do, I give myself what I want.

With a slow, steady breath, my hand trails down to where I'm hot and ready.

I don't allow myself to stop, thrusting two fingers deep within, plunging them inside me, thrusting in and out.

Gasps of air.

I'm so close.

It's not enough. I need more.

My thumb begins to circle as I push deeper inside me, hooking my fingers up until they find the perfect spot, mimicking the ministration of a skilled lover. With my head thrown back, my vision blurs, and I crash over the edge.

It takes a minute for my breath to regulate, but when it does, I can't believe what I just did. It's not that I touched myself; it's the fact I thought of him when I did it that has me mortified.

My face feels flush, much warmer than just a moment ago.

How will I be able to look at him tomorrow?

*Shit.*

———•——

Ever since my dirty fantasy of Mr. Lancaster last night, I'm embarrassed to see him. It's not like he knows he's the star of my own personal porno, but I still try to keep busy all morning, not to accidentally make an ass of myself by turning beet red in front of him. So instead, I bury myself in work. When I look up from my computer, it's a little after eleven. I can't believe how fast the day has flown by. The good thing, however, is things with Grant are not as tense as they were before. Progressively they've gotten better as if our silent war is now at a truce. We've established a fairly consistent routine, which helps ease the tension. He arrives before me, getting the day set up, and when I arrive, I can usually get through a handful of emails before he calls me into his office.

With the exception of today.

I thrive on routines, and with his habitual mood swings in the past, I'm wondering if I've done something to set him off on the warpath again. I stand up from my chair, a pile of folders in hand, and head toward his office. When I walk in, he's on the phone. I don't want to disturb him, so I walk to his desk and place the pile down. Just as I lift my hand his rises and we touch. It's a whisper of a touch, but it lingers, sending my pulse to beat erratically. How can such a small touch be so inflaming? I pull my hand away quickly, my cheeks flushing.

"I'm sorry about that," I mutter. My eyes rise and lock on

his. I expect to see the typical indifference, but instead, I'm met with the same heated gaze I've seen before. He's affected, just like me. He says something into the phone, but I don't hear his words. I'm too fixated on him.

I turn to walk away, needing to get out of this situation. It isn't good for either of us to want something we can't have. I'm almost at the door when I hear my name called out.

"Bridget."

I turn my head over my shoulder and meet his gaze. "Yes?" My heart pounds in my chest, crashing into my breastbone and making my breath accelerate.

"Have you had lunch yet?"

Disappointment washes over me. I don't know what I was expecting, but that was not it. "No, not yet. Did you need me to get you something?"

"If you wouldn't mind."

"Sure." I move back toward his desk. "What are you in the mood for?"

"Your choice, since you're grabbing it," he says, and I see his lip lift. Is he smiling? A small dimple forms on his right cheek. He *is* smiling. Wow, I'd forgotten how handsome he is when he smiles. But now he reminds me of the night at the bar.

My own lips start to spread. "I bet you think I'm going to say salad."

He nods, and I laugh.

"I'm not."

"You're not?" His eyebrow lifts.

"Nope."

"So what are you gonna have?"

"I could kill for a hamburger and fries."

With that, his eyes open wide, and what was once a small smile now spreads across his face into a full grin. "A hamburger." He laughs. He actually laughs. In all the time I've known him, I've never heard him laugh. Maybe he laughed the first night, but I was too drunk to appreciate the sound.

"Does that surprise you?"

"You have no idea."

"Good. I like to surprise." My tone is a little flirty. I'm talking to Mr. Lancaster as if we were at the bar not at the office. The revelation has my cheeks warming again.

His smile falters, but he keeps his cool.

My stomach tightens. *Shit.* Just when we were getting along, I had to go fuck it up. I stare at him for a beat, willing myself to speak. I need to say something to ease the embarrassment. As I open my mouth, he beats me to it.

"I'd love a hamburger."

---

Forty-five minutes later, I enter Mr. Lancaster's office with a very heavy bag of the best burgers in New York. I place the bag with his food on his desk.

"What do we have here?" he asks, not looking up from his desk. "It smells amazing."

"Just a family favorite," I respond.

"Is this family favorite a secret?" he muses, still typing on his computer.

"Yes, and if I tell you, I have to kill you."

"That so?"

"Absolutely. We wouldn't want the place to get too popular. I like not having to wait for my food. Nobody wants to meet up with a hangry Bridget Miller."

With that, he looks up from his desk. A half smile appears on his face. "Hangry?" He chuckles.

"That's right. I'm angry when I'm hungry."

"Duly noted."

He doesn't look up from his paperwork when he says that. I take the moment to study him. The scruff on his face and the circles under his eyes tell me something is up. He appears tired as if he hasn't slept.

"Are you okay?" I ask timidly, not wanting to overstep and piss Mr. Moody off.

"Honest answer?"

"Always," I say.

"I'm exhausted. I have a lot riding on the opening going off without a hitch."

I nod, not knowing what else to say. He doesn't look up at me, and I take it as my cue to exit. I'm halfway out the door when I turn around. "It's a little diner down the road from my apartment."

Grant looks up, confused. "What?"

"The hamburgers."

"You live nearby?"

"Define your definition of nearby?"

He angles his head as if he doesn't understand, and I laugh.

"I live in the West Village."

"You went to the West Village to get me lunch?"

"It's really not that far, and besides, I didn't just go to get you lunch. I went to get *us* the best lunch." I put the emphasis on us. I need him to know I haven't eaten yet either. I just hope he's not mad that I went so far.

"I did it all in under forty-five minutes. I figure that still leaves me time to eat as well. Hope you don't mind. Technically, I still have fifteen minutes. I promise to eat quickly."

He opens the bag and inhales. I can tell by the way he licks his lips that he understands why I say these burgers are the best. The smell permeates through the space, making my mouth instantly water. "Sit," he orders, and I stand like a deer in headlights.

"You want me . . . You want me to eat with you?"

"Yes."

I don't move. I can't. It's as if I'm cemented in place.

"Please." His voice dips with sincerity.

The tone is my undoing. I walk back over to his desk and take the seat across from him as he removes the pile on top of the desk.

"Do you want anything to drink?" he asks.

"You don't have to worry about me."

"Maybe I want to." His words hang in the air uncomfortably. What does he mean? I don't want to think too much into it. "You did go to all this trouble to get the best burger . . . for me."

I smile shyly.

"So what do you want?"

"I'll have a Diet Coke," I reply.

He stands and walks out of the office. About a minute later he returns with a Diet Coke for me and a water for him.

"Thanks." I smile, earning a smile in return.

Neither of us talks as we devour our food. The only sound is the occasional moan we each make as we eat. It's easy. Comfortable. It's shocking how right it feels eating together in silence. It brings me back to our first meeting. To the Grant I met at the bar. As I take my last bite, I want to savor it. Make it last. I'm not ready for this reprieve to end. But eventually we're done, and Mr. Lancaster looks up at me. He stares at me for a second, studying me.

Assessing me.

"You've been here for a few weeks now. How do you like it?"

I about choke on my burger at the directness of his question. How do I answer? If he had asked me only a few days ago, my answer would be quite different. "Well . . ." I stop, and he feigns distress.

"Don't tell me your boss is a tyrant," he says seriously, but his green eyes give him away as they sparkle brightly with humor.

"I wouldn't say tyrant."

"What would you say?"

"I'd say he's tough but fair."

"Tough but fair," he repeats my words. "Sounds like a tyrant to me." He grins.

"If I'm being honest, the verdict is still out. It's different from what I was looking for."

"What was that?"

"I love marketing. It's what I really want to land a job doing. Assistant work is fine for now, but it's not my long-term aspiration."

"Perhaps we can incorporate some time with the marketing department while you're here."

"Really?" I say excitedly.

"Once we get through the opening, I'll see what I can arrange."

Our eyes meet, and I'm happy to find kindness in his. The animosity from before seems to be gone. I can only hope it stays that way. I could get used to working with *this* Grant Lancaster.

# CHAPTER SEVENTEEN

## Bridget

"You're here early," I hear from across the room. Grant is standing just inside the doorframe. His presence is overpowering in the small space, sucking the oxygen right out of the room.

I shrug. "I figured I should get an early start today."

"Smart." His head is inclined as he speaks. "You want coffee?"

Did Grant Lancaster just offer to make me coffee? I can't help the smile that spreads across my face. "I'd love a coffee."

He nods, then walks out the door. A few moments pass before he reappears. This time, he's holding two mugs with steam curling up from them. I'm surprised when he sits in the chair that fronts my desk, looking relaxed and happy. This is the first time in the few weeks I've worked here that he's come into *my* office for a purpose other than to stand at the threshold barking orders. A glimmer of hope spreads through me. Have we finally turned a corner? Who would have thought a burger could do this . . . although it was a pretty damn good burger. My lips spread, but I refrain from laughing at my ridiculous inner monologue. He leans forward.

"What are you working on today?"

The warmth of a crimson flush rises up my neck and colors my cheeks. I'm working on something that was never asked of me. Something that could potentially overstep the boundaries of my job. The idea of telling him has my heart racing and the trembling in my hands causes my coffee to slosh. I've worked hard and I'm proud of what I've accomplished, but what if he thinks it's dumb?

"I'm compiling a list."

"A list?"

"Yeah. A list of influencers."

"What type of influencers?"

I bite my lip. *Here goes nothing.* "Instagram travel influencers. I'm compiling a record of Instagram profiles that revolve around travel and have over one million followers."

He bobs his head up and down as though he's considering what I'm saying. The corner of his lip rises as though he's impressed. Leaning forward, he places a folder on my desk. I look up and then down at the large stack now sitting in front of me.

"For when you're done," he says before walking out the door.

*Uh . . . That went well?*

Not that I expected some huge show of gratitude for my ingenuity, but I was thinking we'd have a conversation.

Something that gave me a chance to explain my idea. I guess at this point I should be glad he didn't shoot it down.

I look down at the papers he laid in front of me. The stack is overwhelming, but once I open it, it's really not that bad. I set to work and not even an hour passes before I'm at the end. Truth is, I'm a fast worker. Most people would have taken double the amount of time, but I'm not most. I don't stop until I get what I want, and right now what I want is to impress Grant Lancaster.

Why?

Pride. I refuse to be seen as a mere temp. I need a glowing recommendation and to do that, I need to *wow*.

If I'm being honest, it's also a little self-preservation. I don't want to be another mistake. I want him to remember me long after I'm gone. It doesn't matter whether it's for the kiss or the work, as long as I'm burned into his memory.

I step into his office, standing tall in front of his desk. His eyes lock on mine. Neither one of us says a word. I came in here with the intention of impressing Grant with my work, but in these few moments, something has changed. There's a shift in the air, and I see something brewing in his eyes. I feel naked under his gaze.

"All done." The words come out husky. "Anything else I can do for you?"

Grant drags his teeth over his bottom lip again, grinning at something I said. I can't even dissect what he could find funny because my attention is locked on his lips. He clears his throat, bringing my attention back up to his eyes.

"I didn't think you'd get through it all."

I shrug. "I'm good at my job."

"Bridget, you're incredible at so many things."

His words turn my legs into jelly. All the air in my lungs whooshes out of me. This man is so good. So good at his job. So good with his words. So good at making me feel so, *so* good.

"Thank you," I whisper back, wanting to reach out and touch him, but knowing better.

His phone rings and our connection is broken.

"I do have more work for you. But it's not urgent, so take your time with these." He motions to a stack in front of him.

I grab the new set of papers, then head back to my office. About thirty minutes pass when my phone buzzes.

"Bridget Miller."

"Hey, Bridget." Grant's voice echoes through the earpiece of the phone. The sound of the rasp of his voice has little butterflies taking flight in my belly. "Can you please come to my office? I want to go over some work I'll need done in the next few weeks before the launch."

"Okay. I'll grab a notebook and head your way."

A few minutes later, I enter with my pad in hand. He furrows his brow, and for a moment I'm afraid I did something wrong. He's just staring at me, not saying a word. Until he does.

"Look, I . . ." he starts, and I know it's serious. "About that first time, at the bar—"

I hold up my hand. I don't look at him—too

embarrassed. "No need," I mutter. My face has grown hot and my hands are shaking slightly as I pretend to write in my notebook. "Don't worry about it. Honestly, it's forgotten. I don't hold it against you, and I don't think you're a bad person," I say without making eye contact. *Good*, my heart hums in my chest. That's the first word I think about when I look at him.

"Don't you dare say sorry," he hisses, and at the tone of his voice, I force myself to look up at his tormented expression. "I'm the one who should be saying sorry. You had every right to be upset with me."

"It's okay," I promise earnestly. I don't want to disregard his feelings or his sincere apology, but this isn't a conversation I'm comfortable having. The memory of being left in that alley is embarrassing no matter how much time has passed.

"It isn't. I can see it in your eyes, Bridget. Please don't lie to me."

"Honestly, Grant, I'd rather not relive that night." I lower my gaze, hoping he sees how over this conversation I am.

"Bridget—"

My eyes meet his and I hope he hears my next words. "No. Please. Things are good right now. Let's not make it more complicated."

He nods. "Fine."

Yesterday didn't go well.

Yes, he respected my decision to shelf the conversation of that night, but I can't help but feel bad. As much as I didn't want to talk about it, I could tell he really did, so today I'm second-guessing my decision to push the memory to the side. Did I ruin our easy work atmosphere? Will things be stifled and awkward again today?

When I arrived today, Grant wasn't in his office yet. I decided to grab the items I needed from his office before he got in. Maybe I can buy myself a couple of hours before I have to face him.

I'm in the corner of his office bent over riffling through files when Grant sneaks up behind me. "Bridget," he calls, causing me to jump a mile.

"Jesus, Grant. You scared the ever-loving shit out of me."

He chuckles. "Sorry about that. I probably should've announced myself in my office."

"Hardy-har-har." Relief. That's what I'm feeling. The fact we're able to fall right back into this easy conversation makes me happy.

"Could you check in the bottom drawer to see if there's a file called Access? I can't find it anywhere," Grant asks.

I pull the lower drawer open and look through all the files, but it's not there. "I'm not seeing it," I say, looking over my shoulder at him. He's staring at me intently. I know that look. Lust. He likes what he sees, and God if I can help it, but I feel the same damn way every time I look at him. "Um, let me check one more spot," I say, breaking our stare. This train of thought isn't healthy for me.

I move a few things around until I spot a misfiled item tucked within another folder. Access. *Bingo*. I lift the file, but as I do, I notice there's also a framed photo in the file. I take both out and look up at Grant. He narrows his eyes as he spies what's in my hand.

"I forgot that was in there," he states with a hint of sadness.

I look down at the photo. In it, Grant looks much younger and much happier. He's smiling into the camera, looking carefree. It's a look he definitely doesn't wear often anymore. Next to him is a young woman, and in his arms is a little girl.

"Your family?" I ask hesitantly. For as long as I've worked here, I've never heard of a daughter. I obviously knew about the wife, of course, but not the child. There's a lot about Grant I don't know, and right now that thought hurts. We've spent so much time together in this office and he hasn't confided in me at all.

"It was my family. Things aren't the same as they were then." His eyes are hard. He almost seems angry.

"Grant—"

"There are parts of my life I'd rather not discuss."

*And there it is.* Once more I'm shut out. Suddenly, I feel unsure about everything. The thought sours my stomach, but then my uncertainty is replaced with sheer . . . anger. He's acting like I snooped or I'm pushing him into sharing. I'm not, dammit, and I'm tired of always feeling awkward and out of place. Fuck this.

"I'm not asking you to share parts you don't want to

share. I stumbled across this because you left it lying around in places I've been given access to . . . to do my damn job. It's not as though I was digging through your personal items."

"I'm sorry. You're right. It's not your fault. I put it there and truly forgot."

"It's a nice picture. You look happy in it." The words come out before I have a chance to think.

He stiffens. "It was a lifetime ago, Bridget. Trust me, you don't want to know about any of that."

He's wrong. I do want to know about him. I don't know why after everything. I shouldn't care, but I do.

"You're wrong, Grant," I say honestly. "Tell me. Please."

He stares at me for what feels like a solid minute. "That photo was taken two years after I had a falling out with my family. Chelsea was pretending to be a doting wife. I thought things between us were turning around. She *seemed* to be obsessed with our daughter." He huffs. "But it was all a mirage. If I'd look closer, I would've seen what was really going on."

"What *was* going on?"

"A hostile takeover. Soon after this picture was taken, she suggested we take my family head-on by starting our own luxury brand of hotels. It was all an act to butter me up."

He starts pacing the room, toying with his watch absently. He looks tortured, and I can't tell if it's because of his relationship with Chelsea or the fallout with his family. Perhaps it's both.

I need to comfort him.

I approach him like one would a wounded animal. Slow and steady. When I reach him, I place my hand on his shoulder, stopping his movements. He turns to look at me.

"I can't claim to know anything about what happened between you and your family, but I'm sure they miss you too."

He scoffs. "Not after everything I've been a party to."

*What exactly did he do?* What's the hostile takeover that he mentioned? I'm finally starting to get answers, and I don't want to push too hard, so I switch up tactics. "Starting your own chain of hotels seems like a big undertaking. Was it something you'd thought about doing before?"

I know very little about the Lancaster family, but from what I do know, he would have never needed to start his own. In fact, it would be in direct competition unless he was opening another branch or sister hotel, but that's not what The L is.

"I always planned on owning and operating my own hotel. It's my family legacy. It was always supposed to be mine." His tired eyes pierce mine. "I fucked that all up. I'm not a good man, Bridget."

His words strike me. After everything that transpired between the two of us in the alley, I would have been inclined to agree at one time, but something tells me not to judge this broken man. There's something dark and haunting about him. *What's happened to you?*

"You're not a bad person, Grant."

At the sound of his name, his eyes lift to mine. "You give me too much credit, Bridget. You're too good for me."

"No. I've done bad things too. We all do. It's what makes us human. It's what you do with your life after the mistakes that make you good or bad."

"How so?"

"Did you learn from your past? Have you atoned? If not, will you?"

"I haven't done anything but wallow in self-pity and regret. I've let time slip through my fingers and I can't get it back." He shakes his head. "It's too late for me."

"It's never too late, Grant. You have time to change and make things right. You're a better person than you're giving yourself credit for. I know you are."

"You make me want to be better, Bridget."

For the first time throughout this conversation, he smiles and it's a beautiful thing.

"Grant, I . . ."

He moves in close. Too close. "I like my name on your tongue."

Heat spreads through me at his words. Our shared kiss floods my mind, leaving me warm and tingly all over. *Too close.*

He extends his hand, palm cupping my cheek affectionately. "What am I going to do with you?" he says huskily.

I sigh into his touch. It feels . . . right.

Our eyes lock in a heated gaze, far too inappropriate to be occurring in his office with the door open, but I couldn't care less. His touch feels wonderful and I'm reveling in it. Without another thought, I reach up on my tiptoes and bring my lips to his. He pulls me the rest of the way in, smashing our bodies together. His mouth opens, allowing my tongue to enter and meet his. We stand in the middle of his office, lip-locked and embracing, not caring who sees. As much as I want to push this further, I know I can't.

Pulling away, I try to catch my breath. Grant's forehead rests against mine. "I can't infect you with the poison that is my life, Bridget. No matter how fucking hard it's been to stay at arm's length, I have to." He frowns, grabbing my shoulders to keep me in place. "I have to, Bridget," he huffs. "I have to."

"Why?"

"My life with Chelsea is complicated, and you'd be smart to keep your distance."

"What if I don't want to?" My eyes pierce his. I want him to see how little I care about Chelsea in this moment. If he wants me, if he'll allow me to be part of his life, I want that. I'm being careless with my heart, I know it, but I can't stop. There's something about this man I can't resist.

"Chelsea would ruin you just as she has me."

My eyes widen at his words. What could she possibly do? What has she already done?

"What happened, Grant? Tell me what Chelsea has done to you." His tenderness and open attitude give me the courage to finally ask what's been on my mind for weeks.

He tenses and pulls his hand away, leaving me cold and desperate to take back the words. He's closing in on himself and shutting me out again. I feel it as much as I see it. He points at the picture still in my hands.

"Back then, things were easier. She lied, and she lied well. I believed every poisonous word she spoke. I didn't know what I do now." He turns away, effectively ending the conversation. I replace the photo in the cabinet, closing the door on all the questions swirling around in my head.

"I think that's about all I need for today." The tone of his voice has changed. He sounds angry and distant. This Grant isn't the same man who stood in front of me moments ago.

"I'll just grab my things," I say, picking up my stuff and walking out on the one man I want more than anything.

# CHAPTER EIGHTEEN

## Grant

SLEPT IN MY OFFICE.

For three hours after I sent Bridget away, I sat at my desk and stared at papers. I couldn't focus, and ultimately I got nothing done.

I'm up to my eyeballs in work, and I can't concentrate to save my damn life.

That fucking picture.

Everything was going great until she found that photo. Why the hell do I still have that? *Isabella*. She's the only reason. She owns my heart and soul, and that picture reminds me of happier times. Of times when my heart and soul weren't at war with my brain, when things were simple, when loving my daughter didn't come with a price tag that threatened to strangle me alive. I only wish she had any sort of happy in her little life. The few short years she's had on this earth have been full of confusion and abandonment. I work miserably long hours, and her mother doesn't give a shit. Not about her, and certainly not about me. I could make a million dollars a minute and fly a private motherfucking jet every other week, but the truth is, I don't feel like a success story. Not by a long mile. My daughter is miserable, and I know it.

Those few good years came and went quickly. Isabella won't remember any of them. It breaks me to think that this is her life. That this is all she has to look forward to.

The sun has been up now for a couple of hours. I'm tired, and I smell like shit. I'm in need of a shower and about four more hours of sleep. It's almost nine a.m., which means I'm fucked. Bridget will be here soon and I'm not prepared. She tried to get me to open up and I did as much as I ever have with anyone, but it wasn't enough. I could see it all over her face that it wasn't. I shut her down, and in the process, I hurt her.

But it's for the best.

I have to keep her at arm's length. Everything I said was true. Chelsea would ruin her. I can't allow that to happen. I won't allow it.

"Good morning, Mr. Lancaster."

Bridget's voice pulls me out of my thoughts. As I lift my head, my breath catches. She's beautiful and she doesn't even try. Her hair is pulled back into a low bun with loose tendrils hanging around her face. She's stunning.

"Did you sleep here?" Her voice has me clearing my throat and turning away from her.

"I have a lot to do."

"That's not a good excuse." Her voice is stern, but it's not cold.

My gaze lifts to meet hers. "I'm concerned about the opening," I confide.

"Let's take a look at what you have."

My jaw drops at the woman in front of me. After my harsh exit yesterday, she should be avoiding me. Hell, most would have quit by now, but not her. Every day she comes in here more determined than the day before. If I'm being honest with myself, this is the very reason I'm drawn to her.

Her strong will calls to me, and I'm losing the battle with myself every damn day. I know I need to keep my walls up, not let her sway my resolve, but I can't. Her ability to rise above our issues and help me regardless of everything has me no longer able to ignore these desires deep inside me.

# CHAPTER NINETEEN

## Bridget

"I T'S A BIG UNDERTAKING AND I WANT TO MAKE SURE everything runs smoothly."

Grant has his plan spread out across the desk. He regards me expectantly, clearly looking for affirmation that his ideas are good. I smile at him. He isn't so bad when he's like this. He's almost insecure. It's cute, considering he's supposed to be a cutthroat businessman.

"You're not alone," I assure him.

"I'm not?"

"You've got me." I cock my head to the side as though that's obvious. "I'm here to help with anything you need."

My words come out breathy. I don't mean them to be anything other than an offer of help, but they sound like so much more. Grant's eyes darken, and his breath hitches. We're only inches apart, and with him like this, I want nothing more than to forget the last few weeks and break the distance between us. My tongue darts out, wetting my lower lip. Grant's eyes follow my movement. With a deep inhale, he moves marginally toward me.

"Grant," I almost pant.

At the sound of his name from my mouth, his lips crash to mine. All thought about where we are and who he is evaporates. I don't give a fuck about anything but his mouth on mine. It's heaven. His groan alerts me we're on the same wavelength. His hands tangle in my hair, and it's the alley all over again. Hot. All-consuming.

Perfect.

A commotion down the hall has us jumping apart, and just like that, our connection is gone. Frustrated and panting, we both go to opposite ends of the room.

"I need to use the restroom," Grant announces, and I can't help but chuckle under my breath.

I bet you do.

———— ◆ ————

"Hey, sweetie, you look lovely. Have you done something different to your hair?" my mom says the minute I walk in the door of my childhood home.

I laugh. It looks exactly the same. "No, Mom. It's the same mousy blond as always."

"It's not mousy. But if you really feel that way, you could always color it."

"You think I should color it? I thought you said I looked lovely." I wink.

"Can never win with you and your sisters. You three will

make me go gray." She shakes her head, rolling her eyes as she does so.

I lean in and kiss my mother on the cheek. She's extremely protective of me, sometimes to a fault, but the fact she cares as much as she does means the world to me.

"Where's Dad?"

"Where else?"

I start down the hall, knowing exactly where he is.

"Hi, Dad," I say as I peek my head into the open door to find my father sitting in his office in the same position he's always in. He loves this sofa so much that it's starting to sag from constant use. But no matter how many times Mom has told him it's time to get a new sofa, he refuses. I love this about my family. The consistency. What must it be like for Grant to not have a relationship with his? I know how much that would wear on me, and in this moment, I get him. My heart hurts for him.

"Hi, sweetheart," he says and smiles up at me. "How are you?"

"I'm good, Dad. I'm happy to see you."

He pulls me into a hug. "How's the new job?"

"It's . . . interesting?"

"You don't like your job?"

"No, I do. It's great, and I'm learning a lot, actually."

"So, what's the problem? A boy?" my dad says knowingly.

"You see too much."

"I'm wise. Years will do that to a person. Experience will make you wiser."

"I don't want to know anything about your experience," I tease, but I see the look in my dad's eyes at my words. My words, although not intended, hit too close to home.

"I've made a lot of mistakes in my life, Bridget, but they were all life lessons. I wouldn't be where I am today without them. Some people come into our lives to grow with us, and others to help us grow ourselves."

"What I'm hearing you say is don't hold back?"

He chuckles.

"It depends on what we're talking about. You haven't really told me anything concrete."

"I'm not ready to talk about it, Dad, but I hear what you're saying."

He nods. "All I'm going to say is take chances but make sure you guard your heart as well. You're young, and you have plenty of time to meet the right person. Don't chase, be chased."

"Solid advice, Dad."

"That's what I'm here for," he says, placing a kiss on my forehead.

"Anything interesting on?" I ask, wanting to change the subject.

"The same old stuff."

"Well then, I'm going to go help Mom. I just wanted to say hi."

"I'll join you when dinner is ready." He smiles.

I walk back toward the kitchen. "Are Lynn or Olivia coming?" I ask my mom.

"Neither could make it. Olivia's traveling with Spencer somewhere. You haven't heard from her, have you?"

"I haven't."

"I think he's the one." She shrugs. "Just a feeling I get."

I roll my eyes. My mother always says stuff like this. She thinks being a mom gives her superpowers. "You read crystal balls nowadays?"

"Hey, wait until you have children and you'll understand what I mean. You get a feeling with your children. Mark my words."

"Whatever you say."

"Help me set the table."

I laugh, grabbing plates and setting them around the table.

"Smells good in here," Dad says, entering the kitchen.

"Thanks, Dad. I've been slaving away all day," I say, placing the last plate in place and taking my seat with the others.

"Ha! You'd poison us with your cooking."

"I don't even have a comeback for that. You're absolutely right." I turn my head toward my mom. "How come my cooking is so bad when yours is so good? I didn't get your culinary genes at all."

"There's no such thing as culinary genes. It's all to do with hard work and practice."

"Ah, well, there's my problem."

"You have so much determination in other areas, why not the kitchen?"

"Not interested, I guess," I say, scooping food onto my fork.

"Now, there is the truth."

"Thanks, Mom," I roll my eyes, blatantly. "This is delicious." I chew my first mouthful of the chicken curry.

"So, tell us about work. How's it going?"

"It's good." I haven't told them where I'm working and I hope they don't press. They probably think I'm still working at Axis, and seeing as I haven't told Olivia where I work, I have no intention of breaking the news to them first. "It's going great. I'm really enjoying it, and I'm learning so much. I'm making some great connections."

"I'm glad to hear that. What's your boss like? I remember you said he was quite hard."

I choke on my food.

"Bridget, are you all right?" Mom asks, brows pinched.

"I'm fine. You just hit the nail on the head," I lie. "He's tough all right. But I can handle it."

"Lynn said you were very unhappy," Dad retorts.

"Actually, he's been a pleasure to work for. He's been teaching me the ropes and has finally opened up quite a lot to me. You know, I think there's more to him than meets the eye. And naturally, it does help that he's so good-looking," I joke before thinking better of it. *I've just opened up a can of worms.*

"He's good-looking? I didn't know that." Her downturned lips and creased brow tell me she has something to say, but then she shakes her head and just nods. "Nothing wrong with a bit of eye candy. Well, I'm glad you're enjoying it, dear."

*Eye candy? Dear God.*

"This boss better be treating you well, or he and I will be having a chat," Dad says with a stern face.

Damn my big mouth. I said too much earlier when we talked. He's a smart man. He's piecing it together.

"He's a boss, Dad. A giant prick, but good at what he does."

He nods and that seems to pacify him, throwing him off the scent of Grant Lancaster and me.

After dinner, my father returns to his office—*as usual*. I help my mother pack everything away in the kitchen, and she's unusually quiet. She puts down the dish she's holding and looks at me.

"You need to be careful with your boss," she says.

"With my boss?" Not what I was expecting. *At. All.* "What do you mean?" I try to play dumb, but there's no use. My cheeks burn.

"Is there something going on between the two of you?"

"No, there's nothing going on at all. Why would you say that?"

"I don't know. It's another one of my feelings, I guess."

"Well, this time you're wrong. He's just my boss, and I'm overly enthusiastic because I really enjoy what I'm doing. I mean, this is the first time I'm being consulted on things. I was worried I might end up sucking at it, which would've been awful. But I'm actually good at it. And yeah, he's good-looking, but that's just a fact. Nothing else. Plus, he's married."

"Just be careful, darling."

"Mom, you honestly don't have to worry. Thank you for

137

caring. I know you only mean well. But you're stressing for nothing. Anyway, I'm only going to be working there for a few more weeks. Then I'm out of there and I probably won't ever see him again."

She picks up a dirty glass and takes it over to the sink. "I just don't want to see you get hurt. Nothing good can come from you falling for some hotshot businessman you work with, Bridget, especially a married one."

She's transferring her issues with Dad to me. He was a career-focused man who worked all the time and ended up in an affair that almost rocked my family. She's worried I'm going down the same path.

"I won't get hurt, Mom. I'm a big girl and I don't have a family to worry about."

She stiffens. "I wasn't . . . I'm not—"

"Mom, stop. You don't have to say anything."

She drops her head. "I'm sorry. It's not fair." She frowns. "You just remind me so much of your dad. No two people were ever more alike, and I worry, is all."

"Aren't you happy with Dad, Mom?"

"Of course, but that doesn't mean I can't recognize his faults. And we all have them, Bridget. You and your father are prideful people who wear your hearts on your sleeves. I don't want you to be taken advantage of."

I smile, walk to her, and pull her into a hug. I don't want to have this conversation anymore, and I can tell it's upset her. Right now I'll ignore that she compared me to the worst of my father and just hug her.

# CHAPTER TWENTY

## Bridget

WITH THE GRAND OPENING OF THE HOTEL RAPIDLY approaching, I've barely had time to breathe during the last few weeks. Long hours and early mornings monopolize my existence. Grant and I have fallen into a routine, but the aftermath of that day and almost having been caught still lurks in both of our minds. It's evident in the way I catch him watching me. His hungry eyes promising me he'll eat me whole if I get too close, so I keep my distance, heeding his unspoken warning. It wouldn't be good for either one of us to get caught, and the reality is, once we start, I won't be able to stop. I'll want him in every way possible.

"What are you working on?" I ask as I pop into Grant's office at half-past four.

"Actually, nothing. I got all my stuff done."

"See. I told you. Pays to have a kickass assistant who does half the work," I joke.

He stands, walking toward me. I take a step back, my

earlier thoughts running amuck through my head. *Don't be weak.*

"You're right. I couldn't do this without you." His hand darts out, moving a piece of hair behind my ears. "You're beautiful, Bridget."

I'm holding my breath. His hand on me is too much. "Grant," I croak. "We—you can't touch me."

He chuckles. "Is this affecting you, Bridget?"

I inhale, taking in his masculine scent. Mint and sandalwood do nothing to help calm my raging hormones.

"Do you want me to stop?"

"No." I don't need to think about his question. I don't want him to ever stop touching me.

He leans in, whispering into my ear. "You're all I think about, Bridget. Your lips on mine, my hands all over you."

An unauthorized moan escapes my lips.

"What you're feeling, I feel too. Don't ever question that," he commands. "Right now, though, I have to step away."

He does, leaving me cold and wanting . . . more.

"I'm sorry. I don't want us to find ourselves in the position we were last time. I don't give a fuck what people think or say about me, but it's not fair to you. I won't have anyone say anything about you, Bridget. Ever."

"Thank you." It's all I can say. I don't want to be the talk of the office and the fact he's thought about that warms my heart. He cares.

"Listen, I'm taking a few big potential investors out. I want you to come."

"Really? You're inviting me to meet with investors?"

"Potential investors, but yes. I'd like you there with me."

My mouth must drop open at his words because he chuckles.

"I don't know why you're so surprised. Temp or not, you're part of the team, and honestly, Bridget, I'm not sure what I would've done without you."

My face begins to warm as if it's on fire. My mother's words come crashing down on me.

"Do you think that's a good idea?"

He smirks. "Why wouldn't it be? You're my intern, and this is a good opportunity to learn, right?"

"What would people in the office say? I don't want to cause problems."

"I don't give a fuck. This is my company, and I don't need permission. You've earned this, Bridget."

I chew on his words. How would Chelsea react to him taking a woman to dinner? Would she even care? Should I care what she thinks? The whole thing makes me uneasy.

"What would it look like to your wife?" My question comes out meek. I don't want to sound like a prying woman, but after everything that's happened between us, I think my asking is called for.

He stiffens at the mention of Chelsea. His eyes darken, and his face hardens. "Quite frankly, I care about her opinion least of all."

"I'm sorry, Grant. I just had to ask. This whole situation is out of my comfort zone."

His face softens. "Let's not talk about Chelsea tonight. Let's focus on work and enjoy ourselves. Can you do that?"

I nod.

"So, will you join me?"

I consider his offer. It would be great experience to sit in on a potential investor dinner, and if he doesn't care, why should I? This is a learning experience, right? My answer is obvious. I'm not skipping. No way in hell. I want to learn and I want to be near him. God help me, but I do.

"Of course I'll join you."

He smiles wide.

"Thank you." He seems relieved, his shoulders less tense, and the lines on his forehead have disappeared. "It's tonight at seven. If you want to head out and get ready for dinner, you're welcome to do so."

I take in my work attire and frown. This definitely won't do for a dinner with potential investors.

"I'm going to take you up on it."

I walk toward him, lean up on my toes, and kiss his cheek. "Thank you again, Grant."

Without another word, I gather my stuff and I'm out the door. I need to impress, and right now, I'm less than my best.

———•———

With the hotel not yet open, the gathering Grant planned for tonight with Ace and Ethel Knapp is set up on the roof-top terrace. I admire the breathtaking view all around us.

From the hotel rooftop we have a panoramic view of the entire city. Goose bumps pepper my arms as I take it all in. It's magnificent.

"Thanks for inviting me tonight, Mr. Lancaster."

I decide to go with professional, feeling a little out of my element in this moment. I turn my head to look at him and find him watching me intently.

"Grant. Call me Grant, Bridget."

My name rolls off his tongue, his voice throaty with seduction. I find it hard to breathe with him around. He's told me repeatedly he doesn't care about his wife, but I can't help but still feel what we've done is wrong. He's married. He's a father. I'm not a hussy.

At least during the day, I can concentrate on work, but here, even though we're talking business, it feels like we're not boss and employee. Right now it feels like I'm a woman and he's a man. A very delectable looking man, indeed. For one night, I don't want the warring voices floating around my head to compete. I don't want awkward or stifled conversation. I'm an adult. He's an adult. We can both be professional.

An hour into the discussion of plans for the hotel and expansion in the future, Grant has hit his stride. His suit jacket is discarded, shirt sleeves pushed up to his elbows, and he's leaning across the table, assured and powerful.

"Why Europe?" Mr. Knapp, Silicon Valley, venture capitalist and possible investor for foreign expansion of The L, asks while sitting back and crossing his arms.

"Why not Europe? The piece of property we're looking at

is in a provincial location that could benefit from additional tourism. The place is stunning, but without nearby accommodations, it's virtually nonexistent to tourists. With luxury accommodations and the right marketing, we could put this town on the map."

"You won't disclose the location, so how can I possibly understand what you're proposing?"

"Yes, won't you paint us a picture, Grant?" Mrs. Knapp bats her eyelashes, clearly taken by my companion for the evening.

Grant gives a short nod. "From one side as you're perched atop a hill, you have views of the cobblestoned streets of a town that has some of the best pastries in Europe, wonderful cafés, antiques, and one of the best farmer's markets in the area. On the other side, you'll have a panoramic view of the sea for as far as your eyes can see. The clearest blue waters will have you thinking you're in the tropics."

"It sounds lovely."

"Throw in the first-class service of The L, and you'll have no reason to leave. It'll create jobs for the small village and bring more money through from tourism."

His excitement for the hotel is evident to everyone sitting at this table. The air is electrified by his charisma. Grant talks for what feels like another hour about the possibilities with expansion into Europe, and Mr. Knapp is eating out of his hand. He's secured enough interest that further expansion is a big possibility for The L.

"Lancaster, you've sold me," Mr. Knapp states. "Big things

are ahead for The L and Knapp industries wants in. Count on our funding."

Grant sits back, putting his hand under the table. His large palm brushes against my bare leg and a shiver runs down my spine at his touch. He looks over at me. He doesn't move his hand and I can barely handle the tension crackling in the air between us. Watching him talk about The L was one of the biggest aphrodisiacs. Now that he's touching me, I can barely breathe.

"How's Chelsea doing?" Mrs. Knapp's words cut through the tension like a dull knife. The reminder of Grant's wife ruins any chemistry between us and makes me feel like an interloper. I'm not here as his date. I'm here as an associate.

Grant stiffens beside me at the mention of Chelsea and then removes his hand from my skin. The void of his warmth makes me feel cold and insecure. He doesn't look my way, and for that I'm thankful. I'm trying the best I can to smile and act interested in the question so to not give away my true feelings.

"She's doing well."

"That's wonderful. Such a lovely woman. Please give her my best."

He nods, and with that, I find the perfect time to make my departure.

"It was so nice meeting all of you, but I must head out," I say, not focusing on any one person as I collect my things. "I apologize for having to cut the night short, but I have a lot of work to do." I stand on shaky legs.

Three pairs of eyes meet mine. "It was lovely to meet you, Bridget. Good luck with our Lancaster here. He's going to make you a very busy girl," Mrs. Knapp says.

I give a tight-lipped smile to her, just wanting to be gone. *You have no idea, lady.*

"It was wonderful meeting you, as well." I turn to Grant. "I'll see you in the morning."

I hurry downstairs and out of the hotel. My exit was so awkward, but I had to get out of there. I was ready to combust. I'm halfway down the sidewalk when I hear Grant calling my name. I turn to see him jogging toward me.

"Grant? What are you doing?"

"I'm sorry about back there. I shouldn't have touched you. I'm sorry she mentioned Chelsea. They go way back and—"

I throw my hands up in the air to stop him. I don't want to talk about Chelsea. Her name alone can ruin the night. It's a reminder that no matter how strongly I feel, he'll never be mine.

"It's fine. I'm just tired."

I begin to walk away toward my place.

"Bridget, don't lie to me," he says, grabbing my hand to stop me. "Let me walk you home."

I twist around to look at him. "Oh, no, you really don't have to. Honestly, it's not far." I try to not sound desperate for space from him, but I am. His very touch has the effect of a tsunami on my insides. With one simple brush against me, my will to fight him would disappear and my body would melt into his.

"Well, then, you shouldn't mind." He smiles. "I told them you had my keys so I said goodbye and ran to catch you."

"You shouldn't have. I'll be fine, Grant."

My tone is a little harsh. I need to get away from him so I don't do something stupid. Something like push up on my toes and press my lips against his in the middle of the street for anyone to see—*including his wife.*

"Please, Bridget. After all the help you've been, I don't want you to walk home in the dark. It isn't safe. I won't hear of it."

I throw my hands up in surrender. "Fine," I say in exasperation.

We walk in silence for a couple of blocks. "What do you think about the idea for the fountain in the middle of the lobby?" Grant asks awkwardly from beside me.

The fountain? Is he serious?

"Um, I'm not sure it's needed. The hotel is so beautiful and modern looking. A fountain would take away from that and completely throw off the feng shui."

He looks at me. "Feng shui?"

"Grant, you can't tell me you don't know what feng shui is. You own a freaking hotel, for shit's sake."

He laughs at my outburst, sidling up beside me so our shoulders are touching and his hand brushes mine. I warm instantly at the slight touch. "Enlighten me."

"It's about centering and balance to make an environment pleasing to all," I scoff. "From the details I saw, that designer of yours doesn't even have the damn fountain balanced.

Besides, fountains are more old-world in my opinion. The hotel has absolutely zero old-world vibe. It wouldn't go at all. I'm shocked you even considered it." This conversation is . . . *different*.

"Interesting," he muses. "The decorator was Chelsea's idea. I think you're right. We need to pass on it."

There she is. No matter how much I want to avoid her, she creeps in. The muscles in my back tighten. My jaw clamping tight as I grind my teeth.

"Don't do that," Grant commands. "Don't make that face. I'm sorry I even said her fucking name, but you're right, the idea was ridiculous. I don't even know why I entertained it."

I smile to myself. I'm finally being heard by Grant Lancaster, and chosen in some small capacity over *her*. It's childish and the very definition of ridiculous, but I can't help it. When I finally see my apartment, my shoulders sag in relief.

"Well, this is it. Thank you so much for walking me home," I say lamely.

I lean forward, placing a kiss on his cheek. I turn my head and his lips lightly brush over mine.

*What the fuck did I just do?*

He pulls me into him, deepening the kiss. I sigh into it, needing this more than I realized. Standing here on the curb of my building, I allow myself to melt into him. A moan escapes my mouth and it only fuels him on. We walk backward toward the wall where he pins me in place, bringing his hands up my sides, just below my breast. My knees go weak and I need more. More of his mouth, more of his touches, more of him.

He strokes my breast through my dress, making my nipple pebble and my core tighten. "Bridget, you're beautiful."

"Oh, God . . ."

He grabs my leg, placing it around his hip, pressing his erection into my core. I whimper at the feel of him through my clothes. I'm on fire, and the need for release is growing by the second. I'm about to ask him into my apartment when his phone begins to vibrate in his pocket.

I pull myself away, breathing raggedly. I'm pathetic.

"Don't say a word, Bridget. We both wanted that, and I won't let you make this awkward."

"Too late," I groan.

"No. It doesn't need to be. Get out of that head of yours."

"I'm sorry. I don't know what else to say."

"Don't say anything." Moving a stray hair behind my ear, he leans in and kisses me once more, leaving me speechless. It's such a tender thing to do. "Go. Get some rest. I'll see you in the morning."

I nod, smile, and walk toward my apartment, every doubt from moments ago forgotten by his actions. I'm on cloud nine and I hope the fall is worth it.

# CHAPTER TWENTY-ONE

## Grant

FOUR DAYS.

It's been four days since the kiss outside Bridget's apartment. I've found that I count my days based on moments with her. It's fucking stupid for a number of reasons, but I couldn't care less. For once I feel something other than the typical animosity, regret, and self-loathing.

My phone rings and I answer an unknown number. "Grant Lancaster."

"Mr. Lancaster, it's Margret."

My stomach shifts uneasily at the sound of my daughter's nanny calling. The woman sounds like shit.

"What number are you calling me from?" I bite out, annoyed that not only is she calling me at the office, but where the hell is she? She better not have taken my daughter somewhere.

"I just got a new phone. I'm running a fever and vomiting. I'm going to have to leave."

"Why are you calling me? You're supposed to call Chelsea

if you ever need to leave early. Contact her."

"I can't get in touch with Mrs. Lancaster, so I'm calling you."

Fucking Chelsea. She's probably off causing me more issues. "Did you call her?"

"Yes, but she's not answering."

"All right, I'll get my stuff together and be right there."

"I'm sorry, Mr. Lancaster."

"It's not your fault. I'll hurry."

I hang up without another word. The soft opening is a few weeks away and I have a mountain of things to do. The last thing I need is to quit my day early. I stand and pace my office.

"Everything all right?" Bridget asks from the doorway.

"My babysitter is sick. I have to go home, but I have shit to do."

"Can your daughter come here?"

"We won't get anything done here with her." I get a crazy idea. "Would it be all right with you to work with me from home?" *Shit, I didn't think that through.* Having her in my home is a bad idea for so many reasons.

"I don't know if that's a good idea."

It's not, but we don't have any other options. Bringing Isabella to the office isn't an option, and we can't lose a day with the opening approaching. In truth, the only person who would have an issue with it is Chelsea, and she's the reason we're in this predicament to begin with, so I don't give a fuck what she thinks.

"It's the only option we have. There's too much to get done and I need you, Bridget." My eyes penetrate hers, begging, pleading for her to agree.

"Okay." Her head nods as she contemplates my suggestion. "Sure. I mean, I need to be flexible, right?"

My body relaxes. "Yeah?" I should have known Bridget would rise to the occasion. She's amazing and I don't deserve her in my life.

"Let's go get your daughter."

She strides out of the room like she's on a mission, and I watch in awe of the beautiful woman. She's willing to sacrifice her own comfort to help my daughter. She's everything Chelsea never was, and in this moment the thought of never truly making her mine causes a stabbing pain in my chest.

# CHAPTER TWENTY-TWO

## Bridget

MY HANDS ARE SWEATING AS WE WALK THROUGH the doors of Grant's home. On the other side of this threshold is his daughter. *Oh, God. What the hell am I doing?* This is a bad idea. I can't meet his daughter. I've practically been the other woman.

*I am. Present tense. I. Am.*

I turn to walk out, determined to fix this fucking colossal mistake before it gets to the point of no return, but I feel Grant's large hand grab me at the elbow, halting my move. "Bridget, calm down. Where are you going?"

I turn my head to look him in the eye. "This is such a bad idea, Grant. I can't be here. I've kissed you," I whisper. I've kissed him plenty, but this is a step too far. This is their home. Their daughter is here. I think about my parents, and what my mom has felt all these years with the betrayal of my father, and I instantly feel sick. I'm the other woman. I'm the interloper.

"Bridget, I might technically be married, but that

relationship has been over for years. I don't give a fuck about Chelsea. It's Isabella I want to protect. Do you understand that?"

"Of course. That's why I think this is a bad idea." I can't do this to her. What will she think of me?

"You're my employee. She won't know anything beyond that. Ever."

His words sting. He's right and I know what he says is true, but it still hurts. No girl who's been kissed by a man wants to be referred to as just *his employee*. Especially not one who's finding herself falling for her boss.

I'm the loser in this equation.

"You're right. I *am* your employee, and you *are* my boss, and we have work to do. Let's get things going. I have things to do tonight." I walk past him, tall and determined.

"Hold on. I didn't mean to hurt your feelings."

I stop and turn to him. "You didn't hurt me, Grant. I'd never let you."

He flinches slightly at my harsh tone but doesn't say another word as he leads me toward a closed door. "This is my office. If you'd like to get set up, I'll go check on Isabella and relieve the nanny."

I nod.

Ten minutes later a concerned Grant comes barreling through the door. "Isabella is running a fever too. She failed to mention that. She's been such a great nanny up until recently."

"Where is she?" I ask, standing to follow him. I have very

little experience with children, but I remember what my mom did for me when I was sick.

Grant walks us down a hall, stops outside an open door, and moves aside for me to enter. The room is beautifully decorated in pale shades of pink. A large canopy bed is situated in the middle of the room, and lying atop a mound of fluffy covers is a little girl. I move toward her sleeping body. Putting my hand to her head, I find that she is, in fact, running a fever.

"Do you have a thermometer?"

"I have no idea."

"Does Chelsea have a medicine cabinet for Isabella's medications?"

"I believe Margret has a cabinet in the kitchen with Tylenol and some other things."

"Great. Grab me some children's Tylenol, a thermometer if you have one, a towel, and cool water."

He nods and leaves. Several minutes later he comes back with a box full of the items I asked for, thermometer included.

"Her fever is high, 103.5."

"What does that mean?"

"It means we need to get meds in her and get the fever down." I shake Isabella lightly to wake her. When her little eyes blink open, she's confused and a little alarmed to see my face first, a stranger. "Hi, Isabella. I work with your dad." I motion my head toward him so she can see he's there. "I came to help you feel better. Can you sit up for me?"

She shakes her little head. "Who are you?" she questions.

"I'm Bridget. Can you open your mouth and take this for me?"

She opens her mouth and I dispense the Tylenol. "Good girl. Okay, now I need to put this towel on your forehead. It will be a little cold, but it will help you feel better. Is that okay?"

"O-Okay," she whispers in a little voice.

I position the damp towel on her forehead and help fluff the pillows so she'll be comfortable.

"Can you read me a story?"

I look at Grant, hoping he'll help me, but he's no longer there. "Sure," I say, not wanting to upset this poor little girl. "Do you have a favorite?"

She nods. "Can you read that one?" She points to a small table and on top is a book called *Fancy Nancy* something or other.

"Of course."

She scoots over and pats the bed for me to sit with her, so I do. We get comfy and I begin reading the story. Before too long, Isabella is asleep, her head resting on my arm. I look down at her and smile. She's such a cute kid. When I raise my gaze, Grant is standing against the doorframe with an odd look on his face. I can't tell whether he's upset or not. I immediately feel awkward and out of place.

"She's asleep. Can you help me move her?"

He comes to my side and obliges. I tuck her little body in and check her forehead. The fever has gone down.

"She'll be good."

"Thank you, Bridget. I don't know what I'd do without you." He leans in, placing a small kiss on my cheek. My body heats at the gesture.

"I'm happy to help."

Our eyes lock, and there's no mistaking the fire burning in Grant's eyes. If I just leaned in a little more . . . Before I have another second to contemplate it, Grant moves, his lips gentle on mine. I pause for only a moment before opening to him. Our tongues caress each other, losing ourselves in the moments, neither of us gives a thought to his sleeping child or the fact we're in his home . . .

*Chelsea's home.*

As soon as that crosses my mind, the moment is broken. I quickly step back, breaking our connection. "I-I'm sorry. That was . . . a horrible thing to do."

"Bridget, please. You did nothing. I initiated the kiss. I *needed* to kiss you."

"Why?"

"The way you were with Isabella. You were so caring. Chelsea can't be bothered with her and it kills me. I do my best to give her all the love she needs, but I can only do so much. I try. I really do, but it's not enough. I want to give her the world."

His words affect me greatly. How can a mother not care for her child? The thought makes me sick to my stomach, but his love for his daughter warms my heart at the same time. I can see how much he loves that little girl and it endears me to him.

"I really am sorry, Grant. She deserves better than that. You deserve better than that."

"She loves you," he says, motioning toward the sleeping Isabella.

"She's a kid. I read her a story. Of course she likes me." I laugh.

"It's more than that. She takes a while to warm up to people, but she didn't with you."

"I like her. She's special, Grant."

He beams. "She's my world. There's nothing I wouldn't do for her."

I want to ask just how much he'd do for her. Would he stay in a loveless marriage? He alluded to the fact they're together but not together in the sense of a true marriage. Perhaps he stays for Isabella. I can tell how much he loves her, and it's clear nothing would ever come between them, especially a woman. I know how important a father is to a little girl. She needs him as much as he needs her.

"Since you're here I have a few papers in my office I'd like to go over with you. Can you stay?"

I nod, and he inclines his head before walking down the hall. I follow, eager to get my mind off him and back to work.

---

"Can you hand me the blueprints for the room?" Grant asks hours later, not looking up from the paper in his hands.

I find the blueprints and lean across the table to hand them to him. In the process, my top gapes at the neck, giving too much exposure to my lacy bra. Grant doesn't hide his appreciation. The smile on his mouth has me believing he likes what he sees.

"See something you like, Mr. Lancaster?" I tease before I think better of it. I'm still very much in his home. The home he shares with his family, including his estranged wife.

"Very much, Miss Miller."

My cheeks heat at his compliment.

He peruses the blueprints for several minutes before letting out a puff of air and putting the papers down on the table with a thump.

"I can't look at these anymore. Let's do something."

"Like?"

"What's one thing you haven't done in a while that you'd like to do?"

I think about it for a moment. There are so many simple pleasures I don't get to enjoy anymore. I've been tied to work practically twenty-four seven, since I started at The L. Even when I'm home I find things to do revolving around the hotel.

"Watch television. I'm so behind on *The Walking Dead*."

"Seriously? *The Walking Dead*?"

"What? It's suspenseful and the actors are awesome."

I'm only halfway through season one, and if I'm being honest, I had to stop because it was creeping me the hell out. There are some things one must not watch while living alone.

"I can't claim to have watched it. I don't watch much television at all. I never have."

"We can start at the beginning. You can't start in the middle of it."

He smiles. "You're willing to delay your progress for me?"

"Of course. It wouldn't be fun any other way."

Grant walks me to a room close to Isabella's, not wanting to wander from her. We settle onto a large L-shaped couch and he throws me a comfortable blanket. "Here, in case you get cold."

I smile up at him, loving how he cares for me at times. He turns the large TV on and starts to search Netflix. I can't help but smile at him while he does this. It doesn't seem like much, a simple gesture, but I'm so used to him at the office, to him being larger than life, that seeing him like this, relaxed and searching for a show, acting normal makes me happy.

Once he finds the show he wants, he reclines back. He's so close to me I can feel his leg adjacent to mine. I can also feel the hand that he has placed on his knee. The tip of his pinky finger is gracing the material covering my thigh, and if I move closer, we'll be touching. My heart pounds in my chest.

Should I move?

Should I diminish the space between us?

I debate the discussion in my mind, berating myself for thinking about this when I know I shouldn't.

*I can't.*

Not here. Not now.

I make myself look at the TV and pay attention, instead of

thinking about what it would feel like to have him embrace me in his arms. It's hard to concentrate on the show, but I push through all the resistance in my overactive brain and look up just as a zombie on the screen leans in to kill someone. I twitch in response to the gruesome scene playing out in front of me, and my pulse accelerates . . .

But not from the show.

My silent wishes have been brought to fruition. Grant has pulled me closer. His arm is now around my shoulder, comforting me. All the tension in my body releases as I settle into his embrace. My eyelids lower as my breathing slows. Being in his arms brings me peace, but then I hear the sound of a door opening and he stiffens. He pulls away from me quickly and stands. I look at him in confusion.

"She's home."

My heart lurches in my chest at the *she* he's referring to. "I should go." I want to say before she sees me. But I don't. I can't stand the idea of seeing his wife right now. Of seeing them together in their house. That would crush me. I pull out my phone and order an Uber. "My car will be here in five minutes. I'm just going to wait outside, I have a lot of work to do before tomorrow," I offer lamely and he just nods. A part of me breaks that he doesn't object.

But I knew he wouldn't, so I give a weak smile and show myself out.

———————•———————

The days pass fast. With the opening around the corner, there is little time to think about anything but work. I still find myself thinking about the kiss, but when I do, I busy myself with tasks or call Lynn.

"So, what do you have going on tonight?" Lynn asks me through the phone.

"It's actually the soft opening party."

"Are you serious? Already?"

"Yep."

"You're so lucky. Only you would weasel your way into one of the hottest exclusive parties in the city," Lynn chides.

I chuckle. "Weasel? I've worked my ass off for this. The least they can do is invite me to a party."

Lynn laughs. "You're probably right. That Karen may have been a bitch, but she sure as hell hooked you up."

"You have no idea. She might've thought she was sticking it to me, but what she really did was find me the perfect job."

"You love it that much?"

"I do. I really do."

Working in the hotel industry has been so much more than I ever dreamed. What I've learned in this short time has been monumental for my future. Even if I haven't been doing marketing this temporary job has helped solidify my path, and for that, I'm so grateful. The whole experience has been wonderful except, of course, for the early part with Grant and the consistent uncertainty of where I stand with him.

"You're going to have so much fun, Bridge."

"I can't wait. Although I hope it's not one of those

awkward parties where everyone just stands around looking at each other. That'll kill the whole exclusive party vibe."

"Dear God, it could be epically bad if that happens. You'll end up saying things just for the sake of making conversation and inevitably make a fool out of yourself. Please, don't do that."

She's right. I do have a habit of talking just to make conversation. I really wish she wouldn't point out all of my downfalls. It makes me feel self-conscience. "Thanks for the vote of confidence, biatch. There'd better be champagne."

"This party is being hosted by The L. I guarantee there'll be champagne."

"You're probably right. Listen, I gotta run, but wanna do lunch this week?"

"Yes, totally. Have a blast at the party and call me tomorrow. I want to hear all about it."

"I will."

I put down the phone and stare at my closet. This is my first work party and I'm starting to freak out. This opening, soft or not, is huge for The L. Hell, it's huge for New York. The whole city is abuzz with the exclusive invite-only opening. I don't want to screw up my first and potentially only high society event. My palms grow sweaty and a bead of perspiration settles on my top lip as the pressure mounts.

*Get yourself together. It's a freaking party.*

The internal pep talk works and in the end, I settle on a skintight black dress. One can never go wrong in a little black dress. A pair of red Louboutin pumps that I borrowed from Olivia a while back and I'm all set. I pull my hair into a low, loose knot and allow a few tendrils to fall around my face. I want to look elegant yet sexy chic. Looking into the mirror as I put on the finishing touches of my makeup, I'm pleasantly surprised by how well I was able to throw myself together despite my nerves. With a quick peek at the clock, I see I'm finishing right on time to head out the door.

The whole way by taxi my leg bounces up and down. I feel like Cinderella must have felt being late to the ball, although I'm not late, and I'm certainly not losing a Louboutin tonight. My sister would kill me. Besides, there isn't an available prince waiting to sweep me off my feet. This isn't a fairy tale.

When I arrive, I give my name to the doorman. As I walk inside, a gasp escapes my mouth. The entire place has been transformed and I can hardly catch my breath. The amount of time and work that went into tonight has paid off in spades. This place is incredible. It's straight out of a Hollywood movie. *Great Gatsby, eat your heart out.*

As I blink myself back to reality, a waiter walks by with a tray of champagne. He holds one out to me and I take it with gratitude. Lynn was right. It's the sort of party where champagne will be in abundance. I take a sip and the bubbles pop down my throat. I spot Jared in a dark blue suit, grinning at me. He has a young, boyish charm I generally don't go for, but I can't deny he's cute. With all of the uncertainty surrounding Grant and me, Jared might prove to be a very nice distraction.

"Hi, Jared. The place looks incredible." I beam.

He looks around and grins as if he were the one responsible for the whole thing. Which, as an intern, he certainly couldn't have been. I know he helped plan it, and the proud expression on his face gives him away. "It is. I've been looking forward to it ever since I joined the team." He marvels at the handiwork of the party planners. "I knew it would be nice, but I never dreamed it would be quite so amazing."

"It really is amazing, Jared. Grant will be so thrilled."

Jared's brow rises at my use of Grant's first name. Around here nobody else would dare. I should be more careful. I intend on correcting myself, but Jared lets it go. "I'm happy they let me help pull it together. So, how's work going with Mr. Lancaster?"

"It's certainly interesting, I'll say that. He's tough, and I'm constantly feeling as if I'm going to fuck up big time. But at the same time, I've learned so much from him. It's truly been a great experience."

"He's a hardass. I've heard it from everyone, so don't let it get to you. I'm sure you're doing great."

I shrug. "Yeah, I guess."

"You have to be, or he would've sacked you already. Lancaster isn't known for charity with employees. He fired several before you came along, so I'd take it as the highest form of a compliment from him that you're still here."

"Well, thanks for that," I say dryly. Just how many did he have? And why did he fire them? My mind runs wild with possibilities, and some are not fun to consider. Was there any other assistant he was . . . *close* to?

"Here, let me get you another glass," he offers as he picks up another glass of champagne for me off a passing tray. I quickly down my drink and take the new one.

"He stresses you out that much, eh?" He winks, and I return it with a coy smile.

"Sorry. I should probably sip a little slower." I chuckle awkwardly.

"No need to ever be embarrassed when it comes to over-indulgence in alcohol. I can easily match your game," he says and downs his glass.

I chuckle. "Impressive."

I finish my third glass while Jared tells me all the dirt he knows about the hotel. I wait for him to tell me something about Grant, but he never does. Instead, he lifts his chin to someone he knows across the room.

"Ah, I'm sorry to do this to you mid-conversation, but I need to go say hello to someone. I hope you don't mind. I'll be back a bit later."

"Don't worry about me. I'll mingle." I wave him off with a smile.

The second he's out of sight, the lavishness of The L hits me in full effect. The place is extraordinary. I take a few more minutes to marvel at the detail. Strings of crystals hang from the ceiling, catching the light from the chandeliers. Large vases pepper the room, overflowing with flowers I can't even name. They are beautiful.

My eyes catch Jared, and I watch as he blatantly flirts with the woman he practically mowed over seconds ago. It's clear from here that he likes her and I can understand why. She's gorgeous. Tall and slender, long red hair flowing to mid-back. She looks like a classy version of Jessica Rabbit, and Jared is practically drooling. I'm a bit far, but he really looks like a lovesick puppy.

As if the girl can hear my thinking about her, she turns to face me and from the first time since this whole exchange has started I notice who the girl is. My mouth drops and she must see the shock on my face because her mouth parts into a large smile. The beautiful bombshell is Paige, and it's obvious I'm not the only person to notice the amazing transformation Paige has made. Jared is enthralled.

A small pang hits my chest. It's not as though I want to date Jared, but I envy the two of them as it's clear the feelings are mutual. When will I find someone? More importantly, when will I find someone who is available? *Ugh.*

As if my night couldn't be any more depressing, in walks Grant, and on his arm is none other than his wife, Chelsea. If the pang from moments ago was distressing, this feels like being plowed over by a dump truck. Just the other day I was in his arms. I could feel how much he wanted *me.* Herein lies the issue with my working conditions. I never know where I stand with Grant, but in the end, it doesn't matter. He's married and has a child.

The thoughts running through my head threaten to unravel me. Tears prickle at the corners of my eyes and bile is making its way up the back of my throat. I can't be here. This isn't professional, and I'm a goddamn professional if nothing else.

I spy a quick exit, and without a second thought, dart toward it. I find myself in a secluded hallway, relieved that I've escaped unseen. Marching forward, I search for an exit but I never make it. Someone grabs me from behind, pulling me through a doorway and into a pitch-black room. I whirl around, but the room is so dark I can't tell who's kidnapped me.

"What's wrong?" Grant's voice rings out and I gasp.

"N-nothing. I-I just needed air," I lie.

"Bullshit, Bridget. You're upset. I could tell from across the room."

"Why were you watching me from across the room? Your wife is with you," I spit out.

He grabs me by my elbows, stabilizing me. "Stop. Don't do this. Tonight is important, and for all the work we've done it shouldn't be spent like this."

"What do you want from me, Grant?"

"Nothing, Bridget. I just want you to enjoy yourself. Did I do something?"

I contemplate lying again to get him to allow me to leave, but at the end of the day, I'm sick of this dance we're doing. I'm tired of not knowing what's going on between us. One minute it's clear that his marriage has been over for a long time, yet the next they look cozy. I'm done with it and I want answers.

"Yes, you fucking damn well did something. You kiss me

senseless one day, and the next you show up here looking pretty damn happy with the wife you claim to hate. You tell me. How should I feel?" I pull myself out of his grasp and cross my arms protectively across my chest.

"Bridget, I'm sorry. I never meant to confuse you or make you feel as if I've led you on. I'm married. It might be over between us, but legally we're still together and in the eyes of investors, we're a team. I can't confuse people or give them a reason to question the state of the company. Any unrest could result in them pulling funds, and you know that can't happen right now. Too much is at stake."

He's right. I know he is, but that doesn't make it hurt any less. "Then stop doing this. Stop making me feel like there's a chance when there isn't." I turn to find the door to exit but am turned abruptly by Grant's strong hands.

"I'm just trying to explain why I allowed her to touch me, Bridget. I don't want her anywhere near me, let alone touching me. You have to know that. This is for appearance only."

"I get it, but I hate it." I sound weak and it makes me sick. I'm not this girl. I don't allow men to hurt me. So why is it different with Grant? "This is a mistake, Grant. I can't do this."

"Nothing about us is a mistake, Bridget."

"Tell me why I should stay in this room with you?" I need him to tell me he wants me. I have to hear him say it.

"I need you. I *want* you, Bridget. Not a single woman in that room has my attention. Only you."

All rational thought is gone.

My lips clash with his in a fury. My hands come up to find his face and hold it to mine. We're simply a man and a woman desperate for each other's touch.

"I need you, Bridget." Grant's words come out raspy and heated.

"Take me."

With that, my dress is pulled up to my belly and I'm lifted off the floor, his hands under my ass. I wrap my legs around him, pulling his hardness into my core. The sensation has me gasping and him moaning into my mouth. Removing one hand, he unzips my dress and pulls it over my head. My breasts are pulled free and my back hits a wall. Grant lowers his mouth to pull one of my nipples into his mouth. My head falls back on a moan.

"Grant, please," I beg, needing more, so much more.

He lowers me to my feet and spins me so my back is to his chest. Trailing his hands down my sides, they continue lower until his fingers find my panties and pull them to my ankles. I step one foot at a time out of the black lacy garment. He's on his knees behind me and I'm shaking, waiting for whatever comes next. His mouth finds my wet center. One swipe and I feel undone. He laps at me over and over, bringing me closer and closer to the edge of composure. I'm panting and desperate for release, holding on to the wall in front of me to hold me steady.

"Come for me, Bridget," Grant commands before inserting two fingers. My core clenches and release comes at his command.

Standing, Grant places small kisses on the back of my neck. His hands hold my shoulders as he whispers in my ear.

"You are not a mistake, Bridget, and I'm done staying away." His words send heat through my body. "I need you to understand the position I'm in. Trust me. Trust in us, and I promise one day we won't have to hide in a closet to be together."

It's the only thing I want to hear. He says it so convincingly, too. I want to believe him as I can tell he believes it to be a possibility. The truth is, I know there are obstacles in our way that even he doesn't have a solution for. There are so many conflicting emotions running through me, but tonight I just want to revel in the fact he made a promise of more. A promise of a future. It's more than I ever expected and exactly what I want.

I want him.

All of him.

For tonight, I'll pretend there's hope for a future.

# CHAPTER TWENTY-THREE

## Bridget

WAKE EXTRA EARLY THE MORNING AFTER THE PARTY. Anticipation and nerves will do that. I don't know how to act. He promised me more.

*He wants to be with me.* The thought is both intoxicating and sobering at the very same time.

Even five hours later, it doesn't feel like a new day. It feels as though only seconds ago his breath fanned my lips.

I couldn't sleep well. Heady visions danced behind my lids until they grew so intense I gave up the pursuit of sleep. Eventually, rest found me, but it was short-lived. When my eyes popped open, it was five o'clock. So now I lie here, knowing I can't possibly fall back to sleep. I sit up, stretch out my arms, and shake the sleep from my body. Going to the office early could be smart. That way I can be there before Grant.

Thirty minutes and a shower later, I feel invigorated, like a new person. One who can take over the world, or in this case, be strong and indifferent to my boss for the sake of a future. He's right. The investors have to feel confident. Chelsea is a thorn in our sides, but just for now. It doesn't always have to be this way. If he said we can be together, then he'll find a way, right?

The warm fall air has begun to fade, and outside my building, there's an early morning chill. I have time to walk today, so I will. It's far but not too far, and today I need to think. I need to feel the air against my face. Breathe in the calm. At this time of day, New York City is empty. A few stray cabs rush by but, for the most part, I'm alone with my thoughts. Within the next thirty minutes, the peace I'm finding will be gone. I don't even bother putting in my earphones that I usually use to distract and cocoon myself on a busy weekday morning. Today I welcome the sounds.

When I arrive at the hotel, it's nearly empty. Since we aren't open yet and the workday doesn't start for at least two hours, it's almost desolate in the lobby. I walk to the far elevator—the one designated for the upper floors where our offices are. I scan my key in the elevator pad, it opens, and I ride up. I'm shocked to find he's already here, but I'm not prepared. With an inhale of oxygen, I square my shoulders.

"You're here early," he says. "Again." His lips spread into a smirk. A lethal one. The kind of smirk that has the potential of landing me naked in his office in boatloads of trouble. *Distance. Distance yourself.* The words play a mantra in my head. This is not the place to lose your cool.

"Yes. I have a lot of work to do. If there's nothing you need, I'll start."

His eyes widen a fraction, and then he nods. "Nothing yet."

"Well, then. I'll be in my office if you change your mind."

I head to my office, knowing my words held an innuendo I didn't intend. My words came out husky and inviting. Far too inviting for an employee and her boss.

I busy myself for hours, trying to snuff out the need I have for him. I can hardly control myself, and it's ridiculous. One night should not make a sex-crazed maniac out of me.

Occasionally, I hear the hum of his voice echo from down the hall, implying he's not happy with someone or something. Typically, that attitude would be directed at me, but not today.

I pull up the list Grant sent me yesterday and start to work on the items I still haven't done. *Must distract myself.*

I'm not sure how much time has passed when I hear a discreet cough coming from the doorway. I peek up from behind my desk. Grant is standing in front of me. How long has he been standing there, staring at me?

"Would you like to have lunch with me?" he asks, and as much as I want to, I can't accept. I don't think I can trust myself to be professional today. My body is aching for him.

"I'm sorry. I can't."

A smirk takes over his face. He obviously is not buying what I'm selling. "Are you avoiding me, Miss Miller?" The playful tone of his voice has my need intensifying.

"No. I'm just busy, and you tempt me to want to do things we can't do in public places." I need to think straight, and I can't with Grant Lancaster being charming and boyish. It's a recipe for career and life disaster. He'll be my ruin, but I'm not allowing that to happen today, no matter how much I want to. If I'm alone with him, we'll be caught in the office on his desk. Or maybe on the floor. Who the hell knows, but we'll definitely be caught with our pants down.

He smirks wider. "You are avoiding me."

"For both of our sakes. Now go get yourself lunch and then get back to work." I smile up at him and blow a quick kiss.

# CHAPTER TWENTY-FOUR

## Grant

GET IT. I KNOW WHY SHE'S KEEPING ME AT ARM'S LENGTH IN the office. We can't flaunt our relationship in plain sight. It could cause issues on a number of fronts, and Chelsea is the least of my concerns. Bridget is right, but fuck, I don't like it. Why can't things be back to the way they were before the party, when her guard was down and mine was, too? It's going to be a long few months if I have to pretend she's not important to me.

I pick up my phone and dial her extension. She's not even able to say her name before I'm firing out, "Bridget, my office. Now." My tone is stern but not harsh.

"Oh, okay," she squeaks. Timid, scared. *Good. She should be.* She can't hide from me anymore.

She walks in, her upper teeth nibbling her lower lip. I look at that lip. *One kiss. To taste her just once.* She dangles in front of me like forbidden fruit hanging from a tree begging me to grab it. To taste it. To savor it. Her lips part on a sigh and I can no longer think straight.

"Close the door." She follows my instructions. I stand and march toward her. "This needs to stop." Her pupils enlarge at my words. "I know what you're doing, but it's not what I want."

She straightens her back, and I sense she's trying to appear taller and not intimidated by my voice. "I'm not hiding from you," she says coyly. Now she's intentionally toying with me. I see her smirk. She knows how much I want her—*need* her.

"I should get back to work."

Before I can stop myself, I cage her in beside the closed door. "Like hell you're leaving, Bridget." We're so close I can feel her brushing against me, and then I close the distance. Taking her mouth. Owning it. My kiss is anything but sweet. It's angry and possessive. My kiss demands her to kiss me back. I slide my tongue against the seam of her lips and she parts them for me. *Good girl.*

Her mouth opens wider. Her tongue meets mine and I take a step closer, her back hitting the wall. When her arms wrap around my neck, I'm lost from her touch. I find myself pulling at her, grabbing her. Feeling her. She's compliant in my arms, allowing me to have my wicked way. Before I know what I'm doing, I'm lifting her into my arms and placing her on my desk.

She shudders and I smile. Reaching out, I push her down so she's lying flat, her bare legs dangling over the edge. I trace her thigh, trailing up and continuing the path until my hand is beneath the hem of her skirt. I lift the material slowly, and goose bumps form across her alabaster skin. Each inch the material moves up has Bridget shivering. I stroke higher until I touch the soft cotton covering her. Her heat radiates through the thin material.

*God, I need to be inside her.*

I run a circle over the sensitive flesh hidden beneath. Teasing her. Torturing her, and ultimately tormenting myself.

"Please," she moans.

"You want me to fuck you?" I rub a little faster. A ragged moan leaves her mouth as I push harder to apply more pressure. "Do you? Is that what you want?"

She lifts her hips in answer. I chuckle and remove her thong. With one push of my hand, I spread her legs farther apart. She's a goddamn feast in front of me. Glistening. Begging me to taste her. *Fuck.* My tongue juts out and meets her sensitive skin.

"Oh, God." She pants and I part her with my finger, my tongue continuing its assault on her bundle of nerves. I lick. I suck. I move my fingers inside her.

*One.*

*Two.*

*Three fingers.*

She stretches to accommodate the invasion.

I draw out her pleasure. Making her pant, making her beg until she finally bites down on her hand to silence her screams. When I feel her body tremble around my finger, I know she's ready for more.

With my free hand, I unzip and pull a condom out from my pocket. When I put it in my pocket the other day, I hated myself for wishful thinking, but now I've never been so happy with a decision I made. I settle between her hips, cup her ass, and lift her up, aligning myself with her core.

Thrust.

A ripple of sensation moves through my veins.

I slam inside.

Pull out.

Thrust.

She can't help but whimper every time I withdraw. Her nails grip at my skin. I increase my speed, slamming inside her over and over again until she's shuddering her orgasm.

It's too intense.

It's too fucking much.

I want to taste her, feel her, own her all at the same time. This woman has me undone. Every muscle inside me tightens and I explode, too.

# CHAPTER TWENTY-FIVE

## Bridget

A S FAST AS I HIT MY HIGH, I COME CRASHING BACK TO reality. I just let my boss fuck me on his desk. *Oh my God. What have I done?*

I've been playing with fire for a long time, but there's a big difference between making out and fucking him in the office. Not a huge difference, but *shit.*

*What have I become?*

My eyes shoot open. He's still inside me. We're still intertwined. His body is flush against my chest. I can feel each erratic beat of his heart as he regulates his breathing. As I regulate mine.

I raise my hands and forcefully push him up. He lifts but doesn't leave my body. His brows knit over unfocused eyes. "What's going on? Why are you freaking out?"

"You've got to get off me," I say with more force, and he pulls out.

"Bridget—" he starts, but I raise my hand.

"Don't. Don't say anything. What the hell have we done?"

"I'm sorry. I didn't want the first time to be like this. I just—"

"Stop. We both did this, but we need to pull ourselves together. We're in the office, for fuck's sake."

"Breathe," he says calmly. It's as if he sees nothing wrong with this. How can I be the only one of us who sees what a colossal fuck-up this was?

"We're in the office. Anyone could've seen or heard us." I throw my hands in the air. "What about the fact you're married and we're supposed to keep this under wraps as to not lose investors?"

"You're right. It was careless, but I don't regret it."

"Your wife is in the building. You just cheated on her and she's in the building."

"That's an entirely different matter. One I don't give a damn about and you know it." He steps away from me, pulling his pants back into place. His smug indifference to my freak-out only pushes me farther over the edge.

"Say something," I demand.

"First off, it's not actual cheating when the marriage is mine," he mumbles.

"What the hell does that mean?" I balk.

"It means for all intents and purposes, we aren't married."

"That's bullshit and you know it."

He grabs a tissue and hands it to me, then makes work at removing any evidence of our tryst. I stand there glaring in his direction. He walks to his chair and sits as if we're about to have a goddamn business meeting.

"Sit," he says.

"I prefer to stand," I reply in defiance, suddenly feeling like an insolent child. The truth is, every time Chelsea's name comes into play I get hostile. It's not lost on me that I'm being irrational, but I can't help it. She holds all the cards for my life and I hate her for it.

"I said sit," he demands, but when I don't move, his mouth opens. "Please." His tone softens and a chink in my armor gives way.

I nod and take the seat across from him—the seat I've taken so many times in the few weeks I've worked for him. Now, after everything that happened on this desk, it's hard to concentrate.

"I'm going to tell you a story, and after I do, you can decide how you want to proceed. Okay? Can you do that?"

"Yes. Talk."

He sighs at my indignation. "Seven years ago, I was fresh out of business school and had just started working for my father. He owned and operated Lancaster Holding Company. He was grooming me to take over." His eyes look lost in a past he obviously wants to forget. "When I started working, I met a beautiful young woman there named Chelsea Roberts. She came from a poor family, was hard working, and in the short time I was in college, she'd gone from a receptionist to office manager. She was smart, beautiful, and most of all exotic. She was everything I wanted. I needed her from the moment I met her."

Jealousy coils in my blood as he speaks of his wife. I want

to dash out of his office and cry. His words make me hate him more. They make me hate myself more. Chelsea sounds like a normal girl who fought her way to success. She's someone I can admire, as I'm striving to advance the same way she did.

"I thought I loved her," he whispers out, but there's no mistaking the venom in his voice. "And I thought she loved me. We were going to take over the world." He rakes his hand through his tousled hair. "One day I told my father I intended to marry her. He knew there was something between us, but he never imagined I'd want to marry the girl from the wrong side of the tracks. She wasn't good enough for me in his eyes. He demanded I have her sign a pre-nup.

"When I spoke to Chelsea about it, she started to cry, asking how I couldn't trust her. She broke everything off with me and tried to leave. I was so in love with her, I begged her to stay. I was so young and dumb, Bridget. She had me duped into believing we were truly in love and my father was the enemy.

"I marched into his office and told him I wasn't leaving Chelsea. He tried to reason with me, but in the end, he gave me an ultimatum." Grant grimaces as he remembers the past. "Her or the company. It was black and white. My father had wronged me. He chose business over family, so I did what I thought I should. I chose her."

I sit here nodding, not knowing what else to do. It sounds like something straight out of a Shakespearean play. *Romeo and Juliet* without the double suicide.

"I lost everything that day, but I didn't know it then. It took me six months to realize how big a mistake I made. Six months for the paperwork to go through telling me I was officially written out of everything Lancaster."

"I'm so sorry, Grant. That seems harsh. How in the world were you able to do all of this?" I gesture around to The L in wonder.

"My trust kicked in at twenty-five, so I had money. From that, I had enough money to invest wisely and afford The L."

"Your father took those things away from you, not Chelsea," I point out. It seems he's unfairly blaming her for everything . . . unless there's more to the story. "What does any of this have to do with your current marital situation?"

"We ran off and got married right after my fight with my father. When the paperwork came finalizing my expulsion from Lancaster Holding, Chelsea showed her true colors. She wasn't content with only being my wife. She married me to take over the world, and without my family that wasn't a reality. That's when I realized she never really loved me. She loved the money and power my family held."

"What happened with Chelsea, Grant?"

"She wanted a divorce. As far as she was concerned, I was worthless to her. She'd just reached out to an attorney when we found out she was pregnant with Isabella. After that day, everything changed. The one thing we both agreed on was that we wanted more for our daughter, so we sat down and made a plan. That's when the idea of The L was born. Fueled with rage in my life for my father and for Chelsea, I set out to take over the world and ruin him."

"But—" I'm confused. I didn't even know where to start.

"My marriage to Chelsea is merely for show. We haven't been together in years. We formed a partnership to take down my father and build our own fortune for our daughter's sake. A few months after Isabella was born, Chelsea stepped out on me. That picture you found, that was taken right before I found out my whole marriage was a lie. There have been numerous affairs over the years and I've known about most of them."

"You're okay with your wife sleeping around?"

"That's the thing. I don't see her as my wife, Bridget. She's merely my daughter's mother and a business associate."

"Why would you ever go into business with her? You could've built this on your own."

He nods and then begins shaking his head back and forth in frustration. "We don't have a pre-nup, Bridget. Anything I build is hers too. She made sure of that."

Oh God. With all the money the Lancasters have, a pre-nup should have been standard practice. What the hell was he thinking?

"If all I have is hers, at the very least, she would work for her half. That's the stance I took. There wouldn't be any handouts, especially after she showed her true colors. My father saw through her from the beginning. He knew what she was after, and when he tried to tell me, I wouldn't listen. He was smart to cut me off."

"Have you spoken to him?"

He huffs. "No. That relationship was ruined years ago."

I see the turmoil and hurt in his eyes. The loss of his family weighs on him and it's heartbreaking, but why doesn't he try? Isn't his family worth trying to salvage? I want to ask him all of these things, but getting him to open up has been a feat and I'm not ready for him to stop sharing, so I turn the subject back to Chelsea.

"So, you've both carried on affairs for years?"

He laughs, but it's not humorous at all. "There hasn't been anyone else for me until you."

My mouth hangs agape. "You haven't slept with anyone in—"

"About four years." The words hang in the air, hovering above us. *Four years.* Not since the birth of their daughter, Isabella.

I'm speechless. *How is that even possible?* He's Grant Lancaster. Women fall at his feet. Why wouldn't he sleep with his wife? Fighting aside, he must have still wanted her, at least sexually. What happened there? I shake the thought away. Thinking about him and his wife, even if I know they aren't together like that, makes me sick.

"I hated women for a very long time. I was so burned I didn't want to be with anyone. I surrounded myself with work and raising the funds, securing the location and most importantly being a dad. My whole life has been Isabella and The L. Until you."

"Until me?"

"There was something about you that drew me in. I don't

know, but when you're around, you make me forget. You make me want to move past this feud. You make me hope for a better life, even if it's only for a brief moment. *You* make me believe that maybe one day I can have more."

"So, why is Chelsea still around, Grant? If you want more, why don't you take it?"

He hangs his head. "Chelsea will never let me go."

"I don't understand. She sleeps around on you. You said she wanted to leave."

"She wants the illusion. She wants to pretend we're the perfect power family. She wants the money. The reputation. Trust me. If I could, I'd leave her. But I'm leveraged to the max."

"It's just money, Grant."

"No, Bridget. It's not just money. It's The L. My own achievement. I can't lose it, and even if I were willing, there's so much more. Things that mean so much more."

"What is it?"

"Isabella. I won't allow Chelsea to take her from me."

"Come on, Grant. This day and age, fathers get custody all the time. She can't keep your daughter away from you."

"But she can." His head falls back as he runs his hands down his face. "She has me by the balls. Not only do I have no pre-nup, but she . . ." He pulls at his roots. "You have to believe me when I say I can't. She really does have me by the balls."

There's something he isn't telling me, but I don't press. Today has been chock-full of information overload, and I don't know how much more I can take. Besides, looking at him, I get the sense he's done sharing. There's more to uncover about the Lancasters, but for today I'll throw him a bone.

"I understand."

"You do?" He seems surprised and a bit confused.

"Of course." I know he feels he has no other choice but to stay. I know it all the way through me to the marrow of my bones. *Why? That's the million-dollar question.*

"So, now what?"

"I truly don't know, Bridget. I should let you go. I know I should. It's not right to do this to you. It's not right to put a giant bull's-eye on your back, to bring you into my shit. But Lord help me, I can't stop. I want you, Bridget." He stands and steps around to lean over me. "Don't say no."

My mind screams he'll break me, but I don't care. I can't say no to Grant Lancaster.

---

The next day we're at an impasse. Neither of us is acting normal. It's as if we don't know what we're supposed to do in this situation. Are we doing this? Are we not? I'm so confused. I'm in a fog the whole morning.

By two that afternoon, I still haven't spoken to him. I'm about to go in search of him when we're all called into a meeting to go over the timeline of the launch.

The table in the conference room is empty. I take a seat and one by one employees file in. Most of the seats are taken by the time Grant comes in. There's one vacant seat across from me and another next to me. Before I can consider the ramification of him next to me and what it will do to my nerves, he sits there. I swear I feel the heat of his body, his chair is so close. He begins to speak, but I don't hear the words over my beating heart. Someone from accounting answers him regarding the release day budget.

After her, Alyssa from marketing starts talking. I've been working closely with her for weeks on some ideas I've had. Secretly, I'd hoped to be transferred to that department, but with everything going on with Grant, I can't decide what I want. Alyssa introduces the idea of using social media influencers that I pitched to Grant. As she starts rattling off my work, Grant places his hand next to my leg. His fingers graze the skin beneath my skirt. My breath hitches.

*What is he doing?*

She continues to prattle off details as his hand travels farther up, pushing under my skirt until he's right at my lace thong. *Oh my God.* He wouldn't. *Would he?* I keep my head facing forward, desperate to not give anything away to the people around us. He keeps rattling off questions as if his hand is not on me, as if his finger hasn't just dipped inside the scrap of material separating him from me.

He can't possibly . . .

He does. His finger swipes at my core, almost dipping inside me. Teasing me, barely breaching. My body secretly protests, begging him to enter. He doesn't. He just sits there on the precipice. Circling his finger. My body is on fire and my core tightens in need, but that all changes in an instant. In walks Chelsea and the fire that raced in my veins a moment ago is extinguished by what feels like ice-cold water. She takes the one empty seat at the table directly across from me. I don't want to meet her eyes, but something sick and twisted inside me has me looking up and finding her glare.

She's more beautiful than I imagined. Everything about her screams sex and power. The worst part is, she knows it. She demands attention. Not even in the room for one minute and all eyes are on her.

I'm so distracted by her, I haven't noticed that Grant has slipped his finger inside me. My body quivers in response. Chelsea's eyes widen as though she knows exactly what's transpiring. I want to push him off, tell him he's being obvious, but I'm so lost in his ministrations I don't. I clamp my legs tightly around his hand in protest. Perhaps Mrs. Lancaster deserves a taste of her own medicine. Who am I to protest?

My heart pounds in my chest. I'm going to come. I'm going to come, staring at Grant's wife. I should be appalled. I should be ashamed, but I'm emboldened. He continues to pump his finger in and out, causing me to straighten in my chair. Chelsea's wide eyes have all others looking toward Grant. Just like that, he stops . . . and I'm left hanging, desperate and frustrated. I want to object. I want to beg for him to finish. But I don't. I can't. We were almost caught by a room full of peers and the thought has me mortified.

By the time the meeting is over, I'm a ticking time bomb.

I don't even know what to do with myself. I'm anxious, aggravated, and feeling foolish. I'm not even halfway down the hall when I see Grant and he's not alone.

He's talking to Chelsea and he's not happy. She looks like the cat that ate the canary as she smirks, turns, and saunters in the opposite direction. Her hips sway and her heels click. I watch her like a spectator who can't get enough.

"Bridget." Grant's voice pulls me out of my thoughts. "My office, now," he barks.

I head in his direction and move to sit, but I never make it. I hear the door close behind me, pause, and his body is behind mine in two steps, his hard length pressing against my skirt.

"Is everything okay?" I breathe out.

"It's better now that I have you alone."

I turn to face him. "Grant, stop." I push him away. "What was going on with you and Chelsea?"

"I don't want to talk about her. Not now. Not ever. She's not our concern." He whips me around so my back is against him once more. "You were so close to me that whole damn meeting, soft and wet against my hand. I could almost imagine how you taste. The thought lingered through my mind the entire time. I didn't hear a word anyone said."

"You could've fooled me with all of your tyrannical questions," I tease, liking this. The way we are right now. No estranged wives or room full of onlookers. Just us.

"Tyrannical, huh?" He chuckles and pulls me closer, his mouth coming down to trail kisses on my neck. "I had to pretend I was listening."

It's my turn to laugh.

"I need to satisfy my curiosity."

"Curiosity about . . . ?"

"If you still taste like dessert, Bridget."

Tingles course their way down my spine. My already soaked panties dampen even more.

"I know it will haunt me all night if I don't have you." His hand reaches between my legs and he dips his finger in and out. He pulls them away from me and the sound of him sucking his finger makes me convulse with need.

"I want more, and then I need to be inside you."

I don't object. Just turn around and stare at him.

"If you want it, take it."

He steps forward, caging me in against his desk. He lifts me up so I'm perched before him, a willing prey to a predator.

"Spread your legs," he commands. "Let me see all of you."

I do as instructed, practically salivating with need.

"Lean back on your elbows."

I groan, lifting my hips. Trying to meet his finger.

"What's wrong, Bridget? Do you need more? Are you desperate for it?"

My whimpers ring out. I don't care if anyone hears. This is almost too much. I want him too much.

"I'll take care of everything. I'll give you what you want. What you need."

He does. He gives me everything I need as his tongue

swipes from one end of my core to the other. As he circles my most sensitive spot, my vision gets hazy. He's literally undoing me. His tongue thrusts at my opening, begging for entrance, but it's not his tongue I want. I *need* him inside me.

"Please, Grant. More. I need more."

My words stop him cold. All the buildup of moments ago is snuffed out in an instant. I don't know what I said, but he's gone still and isn't saying anything. I'm confused, per usual, and feeling foolish when he finally speaks.

"You know I want to give you more, right?" He stands and looks at me. "I'm only capable of this for now. I want to be honest with you, always."

"I know. I don't understand everything going on between you and Chelsea, but I know what we have is something more than a fuck on a desk."

"So much more, Bridget. There are things you don't know—"

I cut him off. "I don't care about that right now. I know what I'm getting myself into. All I want is this. You're all I want. As long as you feel the same way, we'll navigate this together. I need this. I need you, Grant."

"You mean everything to me. I'll fight for us if you will."

"Yes."

He pulls me into his arms and seals his lips against mine.

I expect him to take me like he did before. To fuck me on his desk, but he moves away and looks at me with hungry eyes.

"Off the desk."

I follow.

"Turn around."

I do.

"Brace yourself."

I lean forward and comply, my arms bracketing in front of me on his desk. I hear the familiar sound of a condom wrapper. He enters me with fast slams of his hips.

"All day long. All day I've been thinking about fucking you like this. Bridget, you drive me crazy."

"Good," I breathe.

"Just be here." Thrust. "Now." Thrust. "Fuck tomorrow." Thrust. "Fuck everything." Thrust. "Just let me fuck you." Thrust.

Primal.

Primitive.

"I fucking need this. Need you," he groans into my neck.

"Then have me."

I fear my words will come back to haunt me. As much as I delude myself into thinking this is enough, the little voice inside my head is screaming at me.

*I'll lose my heart to Grant Lancaster and I'll never get it back.*

# CHAPTER TWENTY-SIX

## Grant

I<small>T'S BEEN A FEW DAYS SINCE</small> I <small>HAD MY WAY WITH</small> B<small>RIDGET</small>, and we're trying to be more careful, but fuck if I actually care at this moment if we get caught. *I should call her in here right now.* I start to imagine what she'd look like on her knees before me. But just as I'm daydreaming of her mouth around me, the door to my office swings open and someone comes barreling in. At first, I expect it to be Bridget having changed her mind about our agreement, but it's not. The room feels stifled and I instantly know who it is. I'm not sure how he got in, or what he's doing here.

"Spencer," I grate.

Seeing him here in my office feels . . . wrong. My betrayals seem so much bigger than before as he looks around at what I've built. The company built to be in direct competition.

"Grant," he responds back coldly. His hard stare penetrates me, making me feel small despite the fact I'm taller and broader.

"To what do I owe this honor?"

"You've been avoiding my calls."

What would I have said? My wife is trying to take everything from you? I've been a party to it. Dad was right? "Didn't see a point in talking."

"You didn't see a point in talking?" Sarcasm pours over his words. "What about owning up to the fact you bid on multiple properties I was looking into?"

A pit erupts in my stomach. Knowing it was happening and being called on it are two different things. Before this visit I could pretend it wasn't happening. Now, I have to own up to my mistakes and I'm not fucking ready to do that. Call it pride.

"Small world," I draw out, letting my lips part and spread into a smirk.

I know I'm being a dick when I have absolutely no reason to be. I'm in the wrong, but I can't just admit it. This has always been my problem. Instead of owning my mistakes, I hide them under sarcasm and an arrogant attitude. I'm untouchable, is what my actions portray, but inside another piece of me is dying.

"Seriously? That's your answer?"

I shrug.

"You called Addison?"

"I did business with her for years. Or did you forget? I was once in your spot at The Lancaster." My words drip with misplaced contempt.

"You were never where I am," he bites out. His words sting because he's right. I wasn't.

"I would have been."

"But you weren't. And that's not my fault."

It's not. It's mine, but it doesn't make it any less bitter.

"Why are you here, Spencer? Don't you have an empire to run?"

"I came for answers."

If answers are what he came for, he came to the wrong place. I've been trying to get to the bottom of Chelsea's shady dealings for some time. I want to direct him to her, but I can't. I've allowed it. I'm culpable.

"There's nothing to tell, Spencer."

Not unless I'm ready to divulge that my marriage and life are a sham. I'm not, so I level him with a stare, telling him without words that I won't budge on this matter.

"Is this a continuing problem I need to worry about?"

"No. I don't plan on looking into any properties you are," I huff.

He tilts his head, looking at me as though I can't be trusted. The truth is, I can't promise him what I am. Chelsea will do whatever she wants and unless I have someone on her twenty-four seven she'll get away with it.

"That's over, and I think this meeting is—"

"Grant. I have the papers . . ." Bridget stops just inside the door and her eyes widen.

"What the fuck?" Spencer asks. He looks from Bridget back to me. "What the fuck is she doing here?" he screams at me. "As if it's not bad enough you go after my company, now you're going after my family?"

"Family?" I ask, playing it like I don't know. Of course I know who she is, but I don't confirm it. "Bridget isn't family." A sick feeling seeps into my blood. *Possession. She's not his. She's mine.*

"Cut the shit, Grant. It was low enough that you took my property, but to hire Olivia's sister? You've gone too far."

I look at Bridget. She's gnawing the inside of her cheek.

"Was this some plot to gain information on what we're doing at The Lancaster?" Spencer barks at me.

"No. I didn't hire her. She was sent here by a temp agency."

Spencer drills Bridget with a stern glare. "What were your motivations?"

"I needed a job," Bridget yells. "I knew you and my sister would overreact. Karen set me up here and I took it."

"Karen? Are you fucking kidding me? She knows better. This reeks of something sinister and I'm going to get to the bottom of this," he spits in my direction. "Does Olivia know?" Spencer asks Bridget.

"No."

"What the hell, Bridget?" he hisses.

I step forward, walking right up to him. "Don't speak to her," I grit out, standing in front him and ready to pounce.

"I'll speak to her if I want. She's my girlfriend's sister, for fuck's sake."

"I-I needed a job. I knew if I told her she'd be pissed." Some of my anger diffuses at the sadness in her voice. She looks as if she may break. She clearly never wanted to make Spencer or her sister upset.

"I think it's time for you to leave," I say to Spencer.

He looks at her and she nods. He turns back to me. "We aren't done yet. Eventually, you owe me answers. About everything."

I know what he's asking. He wants to know about a distant past I have no desire to relive.

He walks out.

Bridget just stands there. She looks like a scared little girl, one who isn't sure what to do or say. Her response is misplaced and alerts me that something else is going on. She's afraid of something.

"Are you mad?" she whispers.

I walk to her, studying her. *Am I mad?* It wasn't like she lied, and who am I to judge? I lied about knowing who she is. I lied about how she ended up here. Fuck, I lied about being married. There isn't much I didn't lie about.

"No." I pull her into my arms and she sinks into my embrace. "You should've told me," I say, pulling back an inch to study her face.

"I'm sorry." She bites her lower lip. I lift my hand and caress the side of her face. She turns her head toward me, welcoming my comfort.

"I don't want to lose this job. Lose you. Not yet."

I lift her chin with my fingers, their tips caressing her jaw. Her blue eyes hold my gaze. "Me neither."

"Why don't you talk to your brother? Explain to him."

"No."

"Did you go after his company?"

"I did."

"Was it the money?"

"I'm not motivated by money. I'm motivated by success. To prove myself. To show that I can."

"To whom?"

"To everyone," I answer.

"Is that success? Or arrogance?"

"Probably both." I shrug.

"Seriously, Grant." She crosses her arms and narrows her eyes at me. It's cute the way she's bossing me around. "You need to stop being stubborn and talk to him."

"I think you should probably take your own advice. Sounds like you and your sister need to have a talk."

"I will, but not today."

She leans up and places a kiss on my lips, making all thoughts and questions disappear.

# CHAPTER TWENTY-SEVEN

## Bridget

'M NOT EVEN HOME AN HOUR BEFORE I HEAR THE KNOCKING on my door. It doesn't take a rocket scientist to know it's my sister Olivia.

I don't even bother looking through the peephole. I'm actually more surprised that she knocked and didn't let herself in with her key because she obviously let herself into the building, officially ambushing me. I swing the door open and she walks in. Not speaking. And I know she is livid.

"Why?" she finally says.

I look at her, not really able to voice my reason. How do you say, I finally had something that was mine? Something that was solely about me, and it turned out it wasn't. I didn't want her to ruin it.

"It wasn't about you, so I didn't mention it."

The hurt is evident on her face, her eyes dripping agony. "Does Lynn know?"

"Yes."

She looks like she might cry.

"I don't care that you work for him," she says.

"You don't?"

"No. I get it. It's a great job opportunity. My problem is you didn't tell me. Do you know how much it hurts to know my sister doesn't trust me?"

"This is why I didn't tell you. For years it's been about you. About Lynn. I finally wanted it to be about me," I say on a broken sob. Tears stream down my cheeks at the admission.

"Bridge." Olivia's voice cracks.

"I'm fine." I wave her off.

"You're not. You obviously feel a certain way. Talk to me."

"It's nothing." I shake my head, not wanting to answer.

"It's not nothing. I can see it's bothering you."

A tear rolls down my cheek. "I realized I need this for me. Karen gave me no choice, but once I started working, I realized I was good at it. I didn't tell you because I didn't want you to ask me to quit. I didn't want you to take this away from me."

"I wouldn't have."

"I didn't know that," I admit.

"This is more than that. This is about trust."

"I do trust you, Liv. I've just lived in your shadow for so long, I wanted to shine for once. On my own, not as your kid sister. I didn't want to be the consolation prize."

"What does that even mean?"

"Between you and Lynn, it's hard to be seen." I feel awful saying the words. They seem so petty after everything she has been through.

"Why didn't you tell me you felt this way?"

"You were going through so much, I didn't want to seem selfish. I didn't want to burden you."

At my words, she walks up to me and takes my hand. "You're my baby sister. You could never be a burden."

I nod, not wanting to break further.

"So, now it's out in the open. Sit down and talk to me." She walks to the couch in my studio, not taking no for an answer.

"I don't even know where to start."

"How about the beginning?"

"Can't I start at the end?" The laughter dies in my throat.

"Nope."

Thirty minutes later, I've told her everything about Karen and my first job. I tell her all about work, leaving out details along the way—big, giant details. I'm not ready for her to yell at me. I'm also not ready to break Grant's confidence. There's obviously deep-seated resentment between Grant and Spencer. Telling Olivia means telling Spencer, and that's not something I'd do. I'd never give him leverage to hurt Grant.

After I'm done, she smiles. "It sounds like this job is perfect for you."

"It is."

"I'm happy. Maybe it will turn long-term." She gives me a reassuring smile, but I know better.

"I'm not too sure about that," I respond.

"Why not?"

I shrug. "It's only temporary." *Like my relationship with Grant.*

"Maybe he'll change his mind."

"He won't." The thought breaks my heart, but deep down I know we're fleeting. Eventually, this will run its course and once again I'll be alone. I give her a small smile, not wanting to discuss it anymore.

"Maybe." She looks at her watch. "Oh shit. I didn't realize the time. I'm meeting Spencer for dinner. Do you want to come?"

Going to dinner with her and Spencer is the last thing I want to do.

"I'm kind of tired from today. I'm going to stay home."

"You sure?"

"Yeah, but thanks."

She stands up and places a kiss on my forehead.

---

Not even an hour passes before I hear my cell phone ring. I can't find it and frantically search the couch for it. By the third ring I'm sure I've missed the call, but when I slip my hand behind the cushion, I'm met with the cold metal. Without even looking I hit the green button.

"Hello?"

"Bridget?"

"Yes?" I pull the phone away and notice a number I don't recognize. "Who's calling?"

"It's Grant."

Grant. Oh my God! What is Grant doing calling me? Even though we've been intimate at the office, I'm shocked to see him calling me. No matter what happened, this is a line we haven't breached. I'm excited and nervous at the same time.

"Hi," I murmur. "Is everything okay?" I hear him breathe deeply into the phone and instantly I'm on edge.

"Yeah. I just called to check on you."

"To check on me?"

"Is that so hard to believe?"

"I'm just surprised."

"What are you doing?" he asks.

"You'd be bored to tears by my laziness."

"Nothing you could do would be boring to me."

My legs feel like jelly. I shouldn't take his words to heart, but I can't help it. They weave through me, singeing my insides with excitement.

"What have you been doing that's so boring?" he presses.

"Honestly? Earlier was anything but boring. Olivia just left."

"How did that go?"

"It went okay. She's not angry at me for working for you. She's angry I didn't tell her."

"I'm sorry about you being in the middle of my family drama," he offers.

"Not your fault." It really isn't. I could have told her anytime and avoided the whole mess.

"Are you mad at me? About keeping who I was from you?"

"No. I couldn't be mad at you." He stops talking for a minute, and I listen to the sound of him breathing through the phone. "So, back to your current state of boringness." He chuckles.

"I was about to order Chinese."

"Do you want company?"

*Oh my God! He wants to come here?* "I . . . you want to come here?" I ask, puzzled.

"Is that so hard to believe?"

"Kind of. Compared to where you live, my place is a hovel."

"I'm in a different point of life, Bridget. I wouldn't expect you to live in some grand place. You just graduated college."

"It's just . . . I'm embarrassed by it."

"Stop. I only want to be with you. We've both had a rough day and I don't really want to go home yet." His voice is low and full of emotion.

Now that I know a little about him and his life, I understand why he doesn't want to go home. I'm sure it wasn't easy for him to see Spencer after all this time and on such poor terms. It can't be easy knowing his brother is living the good life while his is falling apart.

Jealousy is a wicked thing. I should know. That's the thing about Grant and me, we're similar. I understand. That thought makes something inside of me want him here too. If only to comfort him for a while. I want to be that person for him.

"Come over."

"I'm on my way." We don't say goodbye. We both just hang up. I look around my small studio apartment. It won't be hard to clean, but I'm running out of time. I run around picking things up and stashing them in their typical places. The intercom chimes as I'm fluffing a pillow. With steady steps, I hit the button.

"Hello."

"It's me."

"I'll buzz you up."

As I wait for him to knock, butterflies swarm my belly. As much time as we spent together, this will be the first time we do it outside of the office. He's not my boss. I'm not his employee. We're just two lonely people seeking solace in each other's company. I pace; the beat of my heart picking up with every second that passes, and then I hear the knock on the door.

Grant steps into my apartment, his presence too big for my small space. He's everywhere, he's everything, he's all-encompassing as he levels me with his stare. The energy between us crackles.

"Can I get you something to drink?" I ask, suddenly feeling out of place in my own space.

Crossing his arms in front of his torso, he steps forward and looks at me as if I'm the only woman in the world. As if I'm his savior.

"Later, Bridget. First I need to lose myself in you. Forget about everything." He closes the distance. I take a step backward, my back hitting the wall in the entrance. He leans down, his breath tickling the skin of my jaw. "Will you let me do that?" He trails farther down, his tongue lapping a line as he proceeds. "Will you let me get lost in you?" he mumbles into the crook of my neck. I don't speak. I can't. A desperate moan escapes my lips. "Too many clothes." His hands are pulling at my shirt. Until the button pops open and my breasts are exposed.

"You have too much on too." I smirk.

My hands roam down his chest until I find the hem, and then I lift it. Once removed, I place a kiss on the hollow of his neck, down his collar, and across his breastbone. Slowly I lower my body to the floor. On to my knees until I'm licking and teasing the V of his hips. I unzip his pants, finding him hard and ready for me. With a swipe of my tongue, I place him in my mouth. Engulfing him in my warmth. I stroke him, lick him, suck, until he's panting desperately.

"Up," he orders before picking me up, walking us across the room and then throwing me on the bed. I quickly strip off my clothes as he puts on a condom and then crawls up my body, bracing himself on top of me. He settles in the crook of my hips. Until I feel him tease at my entrance. Slowly, painfully slow, he slides in, joining us, burrowing himself deep inside me. I rock under him as he thrusts inside me.

So deep, my breath hitches in my chest.

He strokes my jaw, lifting my chin so our gazes can meet. His greens eyes bore into me, saying unspoken words I can only dream to hear one day. They tell me how much he cares.

How much I mean to him. How much he wants me.

He shows me with each inch of his body, with each thrust of his hips. First slow, then deep. Soon he picks up his pace.

A deep, primal cry starts to form in my mouth, but he silences me with his kiss.

Deep and passionate.

Our hips buck together.

He pulls me closer until there's no space between our bodies. He begins to move faster than before. Lifting my hips, I match his rhythm.

Fast. Hard. Desperate. Primal.

A storm starts to brew inside me.

One thrust.

Two.

On the third, I come apart. *We both do.*

His body jerks within me, and an audible breath escapes his clenched jaw. In heavy breaths and pants, moans and gasps, we both succumb. We hold each other, our breaths coming out in tandem.

"Do you want to talk about it?" I finally ask.

"Talk about?"

"Today. With your brother. Do you want to talk about it?"

"Not exactly. I'm over it. Most of his grievances against me are valid. It's not really him who has me worked up. It's Chelsea."

I stiffen at her name.

"I know about you and Chelsea, but I know there's more, Grant. Will you tell me?"

"Are you sure you want to know?" His eyes seem to turn darker.

"Honestly? I'm not sure. But I feel like I need to know."

He nods. "I need to tell someone. Sometimes I feel like I'll explode."

"Have you ever thought about seeing a professional?" I ask.

"A shrink? No."

"Well, then, allow me to be your shrink for the day."

"I'll try, but I don't even know where to start."

"The beginning?" I say and he lets out a deep sigh. "I'm sorry."

"Don't be. I've just never told this to anyone. I've never trusted anyone to keep this secret, but I trust you."

"Tell me."

"My wife . . ." he says and then clears his throat. "I know I told you pieces of it, but the rest . . . it's bad. In the beginning, right when her true colors showed, I guess I kept hoping she'd change. Isabella changed everything for me. She's my everything, but she's also my one weakness. That fact is easily exploited."

"I don't understand why you don't just leave. Why not take Isabella and leave?"

"Chelsea won't let me. That's the thing with her. When she wants something, she gets it. No matter what. For whatever twisted fucking reason, she wants to be married to me. If I left, I'd lose my daughter. That she promised."

"How can she keep your daughter from you? I guess I just

don't get it."

"Because she's not mine," he yells.

I jump and my jaw drops at his confession. "She's not yours?"

Grant regards me with sad eyes. Eyes that have been through more pain than I can ever fathom.

"I stay because if I don't, I'll lose her. I stay and I do everything I can to protect my daughter. Biologically she isn't mine, but I've raised her. She's mine and I won't let Chelsea take her from me."

"How do you know for sure she isn't yours?"

"I had a DNA test done when I first suspected. It wasn't going to change anything for me, but I needed to know how deep Chelsea's betrayals and lies went." Sadness fills me to the depth of my soul. The pain he must go through is unimaginable. Once again I'm met with the similarities between my sisters and me. Again I see the people I care about being ripped apart by a selfish woman.

"Does Isabella know?" I ask.

He shakes his head before whispering "No."

"You have to tell her."

"I can't." He looks so defeated. I want to pull him into my arms and tell him it will all be okay, but I know that keeping this secret from his daughter will hurt her in the future. I know what Lynn went through when she found out her father wasn't her father, and Isabella has a right to know.

"I know this is hard to hear, but one day you have to tell her. When I was in high school, we found out my father had an affair, which resulted in me having another sister. My family lost years because we never knew the truth."

"This is different. There is no father. Chelsea won't tell, ever. Keeping him a secret is too valuable to her. If I tell, I could lose my daughter." His words sink in and I nod in agreement. There's nothing more I can say right now, maybe in the future things will be different. Maybe then he will listen and be open to it. But for right now, I'll just be here for him.

"I'm sorry, Grant."

"I have no choice right now. I stay for one reason and one reason only. Isabella. I've thought about walking away a million times, but I'd sacrifice my own happiness to make sure my daughter is safe. Chelsea isn't a good mother."

"You're a good father. Isabella is lucky to have you."

"I'm not as good as she deserves. I work long hours and a nanny practically raises her."

I balk at his comment.

"Stop. Most parents work. You're doing what needs to be done to provide for Isabella."

"I need to be there more for her, Bridget, and I'm not." He huffs.

"You're a good man, Grant. Give yourself a break. You're running a multimillion-dollar hotel chain. You're providing for Isabella's future. Nobody questions that you're a good father."

"How would you know that?"

"Office talk. I hear it all. People genuinely think you're a good person. Scary, but good."

"Scary?"

"Totally frightening."

He chuckles.

"You're something else, Bridget Miller." He smiles.

I watch as his smiles fades and his eyes drill into mine. I'm almost afraid of what's coming next.

"That night, when I saw you standing there, you were the most beautiful woman I'd ever seen. I had a shitty day, and I was so angry, but somehow this stranger in front of me made it all disappear. All the bad of my marriage, my family issues, that fucking day just melted away when I saw *you*."

I'm speechless. That's not at all where I thought the conversation was going. He looked so serious, so brooding. To know that is what he thought when he first saw me is flooring.

"Grant, I-I don't know what to say."

"When I kissed you, I didn't want to stop. I knew you could be my ruin. I had to get away. I should've stayed away."

"I came to you, Grant. I might not have known it that first day, but I did all the same. I have to believe everything happens for a reason. Maybe I was meant to come into your life to help you through this time."

Grant scoffs. "It's just the universe fucking with my life a little more. It keeps dangling you in front of me. The fucking forbidden fruit." His eyes pierce mine. "I want to give you so much more than I can right now. I can't promise you forever and it's killing me."

His words sting, but they aren't new to me. I know this, and although I don't truly want to accept it, I have no other choice. I'll take any sliver Grant Lancaster throws my way, because despite myself, I've fallen for him.

"Then promise me right now," I say.

Right now he's having a hard time seeing the light at the end of the tunnel. Chelsea has his balls in a vise, twisting and turning every other day. Eventually, she'll tire of her own games. Women like that never stay happy long. After a while, all this won't be enough to keep her. I know her kind. Grant can't see it now, but I can. One day he'll be free of her, and when that time comes I'll have my shot. He's worth waiting for.

I walk over to him and kiss him lightly on the cheek. "Let's get that Chinese. I'm starving."

"Anything for my girl." He gives me an all-American smile and I melt.

It's all worth it. He's worth it.

# CHAPTER TWENTY-EIGHT

## Grant

"WHAT'S THIS?" BRIDGET ASKS AS WE LIE entwined in each other's arms. Her finger trails a circle over a small scar on my chest.

"Nothing," I hiss, moving her hand away from my skin. Instantly, I regret the move. I didn't mean to snap at her. I'm just not used to anyone touching me, let alone touching a place that holds a memory like that one. Softly, her fingers touch my hand and give a little squeeze. I lift my head and look at her blue eyes filled with nothing but concern for me.

"Please," she whispers. "Please tell me about this scar. It obviously hurts you, but if you tell me maybe you will find some sort of peace in the memory."

I realize I want to tell her. I finally want to open up to another person and why can't I?

"I was a kid when I got it. I don't remember much, but what I do remember is I'd fallen and gotten stuck and Spencer saved me." My back is stiff as I remember my older brother saving me. He was always saving me.

"Saved you how?" Her voice rises.

"When he recounts the story, he says I fell from a tree and got stuck on a branch overlooking the lake at one of our family homes. The branch was about to crack and if I'd fallen, I would've drowned because I couldn't swim."

Bridget gasps. "Oh my God. That's scary. Spencer must've been quick on his feet to save you."

"He was. Spencer was always looking out for me."

Her face softens. "Please reach out to Spencer," she pleads. "You clearly miss him, Grant."

"Too much time has passed. What would I even say at this point?"

"Be honest. Tell him you made a mistake and ask for forgiveness."

"Why should I apologize? My father kicked me out. My brother stole my rightful position. It's them who should be apologizing."

"Listen to yourself. Do you really believe the words you're saying? It wasn't long ago that you confided in me you made the mistake of marrying Chelsea. So, which is it?"

"I'm done talking about this," I snap.

"Don't let your pride get in the way of a future with your family. You'll never regret saying you're sorry, but you'll regret not saying it."

She's right. I know she is, but hell if I'll say it out loud. Pride is something I have in spades. It very well could be my downfall, but I'm not ready to admit that to anyone. Not even Bridget.

"I'm not apologizing."

"It's a shame. After everything that's happened between us, you still feel the need to lie to me. You and I both know your family did what they needed to protect the family. It might've been harsh and you may not like it, but think about what Chelsea would have if your dad had given in."

The thought makes me ill. If Chelsea had her way, she would've sunk The Lancaster years ago and taken every last dime.

"All I'm saying is think about it. I could tell in those few minutes in your office that your brother misses you as much as you miss him—despite whatever shit Chelsea's talked you into over the years. He'll forgive you."

*It's me who won't forgive myself.*

<hr>

"What do we have here?" Bridget asks, eyes sparkling when I step into the elevator, Isabella behind me clinging to my leg. Hiding from the world. When she sees Bridget her eyes light up.

"Hello." Isabella claps, remembering Bridget.

"Hi, Isabella. You came to work with Daddy?"

"My mommy too," she whispers.

Bridget looks up at me with wide eyes. "Is Isabella joining us today?"

"She's my right-hand man for the day," I say, and Isabella lets go of my leg and steps out to face me.

"But I'm not a man," she pouts.

"You're right, you're not. You're my right-hand girl. Better?" I smile.

A tiny dimple forms in her cheek and my world shifts on its axis. When Isabella smiles, all is right in the world. She's been the one constant over the years. As many times as I've cared for her scrapes and cuts, she's mended me twice as much. My heart would be made of stone if not for her. With all the disappointment, resentment, and anger, she's been the one thing that's grounded me.

All the anger I have from the events of the morning fade away in her happiness. The elevator chimes, indicating we've arrived at my penthouse office. All three of us file out. Isabella runs forward, leaving Bridget and me to follow behind.

"I didn't realize Isabella was coming today," she whispers.

"Neither did I," I hiss, barely able to control my anger. I step past her, but her hand grips mine.

"What happened?"

"What didn't?"

"That bad?" she asks.

"Worse." I groan. I don't even know where to start, and with Isabella in the office, I don't have much time before she's asking for something. "Let's just say the nanny won't work out and my wife is going away on a trip yet again."

"Oh, shit. What can I do to help?"

"Are you completely against babysitting?" I ask with a wince.

"I can do that. You have a few important calls today. I'll keep her occupied."

All the tension in my body leaves at her words. I've seen the way she's cared for Isabella in a time of need. She has this under control and for the first time today I feel relief. What have I done to deserve this woman in my life?

*Nothing.*

The truth of that stings. What I wouldn't give to unabashedly pull her into my arms right now without a single care in the fucking world as to who sees us. My actions in the past make that impossible, now and perhaps forever. I get to live in hell while my *wife* tours the countryside with yet another fucking fling, leaving me to care for our daughter.

She touches her hand to my cheek and I melt into her.

"Go. Work. I've got this." Bridget's voice pulls me from my dark thoughts.

She has a way of making tough situations inconsequential. I have no worries that Isabella will be well taken care of and now I can focus on work. I've got a mountain of it sitting in front of me, so I push aside the events of the morning and get to work.

When the shadows change in my office, I realize hours have passed, along with several phone calls with investors. It's been a productive day, thanks to Bridget. In fact, I haven't seen hide nor hair of either Bridget or Isabella since I left them this morning.

I clean up my email, straighten some documents on my desk, and then go in search of the two best women in my life.

Rounding the corner, I stop short when I hear giggles.

"Ready?" Bridget asks Isabella.

Bridget has Isabella sitting atop her desk Indian style with a plate of food in front of her. Pretending to have a tea party. A few of Isabella's stuffed animals are sitting next to her on the desk and they are both feeding the dolls. After Bridget makes a big show of how much the panda bear is eating, she offers the fork to Isabella, who takes it and places it in her mouth. She chews and swallows, and Bridget rewards her with a large smile.

"Do you think Panda wants more?"

Isabella nods enthusiastically and the routine continues like that for some time. I stand watching how effortlessly Bridget keeps her happy. The two are quite a pair and it does funny things to me. The fact Bridget knows Isabella isn't my biological daughter but treats her as though she's the most important little girl in the world means everything to me.

Isabella spies me gawking and calls me out. "Daddy, look!"

"Hi, princess. Did you eat all your lunch?"

"She did," Bridget says proudly. "We've been having a great time."

"Do you want to come sit in Daddy's office for a bit?" I throw the offer out, hoping to give Bridget a few minutes break to do whatever she may need.

"Nope. I'll stay here," she says, beaming at Bridget.

"We have plans, Mr. Lancaster. Go do your work and leave us ladies be," Bridget teases.

"Yes. We've got plans, Daddy."

I smile one last time before nodding my understanding and heading back to my office. I'll start the second part of the day knowing full well my daughter is in good hands. Isabella loves Bridget and I can't blame her. Bridget is everything.

———————•—————

Seeing Bridget with Isabella yesterday was almost too much. I wasn't expecting to feel such strong emotions watching them together. It made me want her more and that's not something I can want without complication.

My door opens slowly and Bridget creeps in and then closes the door. Something is wrong. She won't look at me as she walks over to place something on my desk, but I notice that her chin quivers.

"Bridget." Her head lifts up and I can see unshed tears in her eyes. "What's going on?"

"It's always about Chelsea," she whispers.

"Where is this even coming from?" I ask, not understanding what's going on.

"All everyone can talk about is her. No matter where I am. It's always how smart she is, how beautiful. She's like a saint"—a tear drips down her cheek—"and she has you. Does she have to have everything?"

"I don't know where this came from. Can you calm down." I stand from my desk and walk over until I'm standing in front of her.

"How could you even want me? I'm not nearly as beautiful or as smart—"

"Okay. Stop. Stop right there." I take a step closer. So close I can feel her breast heave against my chest. I bend my knees to be eye level with her.

"Don't you dare compare yourself to her."

"But—"

"No buts. How could you even think she could be better than you? A woman—no, a mother who can't even find it in her to love her own daughter! No, Bridget. You're everything and she's nothing."

I let my words sink in. I have a sudden need to brand her as mine. What is it about being with Bridget in the office that ignites me? Is it because it's forbidden, dangerous?

"On my desk."

She sits on my desk and peers up at me.

"Elbows," I demand. "Spread your legs."

She's spread out before me like a feast.

I lick my lips and step toward her. Hungry. Desperate to sink into her. To savor and possess every inch of her. It's been too long. Too many days have passed since I've been able to lose myself in her.

"You have a thing about me on your desk. We really need to get a new place for foreplay," Bridget teases.

"You like to torture me." A statement. Not a question. Not that I mind particularly. I'd take everything she is willing to give me, torture included.

Her chest heaves. "I don't know what you're talking

about," she says, but she's not fooling anyone. She's been torturing me. Swaying her hips, bending over. Pure torture. All so I'd fuck her. I know the game she's playing and I'm happy to oblige. I pump in and out of her but stop short when my office door flies open to reveal Chelsea.

"Oh, what a tangled web we weave," she says as her lip snakes up, showcasing her pearly whites. The smile is wicked. Plotting.

I almost want to smile back at her. Ask if her black heart is crushed even slightly, but I'd have to care to ask that and I don't. If not for wanting to protect Bridget, I'd laugh in Chelsea's face.

"So this is how you spend your nights, dear husband?"

She slithers over and looks at us still joined together. I can't pull away from Bridget, not in her state of undress. I can feel her shaking below me, clearly petrified as to what's going to happen. I stroke my hand down her arm, hoping to soothe her. I won't let this bitch get anywhere close to her.

"Oh, please. Don't stop on my account. I'm sure my husband won't last much longer," she says to Bridget, and that's enough for me to pull out, the evidence front and center.

"Get out."

"Temper. Temper. And in front of the help." She *tsks*.

"*Out.*"

My words bounce off the walls, making Bridget cower underneath me and Chelsea actually look shaken. She turns on her heel and marches down the hall, leaving my door wide-open.

"Fuck," I bellow. "Fuck!" I pull my pants up and throw my shirt on, ready to storm after her. "Here. Get dressed. I'll be back after I take care of her."

Bridget doesn't say a word, only nods.

Now to deal with my wife and her lack of respecting my space.

# CHAPTER TWENTY-NINE

## Bridget

TIME STRETCHES LIKE AN ETERNITY. A NEVER-ENDING loop as I wait. The only problem is I know the truth. The sands of my clock have run out. Grant will be here soon and I know what he's going to say. Our time has run its course.

No matter what we did, how he kissed me, how he touched me, and how good he felt inside me, it will never matter how I feel. He'll never be mine. I saw it in Chelsea's eyes. She'll hold him hostage in his life forever and for Isabella, he'll go along with it.

After being caught in epically embarrassing fashion, I gathered my things and hauled ass to the safety of my home. I didn't want to be anywhere near the showdown between Grant and Chelsea. I didn't want to bear witness to the threats and demands she was inevitably doling out.

When the buzzer echoes, I pretend to not hear it. I'm not ready. I don't want this to end.

*Buzz.*

*Buzz.*

Broken and despondent, I finally answer. "Hello."

"It's me."

I press the button without responding. My stomach slowly bottoms out as I open the door and wait. As soon as I see him walking toward my door, I know my suspicions aren't wrong. This is it. He doesn't kiss me. He doesn't smile. I step aside. He walks past. The sound of his feet hitting the hardwood floors resonates within me. Like the ticking of a clock. One about to expire.

*Tap. Tap.*

I look down to see my own foot has started its own beat, nervously drumming on the hardwood floors. I'm desperate to delay this conversation, yet desperate to get it over with just the same. I close the door and pause for one minute to collect my bearings. I won't let him see me break. When I've willed myself to be numb, I go in search of him. He's sitting on my couch, head buried in his hands.

"Grant," I whisper.

His head pops up, his gaze meeting mine. My vision blurs. My eyes rapidly fill with unshed tears that I smash down. My pride won't allow it.

*Don't let him see you break.*

"I thought we'd have more time." I try to smile.

"I thought so, too," he mutters more to himself than to me.

"What did she say?" I ask, more because I don't know what else to say. Truth is, I don't really want to know.

"Does it really matter?" It doesn't and we both know it.

"I'm sorry," he says, and I can see the remorse etched in his face. It's there in the stiffening of his jaw, the unshaven skin dusting his face.

"It's not your fault. You warned me and I didn't listen." I shrug.

"I don't want this."

"But you have no choice."

"No," he responds with a sigh.

I want to scream. I want to bash my hands against his chest and say there's always a choice. That if I meant more he'd find a way to fight for me, for us. He won't, though, because I'm a passing fling. A woman to lose himself in to feel less pain. I was his own personal bottle of Xanax, but it's being ripped away. The choice isn't ours to make.

I nod, more to myself than to him. Several minutes pass without a single sound or word uttered. What's left to say? Why drag this out?

"I think you should go."

*Self-preservation.*

"I really—"

"No, Grant. Let's not do this." I muster the bravest smile I can manage. "It was fun, but it's over."

Pause. The silence is suffocating us. It is suffocating *me.*

"It was," he finally says, looking as if he wants to say more, but he doesn't. I step past him and his hand moves to reach up, but I move away. He can't touch me. I'm holding on by a small thread. "Will you be okay?"

"I knew from the beginning what this was. You didn't lie about that." It's a half-truth. I might have known what I was getting into, but that didn't stop me from forgetting along the way. Hoping things would change.

"Will I see you tomorrow?"

"Yes," I say to appease him.

I know what I need to do. I have to let him go. I have to let it all go. I have to move on. I open the door to the apartment.

"Bye, Grant."

He steps through without a word. He walks out the door and out of my life.

It's over.

———•———

The next day at work I head straight to HR to request a transfer. When I arrive, Paige doesn't seem at all surprised to see me.

"Hey there," she calls out cheerily. "Mr. Lancaster sent you down bright and early. Did he already tell you about the change?"

"Change?" I manage to squeak.

"He called this morning and said with the opening coming up, marketing is in need of your help. I'm supposed to get you transferred to Alyssa's department."

My stomach drops. This is better. I know it is, but it doesn't hurt any less. He's truly getting rid of me.

"Sounds good," is all I can manage. I don't want to give

myself away, but it's taking everything to hold it together.

We spend the next thirty minutes going through paperwork and the logistics of the change. Paige escorts me to the marketing department, which is unnecessary since I've worked on and off with Alyssa over the past several weeks. But it's nice having her company.

"Well, here you go. I think you'll love working with Alyssa in a broader capacity."

I smile at Paige, not wanting to dampen her excitement. Truth is, she's right. Marketing is more my thing and getting experience in different areas of The L can only help my résumé.

"Thanks, Paige."

She smiles. "Oh, hey. Would you want to grab drinks sometime with a couple friends of mine?"

The thought of going out doesn't sit well with me. All I want to do is work and crawl in bed and shut out the world, but it's not what's best for me. I need to live. I'm young and I need to mingle with people my age. "Sure."

Paige squeals and walks away, leaving me chuckling at her retreating back.

I walk up to Alyssa's desk. It's trashed with loads of papers spread everywhere. They could use all hands on deck in the marketing department, that's for sure. Alyssa looks as if she could pull out her hair.

"Can you believe it's only a week away?" she asks, not looking up from whatever it is she's doing. "I'm freaking. There's so much to be done." Her eyes meet mine and I see a bit of panic in her dark blue irises. "I'm so glad you're here."

"I'm glad to be here. We've got this, don't worry."

She sighs. "I feel confident about it. I'm so happy Mr. Lancaster lent you to us."

The reminder sends a pang to my stomach. He did the right thing. We need space and this opening deserves all of our full attention. As much as it hurts, it was the right move.

"Maybe I can finish out my time here," I reply.

"Oh, that's the plan." She smiles. "He gave the okay for it this morning."

I don't respond, but I feel my cheeks heat in embarrassment. How could he not have prepared me for all of this? It's a kick in the gut, and the feeling of being unwanted circulates through me without permission. This hurts horrifically.

I could call him out on it. I could demand he speak to me directly, but I won't. My fucking pride, as usual, pushes me forward. Not backward, never backward.

"Is there anything you need from me right now? I need to use the restroom," I respond, needing air.

"Nope. You're good. When you get back, we can talk about ads."

"Yay." I force an awkward laugh, but she doesn't seem to notice.

I push through the door and almost collide with Chelsea. Her lip curls into a wicked smile.

"Miss Miller, I see you've been demoted. Can't say I didn't see that coming." The jab goes straight to my heart, nearly plucking it out of my chest and throwing it on the floor between us.

I practically snarl but know better than to say a word to the viper. It won't do me any good, and right now I have a career that takes priority over getting into a pissing match with the she-devil.

I quickly brush past her and rush to the nearest exit. When I get into the fresh air, I breathe deeply, willing my lungs to open and take in the fresh air . . . and wipe away the toxins of Chelsea. After several minutes of heavy breathing, I calm down and force myself back to work. There's a grand opening happening soon and I need to shine.

# CHAPTER THIRTY

## Bridget

I'T'S BEEN DAYS OF WORKING IN THE MARKETING DEPARTMENT and I'm finally settling into a routine. Being transferred has been a godsend. I haven't seen Grant since he left my place and I want to keep it that way for as long as I can.

Paige invited me to lunch with her today and I happily obliged. We've been hanging out on our lunch breaks and I've really grown to like her. I act the same. I look the same. I talk the same.

*I am not the same.*

Grant changed something in me. Something fundamental, yet subtle. Being away from him is pure torture, but I know it is for the best.

"Okay, so you need to meet this friend of Jared's. His name is Ryan and you two would be so super cute together."

I groan. "I'm not really on the market."

"You're seeing someone?"

I shake my head vigorously. "No. I just don't need to get tied down with anyone right now. I want to focus on landing a job."

"Fine. You don't have to double-date, but could you come hang out with us? We're all going to dinner tonight, and I really don't want Ry to feel like a third wheel. He always does and I'm starting to feel bad."

I purse my lips at my new friend. "Sounds an awful lot like a date."

"No matchmaking . . . promise." She lifts her fingers in the Girl Scout salute, which makes me laugh.

"Fine. I'm in."

I'm laughing at Paige's excitement when I lift my head and my gaze collides with Grant's. My smile instantly fades as he walks by our table without even muttering a hello. Paige doesn't notice and just continues.

"You'll love him. I swear he's great. We can all meet beforehand at my place for a couple of drinks."

"Sounds nice. I'm looking forward to it," I lie.

The rest of lunch we discuss our plans, her job, and she gushes on Jared. It's cute that they're hooking up. They're both great people, so it makes sense. When our time is up, we agree on a time to meet tonight and say our goodbyes.

I'm walking toward the women's restroom when Grant comes strolling out of a door in front of me. Without an escape and to not seem childish, I say hello.

"Hi, Bridget. You look well," he responds. I move to walk around him when he grabs me by the arm. "How are things in the marketing department?"

"Fine, but I really need to get back there. I'm running late from lunch." I try to pull myself out of his grasp when he tightens his grip.

"So, you're going out tonight?" His lips are pulled down into a frown. He looks . . . hurt.

"How do you know that?"

"I overheard you."

For as large as this hotel is, it feels really damn small at times.

"You were listening to our conversation?" I ask, appalled.

His head shakes back and forth. "I heard you, but not because I was eavesdropping."

My eyes roll. He damn well knows he was listening in on me. The fact he's even trying to deny it is ridiculous. We're adults. He needs to act like one. We're in this position because of the secrets he kept.

"Either way, I don't find it any of your business." I turn to leave, but he grabs my arm.

"Just answer my question, Bridget. Are you or aren't you?" I'm surprised by Grant's tone. He sounds jealous and angry. Two things he has no right to be.

"Yes, I am." I purse my lips in defiance, standing my ground and looking him directly in the eye.

"Is that really a good idea?"

I bark a laugh, but I'm not at all amused. "It's exactly what I need right now, so yes, it's a good idea." I try not to sound petty but fail miserably. My body is on fire from his touch, yet I'm trying my hardest to feel unaffected and annoyed. I need to get away from him and fast. I don't want him to know how hurt I am.

"It's a little fast."

I pull my arm out of his grasp, throwing my arms into the air in frustration. "What do you want from me?" I say harshly. "You chose this, so let it be."

He steps back, starts to say something but shakes his head, changing his mind and ending the conversation with, "Have fun."

I shake my head and watch as he walks away from me, again.

---

Jared's friend Ryan is as good-looking as Jared. The two are very similar, both cute, flirty, and friendly. It's a welcome surprise to find that not only am I attracted to someone, but I enjoy his company.

"So, what do you think of Ryan?" Paige asks when the guys head to the bar and we're left alone.

"He's great."

"So, why do you seem so uninterested?"

"What? How?"

"I don't know. You're not yourself tonight. I get the feeling you're not that into him. Although, I must say, you're probably making him want you more by being that way. I have a feeling Ryan is the sort of guy who's used to girls falling at his feet."

I laugh. "You're probably right. He has that sort of charm

about him, doesn't he? I don't know. I had a bad day at work and I'm a little out of it."

"Forget about work. Just enjoy yourself."

"I'm having a good time. I really like him, but I'm not rushing into anything because he's charming. I'll see how it goes."

"Okay." She shrugs as if she really doesn't care either way.

"Tell me about you and Jared?" I ask in an attempt to change the conversation. Thankfully it works.

Paige grins. "We're amazing."

"I'm so happy for you. He's a great guy. I totally approve."

The combination of Paige, aka Jessica Rabbit, and Jared equals one hell of a power couple in the looks department. Add to it their stellar personalities, and it's a match made in heaven.

"Look at them, they're trying so hard to look manly in front of us and here we are finishing our cocktails and barely looking at them," Paige says with affection. "The bartender is definitely favoring the female clientele. At this rate, they'll never get us another round." She chuckles. "Come on, let's join them at the bar."

My phone vibrates in my purse and I grab it out to see a text from Grant. Taking a deep breath, I open it up.

*Grant:* **Be safe.**

That's all he wrote. There's a war going on in my head. One side is pissed that he's inserting himself into a space he has no business being. I'm a big girl. This is my time. I'm trying to move on and he's making it impossible. The other side is soaring at the fact he cares and is concerned about me.

I shove my phone back in my purse, refusing to deal with Grant. Fuck him. He chose this. We spend the rest of the evening drinking and laughing. Every now and again my mind turns back to Grant and sadness bubbles up inside me that I never experienced before with anyone. There's something about Grant that pulls me toward him, but I can't allow my mind to go down that path. I try a bit harder with Ryan.

---

It's been a week since my date with Ryan. He asked me out again, but I turned him down. It just didn't feel right to lead him on. At this point, I'm in no place to start dating again. Besides, work demands too much of my time.

My desk overflows with work that still needs to be completed, but before I can dive in my phone rings. I'm not surprised to see it's Paige calling.

"What's this I hear about you not seeing Ryan again?" she asks.

"Wow! Not even a hello."

"I don't understand. You had an amazing time. He really likes you," Paige says.

I groan. "He's very nice, but I don't think he's my type. I don't want to lead him on."

"What exactly is it about him that's not your type? He's charming and thoughtful. I think he's perfect for you. Plus, he's gorgeous. The two of you would make beautiful babies."

"Babies!" I shout and then remember where I am and quickly lower my voice. "I think you're getting a bit ahead of yourself. Look, Paige, he's very nice and, yes, he's very cute, but I just don't feel it."

"Why don't you go out with him one more time? You might find you actually do like him."

I laugh. "Why are you forcing this? Just because you and Jared are so happy doesn't mean I need a boyfriend too."

"I don't know. I guess it would be fun. You know, the four of us." It's not hard to see she just wants another couple to do the whole double dating thing with. I don't want to commit because right now it just doesn't feel right.

"I'll call you later. I really do have to go. Some of us do work in this office."

"Funny. I work."

"You're doing a bad job, then."

She laughs and says her goodbye before the line goes silent.

# CHAPTER THIRTY-ONE

## Bridget

Opening night. *The official opening of The L.* I smile to myself as I look around the room. I can't believe it's finally here after everything I've been through. It feels like an eternity.

"I got you a glass of champagne," Ryan says, pulling me out of my thoughts and handing me my drink.

"Thank you so much." I smile up at him.

"Thanks for inviting me. This place is insane." I had no intention of bringing Ryan, truth be told, I didn't want to lead him on. But I am so happy I did. I let Paige convinced me it would be a good idea and now standing here waiting for Grant to arrive, I realize it is helping . . . *a little.*

"Right? I'm so proud of what we've done. It's fabulous."

"There's a line of people waiting to get in. Is that normal?"

"I don't know, but I doubt it. The buzz surrounding this place has been crazy."

I look around at all the people milling about. Smiles are plastered on everyone's faces. It's clear The L is a success.

"I see Jared. Let me go grab him," Ryan says.

"Great idea. I'll be right here."

Ryan saunters off in pursuit of Jared. He isn't even gone a second before I feel eyes on me.

*Grant.*

Only he can evoke such a reaction from me. It's been weeks, but the pit in my stomach tells me I'm no closer to moving on. I've missed him with every fiber of my being. Not even Ryan's company can lessen the pain. If anything—and this is the worst part, the part that I'm dreading, the part that makes it so difficult for me to live with myself—I always find myself comparing them, and Ryan is lacking. Not because how deep Grant's pockets or eyes are, or because of his dirty mouth, devotion for Isabella or even his shark-like business instincts. Ryan is lacking simply because he is *not* Grant. Only Grant is Grant. And as long as I don't have Grant, I will always feel hollow. Like my body is empty and light and floating in the world without an anchor. Without a home. It hits me fundamentally. Dumpster Dude is my home. I am, therefore, homeless now. Which is ironic, seeing as what we did—what we worked on—was a hotel. A hotel that is about to accommodate thousands of hearts. *Temporarily, of course.*

Grant's gaze is unnerving as he walks my way. Anticipation makes me shiver down to my toes. Time slows and it feels as though it takes hours for him to reach me. When he's finally standing in front of me, the space between us is heady with unsaid words.

"Hi," I say. My voice is lame. My posture is lame. God, my

whole being is.

His sad eyes roam over my body as if they have permission. "You look beautiful, Bridget."

I smile but don't respond to his compliment. If I were to speak, I couldn't hide how broken I am.

"I miss you," he adds, the words somehow like a knife. *My temporary home.* It's not fair that he says that after we threw away the key.

Silence descends upon us.

"I'm sorry, I shouldn't have said that." His eyes are dull as if he's been through a war. I image mine are much the same. His jaw is set hard, holding back words I know he wants to say but doesn't dare.

We still can't be together, so what's the point in punishing ourselves with pleasantries? There's nothing good that can come of this. Only more heartbreak.

He finally speaks. "Who is he?"

"Excuse me?"

"Him," he hisses, glaring at someone behind me.

I follow his line of sight until my eyes rest on Ryan. I shake my head and the green of his eyes pierces me. His stare is so hard it shakes me to the core of my being. If it were possible, the heat of his gaze would singe my skin. "He's no one, Grant."

"Then why are you here with him?"

I've wounded him by showing up with someone else, but what did he expect? The last time we attended one of these events, his wife was on his arm. I wouldn't put myself through that again. No way in hell.

"What does it matter?"

"You shouldn't be with him." His gaze drops to my lips, and it's like a gentle caress across my skin. Ripples of sensation move through me. Down my mouth and across my collarbone until I shiver. "He'll never make you feel the way I do."

"That's not fair," I rasp. "Why are you doing this to me? It's your life that's keeping us apart. Stop torturing me, Grant."

His eyes close as if he's in pain.

"You're right."

He starts to walk past me but stops at my side, leaning into my ear. "Just know that my feelings for you haven't changed. They never will."

Every hair on my body stands on end. Every nerve ending wakens. He doesn't say anything else, simply walking away before anyone spots him. I stand alone in a room full of people, growing colder with every step he takes. I watch him for several minutes from across the room.

It's not long before Chelsea slithers over and drapes herself across his arm. Photographers approach them and snap several photos. From here, they really do play the part well. The L's power couple cozies up for the cameras. I can see the headlines now. My hands clench into fists.

Watching her. Watching them. It kills me to see her touch him, even if I know it's all a lie. She makes a laughingstock of him and there's nothing I can do. There's nothing he can do.

Some time passes and I'm growing tired of being here.

Ryan is off in the bathroom and I decide to grab a breath of fresh air. I need to breathe. Watching Grant with his wife is too much, no matter how fake it is. I'm stepping toward the back hallway that leads to the bathroom and feel a presence behind me.

"Do you want me as much as I want you?" his husky voice asks.

"Not really," I say. "I want you more." I turn around and we lock eyes. This one look . . . He has the power to completely undo me. I won't allow that to happen.

"I asked you earlier not to do this. Not to play games with me, Grant."

"I'm not trying to play games. This is fucking killing me, Bridget. I need you."

His words light me on fire, sending heat spilling to every part of my being. I want to hold onto his words desperately, but in this moment, doubt also creeps in.

Jealousy. It creeps up inside me like a vine, feeding on my insecurities. Playing off my fears. It's hard not to allow it to take over. To not allow it to strangle me. All I can do is tell myself I will not be that person. I will not let it win. *He's not mine to care about.* Stop doing this to myself.

"Seeing you with her is killing me."

He runs his hand through his locks as he stands in front of me. Tall and powerful, his frame towers above me as I move to pass. But he blocks me. Doesn't allow me to move.

"It's not real."

"It doesn't hurt any less."

His hand reaches out, the pads of his fingers skimming over my skin. Across my jaw. Running down the hollow of my neck and across my collarbone.

Tracing.

Teasing.

Like a desperate whisper against my heated flesh.

He moves further, caressing the swell of my breast. The curve of my hip.

Lower.

Lower.

Until he's inches away from touching me.

"She means nothing to me," he states. "All I see is you, Bridget. All I want is you."

"Please don't." I squirm under his touch, desperate for more. Aching for it.

"I want you. That hasn't changed."

"Yet it still can't happen. So why do this?"

"I can't help it. This is my fucking life and I want you," he snarls. "I want to keep you here with me until I've had my fill. I want you begging and pleading, and then I want to give you exactly what you want. Only then will I be satisfied, and maybe I can finally kick this damn obsession I have with you." He says this almost desperately. My chest heaves at his words. "But I can't," he finishes in defeat.

"Why do you keep doing this to me?" My voice cracks with emotion and I think he might touch me, breach me. But he pulls away, taking my hand in his instead. Holding it steady. As if it's the last time he ever will.

"Because I'm a selfish prick. Because I can't stand the thought of you moving on. Because I'm so fucking lost without you, and the only thing I want to find is a way back to you. Because our kismet meant something. Because *we* mean something."

"You're lost, but I am gone. That's the difference between us. I'm done, Grant. Done trying. I might never feel the way I do toward you ever again, and it's breaking me," I say on a sob.

His hand shoots out to wipe away a stray tear that is freefalling from my cheek. "I'm not your perfect love story. There's no fairy tale with me. No happy ending will happen for us, Bridget. You have to come to terms with that. So do I."

His stony eyes have me backing away. "Then stay away from me," I whisper, allowing one final tear to fall.

With those final words, I leave.

# CHAPTER THIRTY-TWO

## Bridget

THE FOLLOWING DAY AT WORK, I'M DETERMINED TO SET my mind on being productive. The opening was a huge success from what everyone in the office is saying. I left after my showdown with Grant. I told Ryan I had a headache and left him with Paige and Jared. Luckily, no one pressed the issue. A part of me expected Paige to call and check up on me, but she never did. I'm so thankful she didn't, because I probably would have broken down. What would I have said? *I couldn't be there anymore.*

Even today, I find myself avoiding her. Faking being happy is becoming more difficult by the day. I only have a few short weeks before I leave The L—and my time with Grant— behind for good, so I'll suck it up. I have no intention of pursuing a career here. I'm not looking to torture myself. I do a good job at staying busy, but every now and then I catch myself thinking about him.

I want to say fuck it. What's one more night with Grant? To feel his lips on mine again. The truth is, I don't only want to touch him, I want to heal him. I want to make him less sad, less empty. I can't, though. I won't. It's not my place anymore.

A few hours in, my stomach rumbles. It's been a while since I've had a decent meal. I don't even want to know how many pounds I've lost during this breakup. I decide to head to the corner deli for a sandwich. Just before I reach the main entrance, a lady walks through the door holding Isabella's hand. I consider hiding, but it's too late. She sees me.

"Bridget," the girl says excitedly.

"Hi, Isabella," I say as she runs into my arms.

The woman introduces herself as Rhonda, the new nanny. "We were in the area and she insisted on coming to see her daddy," Rhonda explains.

"Hey, munchkin," Grant says from behind me. I freeze in place, not wanting to see him but knowing there's no way around it.

"Look who I found. It's Bridget," she tells her father with so much happiness it breaks my heart. I turn around in time to see his sad eyes.

"So I see," he says.

"We're going to the park. What are you doing?" she asks me, her big brown eyes filled with curiosity.

"I'm going to the deli for a sandwich."

"Ooh, I'm hungry. Can I get a sandwich, too?"

Grant's eyes grow wide. "Not today, princess, but maybe another time."

I narrow my eyes at Grant. He knows damn well that'll

never happen. Filling the girl's head with false hope surrounding me is not cool. "Next time I see you here you can come with me for a sandwich. Deal?"

Isabella giggles. "Deal."

"Come now, my girl. Say goodbye to Bridget and then you can go to the park."

"Bye, Bridget," she says, giving me another huge hug.

"Goodbye, sweetheart."

I hold back the tears threatening to spill. In a short amount of time, I've grown attached to Isabella. I understand Grant's need to protect her. She's not mine, but I'd do anything to make her happy after only knowing her for a short time.

I watch as Isabella walks over to give her father a hug. Grant takes her in his arms and kisses her on the cheek. My entire body melts and my heart breaks in the same moment. How long will Chelsea hold Isabella over him? Will he ever be free to love?

# CHAPTER THIRTY-THREE

## Grant

SHOULDN'T HAVE STOPPED HER. I SHOULDN'T HAVE SPOKEN to her. But seeing her with him was too much. So once again, I put my own needs before hers and pulled her aside. I'm not blind. I destroyed her. I destroy everything. For a moment there, I was dumb enough to think that I had a chance at happiness.

I was just fooling myself.

Chelsea would never have let me be happy.

Now, I can't help replaying last night over and over again in my head. It hurt to transfer her to marketing, but I had no choice. It's for the best. No matter how much it sucks.

"Licking your wounds." Chelsea saunters into the living room where I'm downing a glass of scotch. At first, I don't answer. That's how little she means to me at this stage. But of course, Chelsea has mastered the art of poking the bear and is now someone on PhD level.

"Shame. This one was your favorite flavor. A pretty, broken Barbie doll with eyes like saucers and pure intentions."

Right. I'm done playing civil with this bitch. "Leave me the fuck alone. Haven't you done enough?"

"Not nearly." Her smile is sugar, her words venom. I have no idea what she means, but something tells me by the Cheshire grin on her face that she's about to tell me. "The opening was a huge success, shouldn't we be celebrating?"

"I wouldn't celebrate with you if you were the last woman on earth."

"Grant, stop being so melodramatic. She was a child. I let you have your fun. Now it's time to get back to the task at hand."

"You let me have my fun?" I seethe.

"Certainly, you didn't think I hired her just because of Spencer, and I thought she'd be perfect to get you out of your funk. Now that you fucked her a few times maybe you'd be motivated to work. Think of it as a thank you to me for getting you laid."

"You are unreal. You think that's all she was? A quick fuck. She's not some pawn to be used in your devious plan."

"I don't care what she was. I expect you back to yourself come Monday."

"Never going to happen." I slam my tumbler on the table and stand. It shatters beneath my skin, biting into my flesh, making me bleed. With that, I leave the room.

———— • ————

Two weeks. Two weeks of pure hell. I have stayed too true to my word and have left Bridget alone. I thought time would make it easier, but the pain doesn't dissipate. It only amplifies as more time goes by.

Plus without Bridget to calm my nerves, not only am I in pain, but I'm also a ticking time bomb. I never realized just how much she made me believe everything was going to be okay. Now that she's gone and I don't see her every day, it's hard to stay grounded.

I'm angry all the time. But I guess I deserve to feel bad. Knowing I broke Bridget, I deserve to be in constant pain.

Which is why as Chelsea spends my money, I do nothing.

I deserve it.

I'm knee-deep in self-wallowing when my phone pings with an email. I open it up and see that it's an email from Chelsea's account. Once I got the passcode from the investigator, I had her account set up on my phone to monitor her. The email is from an airline informing her that her flight is boarding.

Is her flight boarding?

Since when is she going somewhere and if she's at the airport who's with Isabella?

I dial her number, and it goes straight to voicemail.

Fuck.

# CHAPTER THIRTY-FOUR

## Bridget

S ATURDAY MORNING ROLLS AROUND. I'M SITTING AT home drinking a cup of coffee when my phone rings.

"I need to speak to you."

"Grant, why are you calling me? I thought we discussed this."

"Can we meet? At the park across from the hotel?" He completely ignores me. Alas, it doesn't sound like lack of respect as much as sheer desperation. He is fixated. He is determined. *He is Grant, and he is your undoing.*

"This isn't a good idea."

"I'm begging you to trust me."

I sigh, knowing I've lost the battle in my own head. "I can be there in half an hour."

"Thank you."

I hurry to get ready and practically run to the park. I arrive within twenty minutes of our conversation and find Grant already there, sitting on a park bench and looking out at the pond. He looks nothing like himself. There are bags under his eyes and his clothes are disheveled. My heart lurches at the sight of him.

"Hey, thanks for coming," he says, standing when he sees me approach. I take the seat he offers beside him, but I don't speak. He called this meeting and I'll let him talk.

He sighs. "I'm going crazy at home. I just don't know whether I can do it anymore."

"Chelsea?"

He nods. "Yeah. It's all too much now. Before you, I didn't give a fuck. As long as I had Isabella, Chelsea could pull whatever shit she wanted. Then I met you and everything changed. I changed, Bridget. Living in hell isn't something I can do anymore. Not when I know I could be happy again."

I remain silent. I don't want to jump to conclusions. He's broken me once and I refuse to sit back and let it happen again. I'm stone.

"Chelsea is making a complete mockery of me. I've stayed all these years and now she's throwing it in my face. The only reason I care is because I've given up *everything*. But the walls are crashing down and suffocating me now."

"Did something happen?" I ask.

"She left Isabella again."

"What do you mean 'she left her'?" My voice is lethal. I want to strangle Chelsea with my own damn hands.

"She left her at the house by herself until Rhonda could get there so she didn't miss her fucking flight with her new boyfriend." His words drip with loathing.

"Did you call the police?"

"No, I didn't even know until Rhonda called me in a panic. When she got there, Chelsea was gone. Rhonda called me to find out why the hell Isabella was alone. We're lucky she didn't call them."

"Chelsea's a fucking piece of work. How could anyone do that?"

"She has no regard for anyone and she doesn't give a shit about Isabella. I threatened to take her, and Chelsea kindly reminded me why I can't. I'm powerless, Bridget. Isabella's a bargaining chip to bring me to heel. I'm the only one who truly loves her, yet I can't save her."

"She's disgusting, Grant. She doesn't deserve either of you."

"I don't know what to do." His head falls into his hands. "I feel like my whole world is falling apart. Fuck. I shouldn't be talking to you about this."

I lift his head from his hands. "I'm glad you called me. I want to help."

"I know, but it's not fair. I don't need to bring you into my crazy."

I pull him in and embrace him. For a long time, the two of us just sit like that, holding each other and looking out onto the pond in front of us. We don't say a word, but instead, hold each other as though we never want to let go.

---

When my phone rings on Sunday morning, I'm instantly on edge. Even more so when I see it's Grant calling.

"Grant, what's wrong?" I ask in a panic.

"Everything at home is fine. I'm not calling about that," he says quickly. "It's actually about work. I'm sorry to call you at home on a Sunday, but things aren't going well with the new property."

"Which property?"

"St. Barts."

"I thought they were supposed to start construction." As far as I'm aware, there have been no issues at all and everything is set to go. *What the hell could have possibly happened to change things?*

"So did I. There was some sort of mess up and the whole thing seems to have taken a downward spiral."

"What kind of a mess up are we talking?"

"I don't know. I'm not getting a ton of answers that make sense. I think there's more going on that they aren't telling me. I have no choice but to go there and fix things. It's impossible for me to know what's going on without actually being there."

"You totally have to go, but why are you calling me, Grant? I don't work in your department anymore."

"I called HR and told them about the issues and requested backup in case things go south. Since you've been in on a couple of meetings with me, it makes sense it would be you."

"What?" I ask in dismay. "You can't be serious."

"I know it's last minute, but I need your help. We'll be

gone a day or two at most."

"Grant, this is insane. I can't go to St. Barts with you."

"Please, Bridget. Everything is paid for. I just need backup."

"Why me?"

"I told you. You've sat in on meetings."

"One. I came to one meeting with you, Grant. That hardly makes me qualified to help you clean up a mess."

"I know it's asking a lot, but I really need you. Nobody else makes sense."

I don't buy it at all. Jared, Paige, hell, even one of the other temps would be a better choice than me, but the desperation in his voice has me seriously considering it.

"When do you leave?"

"In two and a half hours."

"Two and a half hours!"

"The sooner I get there the better. I chartered a private plane."

It's a bad idea. A very bad idea, but how can I abandon him in his time of need? Despite our end, I still care about him deeply. The idea of leaving him to deal with things on his own when he's already fragile doesn't sit well with me.

"Fine," I acquiescence. "I just need to throw a few things in a bag and I'll be good to go."

"Thank you," he says, sounding relieved.

I hang up and pack a small suitcase. My hands shake and perspiration builds on my brow. I hate flying, and the idea of having to do it today while also dealing with Grant being close has my anxiety at an all-time high.

It's not long before the car service Grant sent is buzzing up. Sitting in the car considering what I'm doing, I contemplate asking the driver to pull over and let me out. Is helping Grant really healthy for me? No. This is a bad idea. My phone vibrates in my hand, and I see it's my mother. I almost send her to voicemail but at the last second, I think better of it.

"Hi, Mom."

"Where have you been? I've been trying to get in touch with you all day."

"I'm sorry. I'm on my way to the airport."

"The airport? Where are you off to?"

"I'm heading to St. Barts on a work trip. I was packing when you called earlier. I was going to text you when I got there. I was in a bit of a rush."

"What's in St. Barts?"

"I have to help Grant with some problems at the location of the new hotel. It's very last minute."

"Grant? Your boss?"

"Yeah. Um, Mr. Lancaster is having some issues with the new project, so I said I'd go and help. It will be great work experience." I'm rambling, but I can't seem to stop. "So far everything has been going right. It's good for me to be there when something is wrong, too."

"I see."

"You seem strange, Mom. What's going on?"

"So, is it just you and your boss going?" she asks accusingly. She's worried something is going on between me and

Grant. I can hear it in her tone.

"No," I lie. "There will be a few of us going. Anyway, it's only for one day."

"Well, that's good then."

I roll my eyes at her blatant disapproval. She might say it's good, but what she really means is she's not buying what I'm selling her.

"Look, Mom, I have to go. I'll call you when I'm finished, okay?"

"Sure. No problem. Good luck."

I put the phone down and groan. *Why did I just lie to my mom? What's so wrong about going with Grant for something work related?* I should've stood my ground and pointed out that I'm an adult capable of making adult decisions.

"Well, this is it," the driver says as we arrive.

I look up, frowning. My foot begins to tap nervously. I'm not ready for this. "Thank you. Oh, no. I just realized I don't have any cash on me. Would you mind waiting while I run inside to grab some money? I'm so sorry." I wipe the sweat from my forehead. This day can't get any worse. I'm a hot mess.

"No, it's fine. The fare has been paid."

"Oh, really?"

"Mr. Lancaster has it all taken care of."

*I'm sure he does.* The driver grabs my bag and hands it to me, and then I hurry inside to meet Grant.

"Thank you for coming," Grant says when he sees me.

I'm slightly taken aback when I see him. He looks as if

he hasn't slept in days. He has dark rings under his eyes, his clothes look like they could do with an iron, and overall, he looks worn-out. I feel sad for him as I remember how he fell apart on the park bench. His home life is a complete mess. No wonder he looks this way. I force myself to smile so he doesn't see I'm so worried.

"Am I late?"

"Nope. Not at all. In fact, we still have another half hour before we board. Come sit," he orders.

The woman next to us shoots Grant a look and scurries away.

"You're very intimidating sometimes."

"I am?"

"Not to me, but to others. I think people are scared of you." I chuckle at the image of the woman still in my mind.

"You see right through me."

"I most certainly do," I say and grin at him. Then, before I can stop myself, I turn his way. "Are you okay?" I whisper.

He shakes his head. "Not really. But I'll be fine."

"Where's Isabella?"

"She's with Rhonda. Thankfully, she's amazing with her. I only hope everything will be fine tonight."

"It will be."

"I hope so."

We sit for the next thirty minutes and Grant goes over all the concerns he has for the property he purchased on St. Barts.

"Your plane is ready, Mr. Lancaster."

We get up and walk over to the tarmac where the private plane is parked. Once inside, we sit next to each other. My nerves are on high alert for multiple reasons, including but not limited to the man sitting within inches of me. I'm not ready to be this close to him, but I told him I'd be here for him, so here I am.

I grip the seat and close my eyes, dreading the next part.

"Afraid of flying?" Grant asks from beside me.

I nod without opening my eyes. "I don't like taking off."

I wait for him to mock me, but he doesn't. Instead, he takes my hand. I open my eyes to see his hand on mine. He squeezes and I squeeze back, feeling soothed by his touch. When the plane finally takes off I hardly notice. I've been so focused on our hands joined together that I forgot every one of my fears. Nothing matters but the feel of Grant's skin against mine.

"What's going on in that head of yours?"

Grant's voice has me snapping into the here and now. I pull my hand away. I can't allow myself to go down that path again. My heart's too fragile and nothing has changed.

"Nothing. I was just thinking about the mess waiting on us."

"Let's not even think about it for these next few hours. When we get there, we'll get it straightened out."

"You seem much more confident than you did earlier."

"I have you here."

I will my heart not to skip another beat.

"Don't, Grant. It's not fair."

"I'm serious. I don't mean to upset you, but having you here calms me. I don't know what else to say."

"Just don't say anything," I sigh. "When you say shit like that you give me false hope, and it isn't fair."

"I never meant to hurt you. You have to know that. Not then, not now, not ever."

"We're on a work trip. We'll be professional, get our work done, and get home. I'll finish my time with The L and then I'll move on. After that, we won't see each other again unless the universe seriously hates my guts and throws you in my path."

"It would be that bad to see me again?" Grant sounds hurt and I almost regret my harsh tone.

"Yes. It would. I care about you, but that doesn't matter because Chelsea has her claws so far imbedded in your skin you're stuck in place. She'll keep pulling you down, but there isn't anything you'll do about it. And I get it. I really do. Isabella is amazing and she needs you."

"You care about her."

I look him square in the eye. "I do." I take a deep breath. "Let's just do what we came to do and not make this hard. Please?"

He nods and that's the end of further conversation.

I can't help but feel sad when the plane lands safely and we have to get off. I might've shut him down, but I can still feel the warmth of his hand on mine.

We head straight to the address for the project manager without any pit stops. The lady at reception holds our bags while we meet with the unsuspecting man, who's apparently having lunch in his office.

"Fredrick?" Grant asks when we walk into the office.

"Yes? Who are you?"

"Grant Lancaster."

Fredrick's eyes widen. "Mr. Lancaster? From New York?"

"Yes, and I want to know what the fuck you've been doing with my hotel."

"I, uh . . . I was hoping to have it all sorted out by the time you called."

"Not acceptable."

"Uh, well, yes, I-I'm working on the issues as we speak."

Grant leans forward and laughs. "You are? Because it looks to me like you're playing Solitaire."

A bead of sweat drips off Fredrick's face as he gulps. "I'm not. This was, uh, well, you see, it's because I'm having something to eat," Fredrick mutters. He doesn't seem to know what to do with himself. I almost feel bad for him. Almost.

"We're going to figure this shit out today. If you haven't given me a plausible reason for why we haven't broken ground, then you're out."

"You'll fire me?"

"Now you understand."

"Would you like to meet in an hour or so? That way I can gather up everything and we can maybe sit somewhere a bit more comfortable."

Grant looks around. "I'm perfectly happy where we are now."

"Oh. Okay then," Fredrick says, dropping his eyes to the ground, shoulders slumping in defeat.

"Can you stay?" Grant asks me.

"Yep."

I sit and listen to Grant and Fredrick run through everything that hasn't happened. I jot down notes. I can see Grant getting more and more upset and I don't blame him.

Grant stands up. "Right. I think we've seen enough. You're out."

"Excuse me, but you can't fire me." Fredrick grows a set of balls the likes of which we've yet to see from the scrawny man.

"Says who?"

"I'll get my lawyer."

"From what I see, you have two choices: call a lawyer and I'll ruin you or—"

"Or?" His voice shakes.

"Fuck it. You have one choice, and that choice is I'll fucking ruin you either way. Now, get your shit off my site. You have eight hours."

We march out of the office and head to the car parked on the street.

"So, what happens next?"

"We need to find a new project manager, and I have just the man in mind."

"You do? Already?"

"Yeah, there's a guy I used to know in New York who moved here about a month ago. He was hoping to take on the project manager job for me, but I told him I'd already hired someone. I'll call him now and see if he wants to meet."

Grant makes the call and then grins at me. "Looks like he's interested. He started a new job already, but he's far more interested in this one. Problem is, he can only meet with me tomorrow. I'm sorry this delays our departure."

"No problem. What do you need me to do?"

"While I'm meeting with my guy, I'd like you to stop by the job site to make sure Fredrick has gotten his shit off my land. If it isn't gone, call the police."

"Sounds easy enough. Anything else?"

"You'll want to survey the property and make a record of anything that seems unusual. Vandalism is my primary concern. If there are any issues with that, take notes and pictures and we'll take action once I get back to the property. I shouldn't be long."

"Sure, that sounds great," I say, genuinely happy there's something for me to do here. I was beginning to question the reason for my presence. If I'm able to help and learn, the trip was worth it. "Which hotel are we staying in tonight?"

"I have a suite. You can stay with me."

I narrow my eyes.

"It's two bedrooms. I know that might not be ideal, but after all the bullshit here and with the money I'll need to sink into righting all the delays and rehiring Fredrick caused, I'd like to conserve money."

"You can't be serious. You're conserving money? That's the best you can do?" I cross my arms, calling him out on his excuse. Grant Lancaster doesn't need to conserve money. The thought is absurd.

"Okay, that was lame. I'm sorry."

"Totally lame, Lancaster. I told you on the plane we weren't going to complicate this trip, and staying with you sounds like one epic complication." I cross my arms over my chest, waiting for what he'll throw at me next. Instead of more excuses, his head falls, making him look like a wounded puppy.

"I'm not trying to complicate things, Bridget. I just want you close to me. I know that's a lot to ask, but please."

The idea of staying in a room with Grant has my legs shaking nervously. I shouldn't, but God help me, I want to. "Okay. Let's just get back. I'm exhausted."

---

After I check the property to find Fredrick and his crew completely vacated and no signs of vandalism, my job is done. Grant hasn't been away from me for more than an hour, securing a new crew. One he trusts to get the job done right. Then he keeps his word.

We are walking down the beautiful beach of St. Barts, taking in the translucent rolling waters and sun-filled aqua skies. The grains of sand beneath our feet blur out for miles. They lull me into a blissful trance of new beginnings and endless tomorrows. I now get why he'd choose this location as home of one of the newest L hotels.

"What are you thinking?" Grant asks from beside me.

"How gorgeous it is here. You truly picked a wonderful location to build."

"I feel good about it. Now that I have a crew I trust in place, I'm excited for this expansion."

"You really are brilliant," I say, squinting up at him through my lashes.

I'm rewarded with a breathtaking smile. One that fills my heart more than it should.

"Thank you for coming out here. I know it probably feels like it was a waste of your time, but you don't know what it meant to have your support. You're one of the only people I trust."

His words touch me. I wish I could tell him what I'm feeling, but I know better. It will only be met with heartache.

"Our lunch is ready." Grant points to a spot in front of us where a beach blanket is spread out across the white sand. Atop it is a large picnic basket. He motions for me to sit as we get closer, so I do, and he goes about unpacking the contents. I'm in awe. Cheeses, vegetables, fruit, and delicious pastries are all laid out in an assortment of color. Lastly, he removes a bottle of champagne. "To celebrate a successful firing and rehiring," he says shyly.

"How did you do this? When?" I'm literally speechless at the thought he put into all of this.

"I must admit, the concierge at the hotel arranged this at my request."

"It's amazing, Grant." I smile broadly. "Thank you for going to such trouble."

"I'd do anything for you, Bridget."

He wouldn't. If that were true, my heart wouldn't be breaking in two. We'd be planning a future and not saying our goodbyes in a matter of days.

"Can we just enjoy this day? No expectations but good company and conversation? A celebration of sorts."

I nod, needing it as much as he seems to.

Two hours later and we're back at his suite with almost two bottles of champagne emptied. I'm feeling suitably tipsy. Instead of getting more talkative as I normally do, I find myself retreating into silence. Grant is doing the same. Neither of us wants to bring up the one thing that's clearly on our minds.

"I should go."

"I'm not ready," he says, and we both know we're not just talking about leaving the room.

My words were loaded. I need to leave St. Barts, leave The L . . . leave him. I'm a smart girl. I know all these things. But coming to terms with them is something else entirely.

"I have to," I mumble. "I've decided I'll resign as soon as we're back tomorrow."

"Please don't, Bridget. The L needs you."

"I can't work there. Don't you get that? It's too hard."

"I'm going to make sure you get the job of your dreams, Bridget. My recommendation will afford you your choice of employment. I'll make damn sure of it. I might've fucked everything up, but I can make this right. I can do something right."

Tears fall down my face as I study him. He looks dejected and utterly broken himself. Saying goodbye will be the hardest thing I'll ever do in my life, but it's what's best for us both. This push and pull won't go away, and neither will Chelsea's threats.

"Don't cry," he says, taking my hand in his. "Please don't. I can't stand to see you sad, especially knowing I've caused it. It kills me, Bridget. It fucking tears me apart that I can't fix this."

He's sitting too close. I can smell him. I can feel him. He's too close, and if he doesn't move away . . .

He kisses me.

Everything around us disappears. Every ounce of sadness is snuffed out, if only for a moment. This magical mirage begs me to stay forever, to never leave its embrace.

I let him kiss me, and I kiss him back with fervor. Every single part of my body wants more. Craves more. Grant pulls away, looking into my eyes with a fierceness I haven't seen before. It is carnal, it is lethal, and it can ruin every moment I'd spent trying to get over him.

"Give me one last night with you. One perfect night before it's all over."

*One perfect night?* The thought sounds sublime. But can I do it? No. I should say no.

"I know I shouldn't ask this of you, but I'm just a man. A weak man who's desperate for a woman he can't have." His eyes beg me. "A man who's fallen—"

I cut off his words, not wanting to hear any more. Kissing

him again, I smother all chance of him saying the three words I've hoped for. Prayed for. The three words that will surely end me.

"You're beautiful," he whispers as I walk us back toward the bed.

I want to tell him to never leave me. That I crossed the invisible line we set. I want to tell him I did the one thing I promised I wouldn't.

I fell in love.

But I don't. Tears threaten to fall as I move closer to him. I bury my face in his neck and cry.

"*I love you*," I whisper into his skin, but he can't hear me. I don't dare voice the words out loud. "I'll say goodbye. I will. But not now. Now, I just want you to hold me. Touch me."

After we remove our clothes, I lie back with him hovering above me. He widens my legs and positions himself at my entrance, but he doesn't move. "Condom?"

"I'm on the pill. I want to feel you. I want to feel all of you."

"I'm clean," he replies.

"I know."

He thrusts into me. Over and over again. "You're perfect." His passion consumes me. Enflames me. Owns me.

"You deserve more."

*I do*. I deserve a commitment. A future. Things he can't give. I won't settle for less, but I'll give my all to him one last time.

With my body, I offer him all I can't communicate out

loud. With my kiss, I tell him I love him; I tell him I'm lost without him. I make love to him with each pass of my tongue, screaming silently into his mouth all the words I can't say with my lips.

All the I love yous I'll never say.

He makes love to me. Thrusting in and out. Kissing me savagely. Whispering my name against my lips like a benediction.

As if I'll save him.

As if I could.

---

We don't speak as we clean up, neither one of us wanting to ruin the moment. I want to hold onto us for just a while longer.

We lie in each other's arms. The cadence of our breathing is the only sound in the room. With my head on his chest, I listen to his heartbeat. A sigh escapes my lips.

"Bridget . . ." He takes my hand in his and I close my eyes. "I love you."

"You can't," I plead.

"And yet I do. Desperately."

"Grant—"

"No. Let me do this. Let me say this. You deserve to know how special you are to me. I love you. One day you will meet someone, you will fall in love, and have all the things you ever dreamed of. I need you to know, there will never be anyone else for me." He kisses me again. Recklessly. Passionately. "I can't let you go," he mutters against my lips.

"You need to," I whisper.

"I know."

———————◆————————

After heading to the airport and catching the next commercial flight back to the States, I make it home. The first thing I do is call Olivia. For the first time in a long time, I really want to hear my sister's voice. She shows up an hour later, the pain in my voice evident enough to make her come.

"Is it Grant?" she says.

"I'm so stupid," I cry.

"You're not weak or stupid. You're in love with him. That's all."

I cry on her shoulder for the better part of an hour. She doesn't say anything but allows me to feel all the hurt. Live it, own it, embrace it so one day maybe I'll move on. After a while she pulls away, looking me in the eyes.

"This pain you feel will subside, Bridge. I know it doesn't seem so right now, but it will. Someday you'll have the capacity to love someone else." She smiles a sad smile. "One day you'll look back and wonder how you could've ever been with a man who didn't respect you enough to leave his wife for you. You don't want to be with a man like that. You want one who loves you so much he'd move the world for you. Wait for that man to come around. Don't settle for anything less."

"There's so much more to it. I wish I could tell you, but I can't. I owe it to him to keep his secrets."

"You don't owe him a thing."

"It hurts so bad. I don't think I'll ever find anyone like him."

"You can and you will. You're stronger than you think."

"I feel broken."

"You're not broken."

"I am. I'm not strong like you. You rebuilt your life."

"You're wrong. You're the strongest of all three of us. You always have been. You're the glue that has always held us together."

Her words fill my soul. Build me up. Give me strength to believe I'll be okay.

# CHAPTER THIRTY-FIVE

## Grant

MY DOOR FLIES OPEN AND I JUMP TO MY FEET OUT of instinct. Spencer stands inside my door, red-faced and baring teeth.

"Are you kidding me?" Spencer shouts, coming around my desk and thrusting me against the wall. "How could you sleep with Bridget?"

Fuck. I should've known this conversation was coming. As much as I want to fight back and defend myself, I don't.

"You don't understand," I grit through my teeth.

"*I* don't understand? Are you fucking kidding me?" His hands turn white. "You're married and have a daughter and, for fuck's sake, Bridget's a kid."

"She's a grown woman. She can make her own decisions. You know nothing about her." Bridget may be years younger, but she's not a child. She's smart and beautiful and I won't allow him to say anything otherwise. "Not that you're one to talk. How old is Olivia?" I bite.

"You're not good enough for her, Grant. You're a

fucking mess."

My eyes narrow and teeth grind together.

"I don't need you to point out all of my faults, Spencer. You and our father have been doing it for years."

"This isn't about us, goddamn it. This is about you hurting Bridget." His words bounce off the walls in angry waves. He still has me pinned against the wall, so I push roughly against his shoulders. He stumbles back.

"I wouldn't hurt her," I yell back.

"You already have."

My shoulders slump at his words. My hand comes up to my head, wiping the sweat from my face. I knew I hurt her, but to hear it from Spencer is the worst.

"Olivia is consoling her as we speak. She's fucking broken."

"Fuck," I yell, feeling the need to put my fist through a wall. Anything to stave off the pain his words produce.

"I warned you to keep your hands off of her."

"I've never listened to a damn thing you've said, Spencer. Why would I start now?"

*Punch.* "I said I'd kill you." *Punch.* Spencer does as he promised. Putting his fist in my face repeatedly. I should let him. I deserve it.

"I love her," I mutter as the acrid taste of copper fills my mouth.

He stops punching me and steps back. His eyes are pinched and a frown forms on his face.

"What?" he asks as though he can't comprehend what

I'm saying.

"You heard me, damn it. I'm in love with her." I swipe roughly at my bloody lip. "I'd be with her now if *she* didn't have me by the balls."

"Who? You're not making any fucking sense."

"Chelsea," I spit out. "Chelsea is blackmailing me."

Spencer gasps and steps away. Taking a seat, he swipes a hand through his hair. "Start from the beginning."

I tell him everything.

Every word I speak makes me feel lighter than I have in years. I've kept this in with the exception of confiding in Bridget and it feels good to unload years of lies and secrets.

"Let me help you. Put your pride aside and let me help you."

I nod, knowing I need his help. For the first time in a long time, I feel hopeful.

———————•◦•———————

The next day, I find myself at the park with Isabella. I look around at all the families playing, and jealousy seeps into my blood. That's what I long for. I long to be a family. To see Isabella on the swing, being pushed, but I don't see Chelsea's face in this dream. It's Bridget I see. Bridget smiling at my daughter, making her giggle. It hurts to think about it because I can't have it. Not now. *Maybe not ever.*

I watch as Isabella runs toward the slide. Her smile lights up my life. She's always able to pull me from my somber mood. As she rushes down the slide, I watch her face. She doesn't look like Chelsea, but she's so familiar to me. I can't put my finger on why. But to be honest, I probably know who her father is. There's a long line of business associates Chelsea has flirted with over the years. No doubt one of them or maybe multiple ones had an affair with her. I don't put it past anyone in my acquaintance to stab me in the back and sleep with my wife. I don't want to think about it, though. Putting a name to the betrayal would be too much for me. Instead, I watch my daughter and let my love for her be enough. I feel my phone ringing. Spencer.

"Hello," I answer.

"Hey," he responds. "So, about Chelsea," he starts and my stomach drops at her name. "I'm looking into her and your little problem, but I'm going to need a place to start. Do you have any information that might help?"

I rake my brain for anything that could help him and then something comes to me. "Miles, my head of security, has a few files on his computer. Maybe one can be helpful," I suggest. "Also, I had a private investigator a while back get me Chelsea's email password. I'll text you the info."

"Okay. Perfect. I have some people working on it with me. I'm sure we'll find something real soon."

Hearing him say that, I let out the air in my lungs I didn't even know I was holding.

"Great. Let me know if you find something."

"Grant," he pauses, "do you have time to go see Dad with me later today?"

"Yes," I say before I can second-guess my decision.

"About damn time," he asserts.

———————•·•———————

My heart drums a steady rhythm as my father answers the door to my impromptu visit. My foot taps on the ground, my nerves refusing to be pushed down. When the door opens my heart almost stops.

"Dad."

All the emotion of years apart pushes its way through my lips. That one word cracks on my tongue.

"Son." He isn't filled with malice or disdain. There's a deep-seated pain I know I caused. I have a way of hurting the people I love most.

He steps forward, crushing me in a hug. We hold on for dear life, putting years of distance at rest. We don't pull apart and we don't speak, but the silence is welcome. It gives us both a moment to understand the meaning of what is happening. It gives us a chance to digest that after all these years, a truce may come to pass. We might actually move on.

He pulls away after what feels like five minutes, looking me over from head to toe. When his eyes meet mine, I see the unshed tears misting his sight.

"It's been too long," he finally says.

"It has and I'm sorry."

He raises his hand to stop me.

"It's me who should be sorry. I should have never turned

my back on you."

I shake my head. As much as it hurt, he was right to do what he did. So I tell him as much.

"You were right. She was everything you thought she was, but I was too blind to see until it was too late."

He bites his lip and inclines his head. "I was afraid that was the case."

"I was too stupid to listen."

*My pride has always been my downfall.*

"You were young and in love."

I huff. "It was never love. I know that now." The way I feel for Bridget makes that truth painfully obvious. I never felt this for Chelsea. What we had was lust, plain and simple. My love for Bridget proves that.

"I'm sorry, Grant. This is one time I wish I'd been wrong. I never wanted this for you."

I nod, having nothing to say.

"What can I do? How can I help you?"

I laugh, but not because what he's saying is funny.

"There's nothing you can do, Dad. I'm in an unfixable position, one I put myself into."

He purses his lips. "Talk to me."

I spend the next hour filling him in on everything, from the birth of my daughter to the realization she wasn't my blood. I fill him in on the vendetta. The greed fueled by the rage that Chelsea ignited in me, and then I tell him about Bridget. When I'm done speaking, he sits silently for a minute.

"I don't even know what to say." He hangs his head. "I

failed you."

"You didn't. I chose this path."

"Didn't I, though? I never reached out. I allowed you to leave and put this distance between us. What kind of a father does that?"

I shrug my shoulders. "You didn't know."

"Well, I do now and I intend to make up for everything."

"We all know what hell you've lived and why you stayed away." Spencer steps forward. "Enough with the prideful bullshit, Grant. We're family and together we will fix it."

I didn't know how, but I knew together we would.

⸻

*Ring.*

*Ring.*

I reach across my desk and pull my phone to my ear. "Grant Lancaster," I answer.

"Grant, it's Spencer. Can you meet me at my place? We need to talk somewhere private."

He's got something. That's the only reason he wouldn't want to talk on this line. Whatever he has must be good.

"When should I come?"

"Tonight at eight. I have some friends joining us. I just wanted to give you the heads-up that I had to share a bit of your dilemma. Don't get fucking pissed."

I rack my brain for who and what he could be referring to, but I come up short. At this point, I don't give a fuck who he's commissioned if it helps the cause. I'm in.

"I'll be there."

The hours pass slowly, but eventually, I'm knocking on my brother's door. My nerves are all over the place. What am I walking into? When I get inside, my father is there, but what surprises me most is the visitors Spencer was referring to. My eyes widen. The Price siblings, Jax, Gray, and Addison are all present, as well.

The Prices have been family friends our entire lives. Their net worth rivals my father's on any given day and they're precisely the types of friends you want in your corner. Addison is the last person I expected to be in Olivia and Spencer's apartment. Spencer and Addison share a romantic past and let's just say it came to a head between Spencer and Olivia at one point. It was worked out, but with women, those sorts of things never seem to be completely buried. The way her cheeks are sunken in as if she's biting them says she's uncomfortable.

Nonetheless, here she is.

I'm still trying to figure out where they all fit into this equation.

"Come in," Spencer calls, seemingly annoyed at my standing about.

"What are you all doing here?"

"We think we found the solution to your problem," Jax says, reaching out his hand to shake mine in greeting. "Spencer called me in to do some computer reconnaissance." He smiles widely.

Now it's making sense. Jax is a computer genius. He's done work for the government helping to catch hackers. Rumor has it he's one of the best.

"I hope you don't mind," Spencer says. "But since you said Chelsea bid on a few of the Prices' properties, it just made sense for me to reach out to Addison."

Addison is the largest private landowner in the world. She owns property everywhere, making her the perfect contact when looking to expand. Most of the properties Chelsea has bid on have been hers. She's acted as the Lancaster realtor of sorts for properties.

"I was finding it very strange that within minutes of Spencer's team putting in a bid, your team was as well," Addison explains. "With our family's history"—she looks at Spencer before continuing—"I really didn't want to get in the middle of a feud and I just accepted the highest offer, but when Spencer told me what was going on with you and Chelsea, things were starting to add up."

My eyebrow rises, not knowing where she's going with this.

"A hostile takeover," she explains, putting her hands up as if to say, duh.

"I had them look into the transactions and Jax hacked into the accounts you gave me," Spencer jumps in, trying to piece it all together for me.

"Chelsea was very careful in what she said in her emails. She's smart, but not smart enough." Jax wiggles his eyes like the cat who caught his prey. "She led us to the idiot."

I smile, waiting for them to roll it all out. I've wrestled with all the scenarios for years. I'm ready for someone else to take the fucking wheel.

"Apparently, your wife has been shacking up with the help for years."

My brows knit in confusion. Help? What help? Then it dawns on me. Who's the one person we've both had access to for years who could play both sides? "Fucking Miles. The head of security at my own damn hotel." My knuckles clench into a fist at the revelation.

"Bingo," Jax offers.

"That's why he's been avoiding me and Chelsea has always been one step ahead. That fucking rat."

The need to strangle him is intense. I don't give a fuck that he's been with Chelsea. He can have her. It's the fact he's been playing me all along.

"It's not just Miles, though. Karen from the Karen Michelle Agency has been playing both sides. When we would call to have her set up contractors to give estimates on the sites we were looking into, she'd send an email immediately to Chelsea," Spencer adds.

My blood boils at the mention of Karen. She's also the one who placed Bridget at The L. She was involved from the beginning. I make a mental note to destroy her and any reputation she has.

"We'll worry about her another day. She's a small issue in comparison." Spencer reads my mind. He's right. Another day.

Gray steps forward. He's the financial guy in the Price family. He acts as Addison's CPA. "I pulled all the receipts and information for the transactions between Chelsea and the property deeds. The original holding company you used when purchasing the land for The L was a different company than has been used for the last few transactions. We always look into everyone we do business with, but we didn't with you because of our family history. Typically, we would've looked into any changes, but this one slipped through. We had Jax pull up the new company and that's when it got messy."

"Messy how?"

"The new company leads to an off-shore account. One that's not affiliated with you at all."

"She's stealing money and funneling it into an account?" I need to make sure I'm following what he's saying. His nod affirms my understanding.

"It gets worse, though. Off-shore accounts are tricky to infiltrate," Gray explains.

"Not for me." Jax's lips turn up into a wicked smirk. "She's been pulling funds from accounts that weren't hers to pull from and funneling it into this account."

I gathered this much. She doesn't do anything outside of The L to have her own money and we just concluded she's embezzling. How much worse can it get?

"She's been pulling money from Isabella's trust."

I see red. Stealing from me and my company is one thing, but stealing from our daughter?

"Not only is she stealing from Isabella, but she's been 'selling' residential properties in The L."

"We don't have residential properties."

"Exactly. The paperwork she filed isn't legit. If someone from the hotel ever noticed that people actually lived in one of these so-called apartments, The L would have the right to terminate the fake contracts. This wouldn't look good for The L and would surely result in a lawsuit."

"Wouldn't this hurt me and the hotel's image more than anything?"

"Not when we can show proof that all of the funds were siphoned into an outside account that does not have your name attached to it. She was dumb enough to put her own name on it. She's been using those sums not only to try to ruin Lancaster, but she's also been spending an extreme sum of money on herself and Miles Smith."

"It seems she's been having an affair with the head of your security for quite some time," Spencer chimes in.

"She made me hire him. She . . . How long?"

"We dated it back over six years according to Miles' emails and texts."

Jax is a genius.

"Over the course of the six years, she's stolen in little increments as to not raise a bell on your end."

"How much?"

"Over four million, but only a little over one million is still in the account. They've clearly been enjoying themselves."

I shake my head at the audacity of those two. Stealing

from a child. How fucking low can they be? All the trips and fancy clothes have all been on her daughter's dime. The fact that Miles has stuck around for six years floors me. What is he getting out of this? She's had several affairs with different men so why stay? The money? Then it hits me.

Isabella.

It all makes sense. My blood runs cold and my face falls.

Miles Smith is Isabella's father.

"What's wrong, Grant?" Spencer asks, concerned.

"They were stealing from *their* daughter."

The room goes silent as everyone allows me to process this information. It's too much. Way too fucking much.

"How do I fix this?"

"Don't you see? We're saying we got her. We fucking got her. You can use all this as leverage. No way that bitch will want to go to jail. She'll give you anything," Jax explains.

"What about him? I can't risk losing my daughter. Not when he can take her from me."

"Nah, man. We got him, too," Gray says. "He's all over this. The email correspondence coming from his account is very damning. You got them both by the balls now. As for Isabella, he doesn't care about her. What father allows another man to raise his daughter? And for what? Money?"

I let his words sink in, looking up at Spencer.

"So, what are you going to do?" he asks.

"I'm going to show them how it feels to live your whole life at the mercy of someone else. I'm going to get my life back." Not wanting to waste a minute, I turn to face the door and see Olivia Miller blocking my way. She smiles.

"Keep her safe. Make her happy. Love her. And if you can't, let her go." She walks past me and out of the room.

I'll do all of those things and more. Bridget deserves it.

"Thank you," I say to everyone, my eyes concentrating on Spencer and then turning to my father. "Thank you."

What they've done for me is more than I deserve. For years I've been underhanded in my dealings and did my best to take them down. And for what? *My own pride.*

"It's what family does," Spencer replies.

"I want to make things right, but right now I need to get my baby girl."

"Go." He laughs.

A small smile forms on my face and I make my way toward the door. It's time to reclaim my future, but first I need to deal with Chelsea.

---

I stroll into Chelsea's office, standing tall. She's sitting behind her desk on the phone. "I have to call you back," she tells the person on the other line before placing the phone down on her desk.

"You thought you had me. You thought you could manipulate me one more time, but there's something you missed," I say, approaching Chelsea.

"I miss nothing."

"That's where you're wrong. You just don't get it. You don't get family. You never have and you never will."

She laughs the haughty, irritating laugh I've grown accustomed to over the years. It's grated on my nerves forever, but today it doesn't. I'm not bothered by it in the least because I know it's the last time I'll ever have to listen to it.

"What you missed is that a real family, no matter what, is there for each other."

"You don't have a family either. I made sure of that."

"That's where you're wrong." I chuckle. "A real family always has your back. Years might pass, but they never give up on you. They're there for the good, they're there for the bad, they're there to listen to you apologize, and . . . they're there to fix the problem." I let the words hang in the air around us until she pales, and her mouth drops open. "That's right, Chelsea. They're there to fix my problem. Turns out they found a whole bunch of problems."

I shove the papers from Jax in her hand—pages upon pages detailing her embezzlement with her signature on the forms, and his emails detailing everything. Her hand noticeably shakes as she looks down at the paper before lifting her gaze to me. I watch as a myriad of emotions play across her flawless face, confusion, shock, and then her cheeks suck in as she squares her shoulders.

"It's over."

"What do you want?"

"My daughter."

"Or what?"

"Or this all goes to the police. Or . . ."

"Or?"

"I turn a blind eye to what you did to me. To what he did to me."

"I want half of what is owed me," she says with defiance, her hand resting on her cocked hip.

"You'll get nothing. I'd say you've more than collected over the years."

Her eyes widen, and I finally see the fear hiding deep within them.

"You can't give me nothing! How will I live?" she cries.

"I'm sure you can get Miles to help you." I shrug because I don't give a fuck.

"Can't you find it in yourself to go easy on me?"

I look at the ceiling and consider. "You've made a fool of me for a very long time. You made a fool out of my family. I don't owe you a damn thing."

"What about Isabella?"

"Like I said, I want custody. Full custody."

"That's never going to happen, Grant. She's not yours."

"It'll happen. My name is on her birth certificate, and to make sure that never changes, I'll give you one million to sign away all your maternal rights to me."

"Her father—"

"Has never been a father to her. He knew all along and she was right there," I seethe. "Miles is no better than you, using her to his benefit. He's not her father. I am. I don't care what blood runs through her veins. She's mine. I loved her. I raised her. I held her when she cried and I wiped her tears.

When she's older, old enough to understand, I'll tell her the truth about all of you. Until that time, you stay away or you both will find yourselves in jail. Am I clear?"

"One million?"

She's considering it based on her expression. I can almost see the cogs moving in that brain of hers. She's calculating what she can do with one million dollars.

"Yes, and not a penny more."

"One million isn't nearly enough to survive."

"It's more than you deserve. Invest wisely, Chelsea, because you won't get a penny more from me."

She huffs.

"One million. You stay the hell out of my life and you don't contest me as Isabella's father. It's that or jail. You choose, but I'm running out of patience."

I watch as her shoulders fall in resignation. She's not happy, but what choice does she really have? She can't live without the money and she wouldn't last a day in jail. Let's not forget how cramped her life would become if she actually had to take care of her child.

"Fine. I'll take it," she bites through her teeth.

"Leave."

"You're kicking me out of The L?" Her eyes are wide. How in the hell could she have thought I'd allow her to keep her job here?

"Our time is up, Chelsea. Every aspect of this relationship is over."

"Now you're divorcing me?"

I laugh haughtily. "It's been a long time coming. Now get out so I can celebrate the end of my time in hell."

Her mouth drops open. The reality of the situation finally sinks in. We're through. Her reign at The L and over me is through. She stands on shaky legs, beginning to gather her things.

"You can leave all that here. It belongs to The L and you're no longer a part of it."

She goes still, looking lost and confused for the first time ever. I've never seen her so forlorn. It's a different Chelsea entirely. She almost looks . . . human.

A tear falls down her cheek and then another.

I might've actually felt bad for her, but then I remember she just signed over the rights to her child for a measly one million dollars and all sympathy is lost.

"Go," I say in a softer tone, not needing to kick her any farther although she deserves it.

Without a word, she slithers out the door and out of my life for good.

# CHAPTER THIRTY-SIX

## Bridget

RESIGNED FROM THE L AND WAS GIVEN A LETTER OF recommendation that will land me any job I want, as promised.

And I haven't heard from Grant.

I bury myself with various other hobbies but can't seem to concentrate on anything. I won't let Olivia speak of what's happening with Grant, but from the little I heard, I know that Spencer and him along with his father have reconciled. Hearing about him is bittersweet, and normally leads to a tear-filled sob fest with my sisters. Lynn keeps telling me time will heal my wounds, but I don't believe her.

Just because Lynn and Olivia have their fairy tales doesn't mean it will happen for the rest of us. If I'm being honest, I'm sick of hearing it from them. Their words of wisdom are much the same and never help. Nothing will. My life is dull without Grant, and that's a fact I can't live with.

I hear a knocking at the door and jump up to grab it. Lynn is annoyingly consistent with her pounding when I don't answer. My head can't take it today.

"Stop with the noise already," I say as I swing it open.

Grant.

He's here, standing in my doorway. He looks more disheveled and even more handsome than ever before. My legs give way and my hand reaches out to hold on to the doorframe for support.

"Grant," I whisper.

"Can I come in?"

"I, um . . . Yeah. Sure. Come in," I say, moving aside to allow him entry. "Sorry about the place. I've been . . . busy," I lie. I've been heartbroken, but that about covers it.

"You do realize I'm only here to see you, not your place." He smiles.

"What brings you here?" I go for small talk because I'm out of my element. I'm caught off guard and not sure if I'm relieved to see him or about to break all over again.

"I filed for divorce."

The words fill the air and I think I'm about to faint. I blink a few times before finally finding my voice again. "Wh-what?"

"I fucked up, Bridget. I should have tried harder with you. I never should have let you go."

Speech escapes me. I can't form words. Everything I've wanted to hear for weeks, everything I've dreamed every night . . . he's saying it. I want to pinch myself awake, not wanting to delude myself any longer, but not wanting to wake for fear it's only a dream.

"I'm lost without you, Bridget. Please tell me I'm not too late."

My heart seizes, and all the broken parts begin to mend themselves. Hope swells. *Am I hearing him right?*

"God, I missed you so much," I whisper. "More than you will ever know or even understand." I hiccup a sob. "I love you." The words spill out of me, and I suddenly feel very uncomfortable. I lower my head, but then his fingers tip up my chin.

"Don't look away from me," Grant says.

Through tear-rimmed eyes, I peer up into his green gaze. "Promise me right now," I whisper.

"I'll do even better . . . I'll promise you forever."

# EPILOGUE

## Grant

STANDING ON THE BEACH IN ANTIBES, SURROUNDED BY family and beautiful scenery, the only person who holds my attention is my wife. She captivates me in ways I never dreamed possible. She's everything I ever wanted and nothing I deserved, yet she's all mine.

She catches me staring and rewards me with a smile that's just for me. Nodding toward the event taking place before us, I'm forced to oblige. I never thought I'd see the day when Spencer took the leap and asked for a woman's hand. Yet, here we are, watching him on bended knee, vowing his intentions of a lifelong commitment to Olivia, Bridget's sister.

If you had told me the Lancaster brothers would be a family again I would have never believed it, but here we are, stronger than ever. The bond of brotherhood proves to withstand even the greatest of betrayals. To be one of the few to witness this is humbling after everything we've been through.

Olivia squeals in excitement as Spencer spins her around. Lynn and Bridget don't waste time rushing forward to celebrate the upcoming nuptials with their sister. My brother's eyes meet mine and I smirk. The Miller girls have a way of rooting themselves deep into your veins.

Soon after Bridget and I reunited, I made her my wife. I offered her the big wedding every girl dreams of, but she wasn't interested. Too much time apart had us both eager to jump at the chance of forever. The day my divorce was official, about three months after I filed, we boarded a plane, and forty-eight hours later we were married. The only stipulation Bridget had was that our families were there and Isabella was by her side.

Her love for my daughter sealed my feelings for her. There's no better mother for my daughter than Bridget. Of that I'm sure.

Chelsea hasn't even tried to see Isabella since she received her check, which doesn't surprise me. As much as I wanted it that way, it pains me that Isabella means so little to her. I thank God every day that he brought Bridget into our lives, because between the two of us my little girl will never feel unloved. I was nervous at first about how Isabella would take her mom's absence, but she's a resilient and strong little girl. As the weeks and month have passed, she barely mentions her mother's abandonment.

I look away from the sisters celebrating and my eyes catch on Pierce, our youngest brother. He's chatting up some girl in a wheelchair who Bridget introduced earlier as one of Olivia's friends, Lindsay. They appear to be deep in conversation, so I refrain from approaching him. I've yet to forge a solid relationship with him since he was so young when I left, but I need to make an effort. He's been getting into so much trouble these past few years, and it wouldn't hurt for Spencer and me to take a bigger interest in helping him straighten up.

"Hey, babe," Bridget coos as she sidles up beside me.

"Hey, gorgeous. Is your sister excited?"

"Are you crazy? She's over the moon. She's going to drive me batshit for the next few months."

I chuckle.

"I'm serious. She's a bridezilla in the making."

"You can give her all sorts of hints."

She scrunches her nose. "We eloped. Do you know Olivia at all? This shindig is sure to be the party of the century. She's insane with this shit."

"Come here." I pull her into me, needing her close. "Want to get out of here?"

"We're alone for the weekend and our minibar was stocked full of tequila."

"Tequila, eh?"

"Great things start with tequila."

"The greatest, Dumpster Dude."

"Huh?"

She laughs, the wind carrying her magical voice to the ears of everyone around us. "Never mind."

I pull my wife into a kiss, not caring who sees. I intend on showing her how much she means to me tonight, tomorrow, and for every tomorrow after that.

*Forever.*

Thank you for reading Sordid. If you loved Grant and Bridget, click here (www.subscribepage.com/g9t5j0) for an exclusive bonus scene.

If you enjoyed this book, consider leaving a review at Amazon, Goodreads and/or the retailer of your choice to help other readers discover this book.

# BY AVA HARRISON

*Imperfect Truth*

*Through Her Eyes*

*trans-fer-ence*

*Illicit*

*Clandestine*

Pierce Lancaster is coming soon.
Click here: www.goodreads.com/book/show/35617716-explicit
to add to your TBR.

To receive a text alert when *Explicit* is live Text 'Explicit' to
313131

# ACKNOWLEDGMENTS

I want to thank my entire family. I love you all.

Thank you to my husband and my kids for always loving me, I love you so much!

Thank you to my Mom, Dad, Liz and Ralph for always believing in me, encouraging me and loving me!

Thank you to my in-laws for being so cool about me writing books and encouraging it!

Thank you to all of my brothers and sisters!

Thank you to everyone that helped with Sordid.

Write Girl Editing Services

Indie After Hours

Lawrence Editing

Becca Mysoor

Love N. Books

Marla Esposito

Champagne Formats

Sophie Broughton

Lori Jackson

Becca Zsurkán

Hang Le

Danielle Beckett

Thank you Ena from Enticing.

Thank you Rafa Catala and Fabian Castro

Thank you to my beta team! Becca, Leigh, Melissa, Livia, and Christine. Thank you for your wonderful and extremely helpful feedback.

Thank you to my agent Emily Sylvan Kim and everyone at Prospect for believing in me!

I want to thank to ALL my friends for putting up with me while I wrote this book. Thank you!

Thank you to my smut moms!

Thank you to my Phi Girls for always being there!

Special Thanks

To Melissa Saneholtz. You are my sanity! There aren't enough ways for me to say THANK YOU!

Mia you are my plotting goddess, even if I had to change my whole plot!

Leigh. . .Thank you for everything! Especially listening to me complain. . .PS it's my week now. ;-)

Livia . . . Still want to thank you for answering my calls.

To all of my author friends who listen to me bitch and let me ask for advice, thank you!

To the ladies in the Ava Harrison Support Group, I couldn't have done this without your support!

Please consider joining my reader group if you haven't: http://bit.ly/2e67NYi

Thanks to all the bloggers! Thanks for your excitement and love of books!

Last but certainly not least...

Thank you to the readers!

Thank you so much for taking this journey with me.

For future release information please sign up here to be alerted: http://bit.ly/2fnQQ1n

# ABOUT THE AUTHOR

Ava Harrison is a *USA Today* and Amazon bestselling author. When she's not journaling her life, you can find her window shopping, cooking dinner for her family, or curled up on her couch reading a book.

### Connect with Ava

Newsletter Sign Up: http://bit.ly/2fnQQ1n

Book + Main: bookandmainbites.com/avaharrison

Facebook Author Page: http://bit.ly/2eshd1h

Facebook Reader Group: http://bit.ly/2e67NYi

Goodreads Author Page: http://bit.ly/2eNjYwX

Instagram: http://bit.ly/2f5H5RT

BookBub: https://www.bookbub.com/authors/ava-harrison

Amazon Author Page: http://amzn.to/2fnVJHFF

CPSIA information can be obtained
at www.ICGtesting.com
Printed in the USA
LVHW041726170920
666361LV00004B/739

9 781724 616241